Between one eyeblink and the n[ext...] a large craft, easily the size of a troop carrier helicopter. Without making a sound, it stopped dead in midair directly over the city, just outside the reach of the defensive force field. Though it was constructed of some smooth, unmarked metal, its shape was almost organic in design, looking like an internal organ removed under dissection, or some microscopic bacterium.

Alysande turned to her second in command. "Major! Tell the men that I want all safeties off, all weapons hot, but that they are to fire only on my command."

"Yes, sir."

"What's it doing up there, anyway?" Kitty asked, squinting up at the strangely shaped craft.

As if in answer, the craft rotated slightly in midair. Then, it began to *unfold*—that was the only word for it—to unfold, sections opening up and curling back, looking more like the petals of a blossoming flower than anything man-made.

Without warning, from the top of the blossoming vessel, five figures emerged, flying under their own power, for starters. All of them were dressed in strange, metallic, formfitting clothing, but their appearances were anything but uniform. One had wings, another seemed to be covered in a sheath of green flame, another seemed to be made entirely of stone, still another had pointed ears and blue fur.

The lead figure, a massive, heavily muscled male whose skin appeared to be made of highly reflective metal—organic steel?—hovered in midair above the atoll, addressing Alysande and the X-Men on the beach.

"I am Invictus Prime of the Exemplar, augmented clade, and you are hereby ordered to vacate this area."

"On what authority?" Alysande shouted back.

The steel-skinned figure regarded her coolly before answering.

"The Exemplar carry out the will of the Kh'thon Collective, former occupants and rightful owners of the planet Earth."

Also available from Pocket Books

X-Men: Dark Mirror
by Marjorie M. Liu

X-Men: Watchers on the Walls
by Christopher L. Bennett

X-MEN:®
THE RETURN

a novel by
Chris Roberson

based on the
Marvel Comic Book

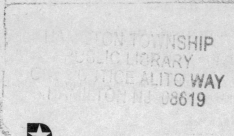

POCKET STAR BOOKS
NEW YORK   LONDON   TORONTO   SYDNEY

An *Original* Publication of POCKET BOOKS

A Pocket Star Book published by
POCKET BOOKS, a division of Simon & Schuster, Inc.
1230 Avenue of the Americas, New York, NY 10020

ISBN-13:   978-1-4165-1075-8
ISBN-10:   1-4165-1075-3

First Pocket Star Books printing May 2007

10 9 8 7 6 5 4 3 2 1

Cover art by John Picacio

Manufactured in the United States of America

For information regarding special discounts for bulk purchases, please contact Simon & Schuster Special Sales at 1-800-456-6798 or business@simonandschuster.com.

To Chris Claremont,
with respect and admiration

Note: This story takes place immediately preceding
the events of *Uncanny X-Men Annual* #10

First Prologue

Peter Corbeau sat in his quarters onboard Starcore One, trying to work out how many seconds remained before the first of July.

Across from him sat two of the station's crew, Colonel Mikhail Kutuzov and Dr. Stephen Beckley, in a heated discussion about something or other.

"Look, Dr. Corbeau," Beckley was saying, "all I'm asking is to retask the array for a few tens of hours, to get the final data I need for the Edmund Project."

"With all due respect, Beckley," Kutuzov said, his tone indicating anything but, "the administration allowed you onboard only as a courtesy to NASA. I refuse to allow your project to disrupt any of Starcore's ongoing experiments or data-gathering efforts."

It was something on the order of twenty-seven million, give or take three hundred thousand, Corbeau estimated. Twenty-seven million seconds before he'd be back on Earth, fishing the waters of the Caribbean from the deck of his yacht, the *Dejah Thoris II*. And in the meantime, he'd be busy playing chaperone to a group of quarreling schoolchildren. Or highly respected scientists. Sometimes he had difficulty deciding which.

It was his fault, ultimately. Not just that shifts on the UN-sponsored solar observatory ran the better part of a year, though he'd had a voice in that decision, as well. No, the whole Starcore operation itself could be laid at his feet. So when it came time to bemoan the fact that he would not be able to fish again for the better part of ten months, he had no one to blame but himself.

He'd had two passions since childhood, linked in his mind: the sun and the sea. Peter had spent years studying the former, and devoted what little free time he had to enjoying the latter. But now his love of the one meant he was denied the other, and he couldn't help but feel that was somehow unfair.

Peter was a scientist, after all. So how did he end up in *management*?

"Dr. Corbeau, I must insist," Beckley said, and Peter found that he'd completely lost the thread of the discussion. He didn't worry too much, though, since if there was one characteristic the two men before him shared, it was an inability to avoid endlessly repeating their own arguments.

Despite having initiated Project Starcore just so he could study the sun in ways that were impossible from Earth, Peter was now personally responsible for overseeing the work of a dozen men and women, scientists of different disciplines and nationalities, each a leader in their field. Collectively they held almost a dozen Nobel prizes, and any one of them could have retired comfortably on the patents generated by their work. And yet they still fought like kids in a schoolyard, jostling for access to the wide variety of monitoring equipment on the station, each with their own experiments to run and hypotheses to test.

And all Peter really wanted to do right now was fish. But that would have to wait until the first of July, another twenty-seven million seconds away.

Starcore had been Peter's idea, his baby from the beginning, and he'd personally overseen the design of every inch of the Starcore One space station, garnering two Nobel prizes along the way. When the UN tapped him to act as director of Project Starcore, it came as a surprise to no one. And yet it wasn't until strapping into the *Starcore-Eagle-One* shuttle, bound for his first tour of duty on the station, that it first occurred to Peter what he'd be giving up, leaving Earth for such long stretches of time.

He was a genius, sure, and had the paperwork to prove it, but too often he missed the blindingly obvious, even when it was staring him right in the face.

His comm pinged, interrupting whatever Kutuzov was about to say. With a sigh of gratitude, Peter toggled on the display, and the face of Talia Kruma filled the screen.

"Yes, Talia?" Peter said. "What is it?"

"Something pretty strange, Peter. A ship of unknown design has just popped up in our sensor data."

"Where?"

Kruma glanced to one side, lips pursed. "It's close."

Peter was already on his feet and heading to the door. "I'll be right there."

• • •

Moments later, Corbeau was on the bridge, Beckley and Kutuzov at his heels.

"Well, Talia, what can you tell me?"

"That's it," Kruma said, pointing to the indistinct image displayed on the overhead monitors. The still was blurry and distorted, but the overall impression was of an immense ship of strange angles and proportions. "It appeared near the sun a bit over four minutes ago, and passed within a few thousand miles of Starcore One."

Peter's eyes widened. "That puts its velocity at a significant fraction of the speed of light."

Kruma nodded. "We figure it at just over .75 c, Peter. And *slowing*."

"What's its bearing?" Beckley asked, breathless.

Kruma glanced over at Alexander Hilary, who was busy collating the most recent data at his station.

Hilary looked up, face ashen, and said a single word: "Earth."

Second Prologue

"I don't know, Cap'n. This seems like a real bad idea to me."

"Well, Frank, maybe if you didn't drink away what little money you don't lose at cards, you could scrape together enough to buy your own boat, and then *you* could make the decisions."

The crewman shook his head ruefully, and left Aleytys Forrester in the wheelhouse. It was her boat, and her decision, but the crew was clearly none too happy about it.

When Frank had gone, Paolo came in from the deck, carrying a steaming cup of coffee in either hand. Lee gratefully accepted one, her attention still on the far horizon.

"Frank's an idiot, Lee, but he's right about this. Let the Coast Guard take care of this mess. Nothin' good'll come of us sailing the Devil's Triangle."

Lee Forrester had known Paolo since she was a little girl. He and her father had been good friends, and when she'd blown her savings on buying the trawler right out of college, Paolo had been the first to sign on to her crew. He'd been onboard ever since, and he knew more about the sea than he could ever teach her. But despite Lee's repeated insistence that there was nothing to the legends of the Bermuda Triangle other than the periodic eruption of methane hydrate deposits on the ocean floor, affecting the buoyancy of ships and the ability of planes to maintain lift, the old man refused to believe that these waters were anything but cursed.

"Heard and understood, Paolo," Lee said, with a weary smile. "But my decision stands. We've radioed it in, but if there's somebody left alive from that crash, we'll be able to get to them long before anyone else can."

Paolo shook his head, but kept silent, taking up his accustomed position at her side.

The trawler *Arcadia* was about five hundred miles off the east coast of Florida, and making its way steadily northeast, roughly in the direction of Bermuda. It had been a few hours since they'd seen the craft arcing overhead. Lee thought it might be some sort of NASA craft, or maybe an experimental airplane. Either way, it was coming in hot and fast, looking like it was going to crash into the ocean somewhere just over the horizon. Lee hadn't needed to think about it too long before she ordered the men to haul in the nets, and headed at full steam toward the place the craft must have gone down.

The vapor trail lingering in the air led them like a beacon, and by midmorning the little atoll came into view. Lee didn't have to check the charts to know where they were. She'd once washed ashore on that little strip of land, after being tossed overboard in a squall. One of her crew had dived in after her, for all the good it did either of them. The two of them had spent days on the atoll, unsure if they'd ever be rescued, until *he* appeared and they went from the frying pan into the fire.

"God preserve us," Paolo said, his mouth drawn into a tight line, his gaze fixed on the shapes hulking just beyond the atoll.

Lee nodded, expression grim. As the *Arcadia* motored around the little island, the strange prominences of the city beyond came into view. The island was Julienne Cay. The city had no name, at least not one that Lee knew. All that she knew was that it was older than civilization, and had not been built by human hands. And the vapor trail they followed pointed directly at its heart.

Over the objections of the crew, Paolo included, Lee made landfall, mooring at the makeshift dock she'd used on her previous visits to the strange, unearthly city.

"Come on, you lunks," Lee said, slinging her pack on her back. "If there *are* any survivors, we're not doing them any favors standing around here."

There were four members of the crew besides Lee and Paolo, and they now gathered around Frank, their de facto spokesman in times of dispute. He was the one who typically brought any of their grievances to the captain, all of them invariably minor and easily settled, and though he'd never done more than win the crew a few more percent of the ship's haul to split amongst themselves, he carried himself like a shop steward facing down the oppressive forces of big business.

"Look, Cap'n," Frank said, squaring his shoulders

and trying his best to look intimidating. "The guys 'n me have been talkin' it over, and we've decided we're stayin' on the boat."

"Is that so?" Lee asked sweetly.

Frank nodded. "Yeah, it is."

"What are you afraid of, guys?" Lee asked "Bogeymen swimming up out of the triangle to drag you down to a watery grave?"

A couple of the younger crewmen exchanged worried glances, and Lee knew that was precisely what they were worried about.

"Well," Lee said, nodding slowly. She stepped back into the wheelhouse, and stepped out holding a rifle, normally kept racked on the cabin wall. A Lee-Enfield .303 that her grandfather had brought back from the first World War, it was euphemistically called the "shark gun." It had been used to shoot more than sharks in its day. Lee planted the rifle's butt on her hip, her hand on the stock. "Unless I'm very mistaken, this is the only firearm on the boat. And its coming with me. So you've got to ask yourselves. Do you feel safer inland with me and my rifle or here on the boat with Frank?"

The crew looked to one another, and with a ripple of shrugs prepared to follow Lee inland.

"How about you, Frank?" Lee said, stepping up onto the ship's railing, and then vaulting to the dock a few feet away. "You coming along, or are you going to stay on the boat all by your lonesome?"

"I'm comin'," Frank said reluctantly, glancing up at the strangely shaped towers of the city. "But I still say this is a bad idea."

• • •

Following Lee's lead, the crew made their way through the labyrinthine concourses of the city, moving through narrow passages and across broad avenues, under the gaze of towering statues depicting unearthly, inhuman creatures. At the feet of many of these enormous monsters were sculpted human figures, lounging in submissive poses in various states of undress. The crew walked in silence, unsettled by the strangeness surrounding them.

At last they found the craft, parked in the middle of a broad plaza without a scratch on it.

"What the devil is *that*?" Paolo said.

"Whatever it is," Lee said, looking at the odd angles and unsettling protuberances of the vessel, "it isn't local."

"Cap'n?" Frank said uneasily, pointing at the strange figures issuing from the craft's open hatch, who began to advance on them menacingly.

"Frank," Lee said, unslinging the shark gun from her shoulder, "I'm beginning to think you might have been right after all."

More of the strange figures were in view now, and some of them had taken to the air, shouting at Lee and her crew in an alien, guttural language.

"Captain?" one of the younger crew said plaintively. "What are we . . . ?"

"Quiet, Joe," Lee said, and tossed the rifle to Paolo, who trained it on the nearest of the figures. She then slung her pack from her back and grabbed the satellite phone from the side pocket.

"Lee?" Paolo said, warily. "These folks don't seem too friendly, I don't think."

Lee finished punching in the number, and held the phone up to her ear. "Come on, come on, pick up, damn it!"

"Cap'n? A little help, here?"

"I'm working on it, Frank," Lee said, and then heard the click on the other end of the line. "Oh, Scott, thank god you're . . ."

"Thank you for calling Xavier's School for Gifted Youngsters," came the voice on the other end of the line. "I'm afraid we're not able to take your call at this time, but if you'll leave your name and a brief message after the beep . . ."

1

This wasn't the slums, or the war-torn streets of some distant city, or a savage and distant land. This was Manhattan, Park Avenue to be precise, somewhere in the upper seventies. Kitty Pryde knew it as one of the swankiest neighborhoods in the city, perhaps even the world, but on this moonless night, the streets strangely empty of vehicles and pedestrians alike, the shadows pooling under every awning and around every door, she felt an inescapable sense of menace.

For the moment, it seemed that the world consisted of nothing but Kitty and the buildings towering on either side. But she knew that was too good to last.

As if in response to her thoughts, a pair of street thugs emerged from the shadows. They looked like rejects from *The Warriors* or a *Street Fighter* arcade game, one of them done up like a B-movie Indian with Mohawk, face paint, and feathers, the other in a battered top hat and tattered tails.

The Mohawk carried a hunting knife, whose blade glinted dully in the low light, while the top hat swung a Louisville Slugger like a batter approaching the plate.

"How do, Chicken Little?" said the Mohawk in a rasping voice. "Ready to have some fun?"

"What's the matter?" Kitty asked, crossing her arms over her chest. "You guys get lost on the way to a Village People tribute?"

"You hear that, Robbo?" the Mohawk said to the top hat. "Chicken Little thinks she's a comedian."

Robbo, the top hat, snickered like a dutiful sidekick, but said nothing.

Kitty sighed, and shook her head. "That doesn't even make any sense, you know. Chicken Little? Since when have I worried about the sky falling?"

"Oh," the Mohawk said, dramatically, "it's gonna fall."

Kitty rolled her eyes. "You need to work on the script a bit. If this is the best you can do, well, it's just embarrassing." She motioned to the two street thugs. "Come on, let's get this over with."

As the pair advanced, menacingly, Kitty sized up her options. *Ninjitsu?* she wondered. *No,* she thought with a smile. *Krav maga.*

The Mohawk attacked first, swinging the hunting knife down in a wide arm, the blade toward the ground. Kitty responded instantly with a simultaneous block and strike, punching the Mohawk in the throat with the heel of her palm, grabbing hold of his wrist with her other hand. As the Mohawk pulled away, Kitty kept her hold on the knife. A brief tug-of-war ensued, ended quickly with a knee to the Mohawk's groin. As he staggered backward, moaning, Kitty sent the knife flying off into the darkness, end over end, finally landing with a clatter some yards away, well out of reach.

The top hat came next, swinging the bat like a club. Kitty ducked under the swing, knocking his arm aside with her left elbow, then went in close with a shovel hook with her right, fist held palm up, elbow tucked down by her ribs, the force of motion coming from her hips. The short-range punch caught the top hat in the soft tissue just beneath the ribcage on his left side, knocking the wind from him. Then, as the top hat reeled, she swung around and followed the body shot with a head shot that caught the top hat in the side of the face.

Kitty kicked the bat away as the top hat dropped to the pavement, just as the Mohawk regained his composure. She set her feet, arms held lightly to either side, and smiled sweetly at him. "Ready for another go?"

The Mohawk looked at his friend, moaning semiconscious on the sidewalk, and without another word turned and ran.

Kitty shrugged, and started to head up the avenue in the opposite direction. Logan would have been proud. She hadn't even had to use her phasing powers.

"This is too easy," she said to the empty air. "I was expecting something a bit tougher."

Just then, a hulking metal figure rounded the corner of 71st Street, blocking her path. It was roughly man-shaped, but towered over her, taller than the two street thugs combined.

"Okay," Kitty said, whistling appreciatively. "*That's* tougher."

Kitty's first thought was that it was some sort of robot. A bit clichéd, perhaps, but more of a credible threat than the Village People rejects of a moment before.

No, she thought, seeing the very human eyes in the faceplate, high overhead. *It's a powered combat suit, like Iron Man on steroids.*

As the towering figure of yellow metal approached, Kitty recognized the design. It was a Mandroid, tech originally developed by Tony Stark for SHIELD, but since fallen into the hands of any number of well-funded criminal masterminds and megalomaniacs bent on world domination. But who the suit's owner might be was of much less concern to Kitty at the moment than what its operator might be planning.

Okay, Kitty thought, dancing backward as the Mandroid slowly advanced, *if this model is anything like the ones I studied, it'll be made of vanadium steel, with a laser cannon mounted on its left arm, a power claw of some kind on the right.*

How well the armaments would be employed, of course, depended largely on the skills of the operator inside, but even a complete novice could be ruthlessly effective in a rig like that.

Delightful.

Kitty phased as the laser cannon sent a gout of coherent light right at her, and though the beam passed harmlessly through her phased molecules, she could still feel the heat of its passage. It felt like stepping out of an air-conditioned plane into a hot desert summer, and Kitty didn't like to imagine what the full intensity of the beam would do to her if she weren't phased.

The Mandroid didn't give her a chance to counter, but swung the power claw at her in a vicious arc. Kitty remained phased, nonchalantly waiting for the arm to pass through her. But just as the metal of the suit's claw passed through her phased molecules, Kitty winced, feeling as if she'd just been kicked in the head. Spots danced in her vision, and the worst migraine she'd felt in ages flared up behind her eyes.

"Ouch!"

Kitty staggered back, suddenly solid.

That is not *vanadium steel,* she thought ruefully. No, whatever the suit was made of, it was something so dense that it sat at the outer range of her ability to phase through it.

The migraine was just beginning to fade, her vision clearing, when Kitty saw the power claw coming back around for another swipe. Still disoriented, she just managed to duck, the arm whistling only inches overhead. In no rush to feel the sensation of phasing through *that* again, she rushed forward, crouched low, and slipped between the powerful legs of the combat suit and out the other side.

The Mandroid wheeled around as Kitty danced out of reach, trying to formulate a plan. She could continue to phase through its laser bolts indefinitely, but whenever the Mandroid closed the distance between them she was going to run the risk of another kick to the head.

I'll be lucky to handle another one or two phases through that muck, at best. And that's if I only have to contend with an arm or leg. If I have to phase through the bulk of the suit, I'll probably end up unconscious on the ground in seconds.

Her only hope was to knock the suit out of commission with her next phase. Unless she was extraordinarily unlucky, the electronics driving the Mandroid would be vulnerable to her ability to disrupt any electrical system she phased through. Her phased molecules acted like a miniature, localized electromagnetic pulse, and if she could get a hand into the suit's power source, she could immobilize it.

The problem was that the suit's power source was bound to be in some protected area, somewhere inside the chest carapace, and she was likely to have only one shot at this.

Sure, she thought, lips pursed. *A piece of cake.*

Kitty tried to think back and remember the schematics she'd studied. The models the X-Men faced years ago had been Stark Industries Mark I and Mark II Mandroids. The one she was facing now was a different design entirely, but seemed to be built on the same basic principles.

Engineers usually don't reinvent the wheel. It's easier to evolve a design from one model to the next. That's why cars almost always have their engine in the front and the trunk in the back. If a design works, why change it? So if this one is built on the same lines as the earlier model Mandroids, its power supply is probably in the same place. Right?

Unless, of course, Kitty realized with a grimace, the engineer had decided to get *creative.* There was always the chance that this was the Volkswagen Beetle of Mandroids, with its power supply squirreled away somewhere screwy, and nothing but a roomy storage space where the power supply logically should be.

So which was it? Simply this year's model, or a new

design entirely? If the former, Kitty's play would work. If the latter, well . . .

I hope my friends remember me fondly.

Kitty crouched low, and waited until the Mandroid lunged at her. At the last possible moment she leapt into the air, legs out to either side, and planted her hands palms down on the Mandroid's forearm, using it like a pommel horse and going into a handstand. Kitty breathed a silent prayer as the Mandroid responded just as expected, swinging its claw upward. Kitty folded her arms for a brief instant, like springs soaking up kinetic energy, and then pushed off, letting the combined momentum carry her upward, doing a tuck and roll in midair that would make Stevie Hunter proud and landing gracelessly on the Mandroid's broad shoulders.

"Here goes nothing," Kitty said, and thrust her phased arm straight down into the back of the Mandroid carapace.

With a sputtering sound and a sudden smell of ozone the Mandroid shuddered once and then went still as a statue.

A blinding headache lancing through her skull, Kitty was barely able to remain phased long enough to pull her arm back out of the Mandroid before going solid, and then slipping unceremoniously down to the ground. She managed to keep her feet beneath her, just barely, and rubbed the bridge of her nose, waiting for the spots in front of her eyes to fade and the ice pick in her frontal lobe to dissipate.

"Ouch," Kitty said, rubbing her temples. "I'm not in a hurry to try *that* again."

The only answer was a deep, reverberating thud. Then another, and another, and another. Sounding like footsteps, but impossibly loud, and getting louder.

Kitty turned, and looked up 70th Street toward Madison Avenue.

A trio of Sentinels were emerging from the direction of Central Park. Purple and gray human-shaped robots, designed to hunt and eradicate the "mutant menace," stood a dozen stories tall, yellow eyes glaring in their expressionless faces, arms outstretched menacingly.

From the immobile mouth on the face of the lead Sentinel issued a strange, inhuman voice.

"Mutant, you are advised to surrender or face immediate termination. This is your only warning."

"Aw, come on, Doug!" Kitty yelled, hands on her hips. "Are you *kidding* me? Why not just toss in Galactus, too, and complete the set?"

The Sentinels were less than half a block away, their hands raised, palms forward, weapons no doubt trained on Kitty and ready to extinguish her life.

And then everything was gone.

All of it, the city, the street, the buildings, the Sentinels. Only Kitty remained, standing in an immense, featureless room of glittering steel. Where the Mandroid had stood was now an oversized humaniform practice dummy of the same featureless steel as the surrounding walls, ceiling, and floor, its holographic cloak now disabled.

Through the window of reinforced transparent aluminum, set high on the wall overhead, Kitty could see the smirking face of Doug Ramsey in the control room.

"Aw, come on, Pryde. Don't feel up to a little challenge?"

Kitty shook her head and stepped forward, lifting her foot as though to put it on a step. The fact that there was no stairway there, just empty air, didn't stop her from slowly ascending, air-walking gradually higher, step by step. It was another interesting side effect of her phasing abilities, one that had taken a while to get the hang of. She often felt like Wile E. Coyote from the Road Runner cartoons when air-walking, and preferred to keep from looking down, for fear that the sudden discovery that there was nothing beneath her but empty air might send her falling to the ground far below.

"Doug, have I ever told you about the first time I was in the Danger Room?"

His voice echoed through the speakers hidden in the walls around her, but the shake of his head was a slight, understated motion. "No, I don't think so. Why?"

"Well, it was just the standard first-timer test, just like all the New Mutants had to do on their first days—present company excluded. All I had to do was walk from one side of the room to the other. I don't think I'd ever been so scared in my life, even after being kidnapped by the Hellfire Club and all of that crazy. So I squeezed my eyes shut and just put one foot in front of the other. And you know what happened?"

Kitty was now only a few steps away from the control room, her eyes fixed on her destination, and not on the hard steel floor dozens of feet below.

"No, what?" Doug said.

"Nothing," Kitty answered with a smile. "I just kept walking. I didn't even realize I was phasing through tentacles, and projectiles, and force beams, and all kinds of nastiness Professor Xavier had cooked up."

Kitty was now in arm's reach of the control room window. She stepped through, feeling the slightest whisper on her exposed skin as her molecules phased through those of the transparent aluminum.

"Of course," Kitty added with a sigh, "then I was knocked unconscious by a psionic bolt, and spent the next few hours in a coma in someone else's body while an alternate version of me from the future of a parallel time line used mine to try to stop World War III, but that's a *whole* different story."

"Heck," Doug said, leaning back and lacing his fingers behind his head, feet propped up on the Danger Room's control panel. "I'd be lucky just to make it through the front door."

"Yeah," Kitty said, dropping into the chair beside him wearily. "I guess the ability to translate any language and talk to computers isn't all that handy when dealing with evil mutants or giant robots."

"I'll just have to get by on my good looks." Doug smiled.

"Well, good luck with that." Kitty punched him lightly in the arm. "I wouldn't count on the next mutant you meet succumbing to your boyish charms, though."

"Um, excuse me?" came a cultured voice from behind them.

Kitty looked to see a stunning woman with purple hair standing in the entrance to the control room. It was

Betsy Braddock, former British fashion model, telepath, and newcomer to the Xavier mansion.

"On the other hand," Kitty said in a low voice, shooting Doug a sly look.

"B-Betsy," Doug said, jumping awkwardly to his feet. "What . . . what can I . . . ?" He stopped, and glanced at Kitty nervously. "You didn't just . . ." He looked back to Betsy. "Did you?"

Betsy regarded Doug for a moment, a slight smile on her full lips, and shook her head. "I'm certain I didn't, whatever it was."

"What can we do for you, Betsy, is what the boy wonder here is trying to say," Kitty said dryly.

"Yes, well, it appears that someone is waiting at the front door. Or so it would appear on the monitors in the corridor. I'd have gone and answered it myself but . . ." A slight blush rose on Betsy's cheeks. "But to be perfectly frank, I couldn't find my way back to the lift, and I've been stuck in this bloody subbasement all morning!"

"No problem," Kitty said, standing. "That'll probably be Scott at the door, and I need to talk to him myself anyway." She strode toward the door, but paused as she came abreast of Betsy and glanced back at Doug. "Hey, Ramsey, why don't you give Ms. Braddock a full tour of the mansion. I'm sure she'd appreciate the attention."

As Kitty walked out, Doug gave Betsy a sheepish grin, looking like a kid at a middle school dance trying to work up the courage to approach a girl.

I don't know who to pity more, Kitty thought, heading up the corridor toward the elevator. *Him or her.*

2

Scott Summers stood at the front door of the Xavier mansion, scowling, eyes narrowed behind the thick ruby quartz lenses of his glasses. He felt uncomfortably like an outsider, like a door-to-door salesman, not like someone who'd lived his entire adult life and almost half his childhood inside these walls. It'd only been a short time since he'd left, but it already seemed a lifetime ago.

Scott remembered the first time he stood on this doorstep, the day that Charles Xavier had invited him to be the first X-Man, and given him the code name Cyclops. It sometimes felt as though he'd spent his every waking moment these last years wearing that uniform, answering to that name. And now who was he? This would be the first time since he was a teenager that he'd be entering the mansion as anything but the leader of the X-Men.

So he wasn't an X-Man anymore. What of it? He and the others, the founders—Hank, Bobby, Warren, and Jean—they had lives of their own these days, and plans that kept them busy in Manhattan and elsewhere. Scott tried not to look back, tried to put his past behind him.

Besides, in a very real sense, the mansion wasn't the place he remembered. Not anymore.

But when he'd gotten Kitty's call, he knew he couldn't refuse. Even though the X-Men weren't his team anymore, and the mansion not his home, he would always answer when they called.

So why weren't *they* answering the door?

As if in response, the knob turned, and the door swung open. Kitty Pryde, face flushed and hair in disarray, stood on the other side.

"I thought it'd be you!" Kitty said, breathless. She tilted her head to one side, looking at him quizzically. "Why didn't you just come in?"

Scott just held up his key, his eyebrow raised. "You changed the locks?"

Kitty smiled, somewhat sheepishly. "Ah. Well, don't take it personally. It was Tom Corsi's idea, to cycle all the security systems once a month. With the number of doppelgangers and alien shape-shifters and mind-controlled zombies we get around here, we figured it couldn't hurt to try."

Scott realized that the long silence that followed suggested that Kitty was waiting for some kind of response. He nodded, and when that failed to get the desired reaction, gestured toward the door. "Can I come in?"

"Oh," Kitty said, eyes widening. She stepped to one side, and added apologetically, "Of course, sorry about that."

When Scott was through, Kitty closed the door behind him, then set off across the foyer toward the headmaster's office.

Scott remembered that once upon a time he'd kidded himself that Xavier might one day hand the school down to him, if circumstances ever demanded. But when the time came, and Xavier chose a successor, Scott wasn't it. Really, if he was honest with himself, that was probably the biggest reason that Scott had left in the first place. They were someone else's X-Men now.

"Anyway," Kitty was saying, "like I said on the phone, just about everybody is still on their way back from visiting Moira and Sean on Muir Island. Logan's somewhere around here, and all of the New Mutants are all out west visiting Danielle Moonstar's parents. All except Doug Ramsey, of course, who's busy following Betsy Braddock around like a lovesick puppy. It's kind of cute, in a sickeningly icky sort of way."

"You said there was some kind of message?" Scott said impatiently.

"Right, the message," Kitty said. "It came in when I was in the shower, and Logan was taking a nap, so the machine picked it up."

"A nap?" Scott smirked.

"So sue me, Cyke," Logan said, coming around the corner, his flannel shirt open to the waist, a beer in one hand and an unlit cigar in the other. "I gotta get my beauty sleep, don't I?"

"Logan," Scott said simply by way of greeting.

Taking a long slug of his beer, Logan shouldered past Scott and into the headmaster's office. He collapsed unceremoniously into the leather swivel chair, propping his feet up on the desk.

"Here it is," Kitty said, and punched the replay button on the answering machine.

The voice message was fragmentary, and laced with static, but the breathless voice was immediately recognizable. She was clearly under stress, but not yet panicking.

"Scott? Or . . . it's Lee. We're here . . . triangle . . . There's some . . . UFO . . . and these . . . others . . . coming closer . . . Help!!"

"Lee." Scott closed his eyes behind his ruby quartz glasses, his hands curled into fists at his sides.

"I figure 'Lee' to be Magneto's old squeeze," Logan said casually. "But I can't make heads or tails of the rest of it."

"Scott," Kitty said, concern written on her features. "Does that make any kind of sense to you?"

"Yes," Scott said, his tone grim.

"Well, what does it mean?"

"Yeah, Cyke, spill it."

"It means," Scott answered, his mouth drawn into a thin line, "that I need to borrow a plane."

3

A short while later, the *Blackbird* was halfway to Bermuda. A Lockheed RS-150 modified with Shi'ar technology, the X-Men's private spy plane was cruising somewhere around Mach 4, and would reach the waters of the Sargasso Sea in only a matter of minutes.

Kitty looked out the window at the sapphire blue waters racing far beneath them. Scott was beside her at the controls. Behind them, Logan sprawled across two passenger seats, his cowboy hat tilted forward, almost completely covering his eyes.

Logan hadn't said a word since they'd boarded, and Kitty was sure he was asleep, but then he surprised her by breaking the silence.

"You know, Cyke, you seem awfully hot and bothered over a call from Mags's ex-girl." Logan reached up a single finger and tilted his cowboy hat back fractionally, looking up under his brows at the back of Scott's head. "Am I wrong in thinking maybe the two of you had a little something on the side?"

"Logan!" Kitty snapped, wheeling around in her chair.

"No," Scott answered, glancing back at the diminutive

Canadian. "Logan's right. Lee and I were . . . involved."

Kitty gaped at him. "When?!"

Scott? Two-timing with Magneto's girlfriend?!

Kitty'd met Lee Forrester only once or twice, and only at Magneto's side. Lee had always seemed a bit shy and standoffish, though Kitty could tell there was real iron in her. She'd initially thought that she might be some kind of mutaphobe, but quickly dismissed the idea. No one with a pathological fear or hatred of mutants could be in a romantic relationship with Magneto. That would be like a white supremacist snuggling up with Malcolm X. Still, there was something about the way Lee carried herself that suggested that, while she might have been the mistress of her domain at sea, when elbow to elbow with people who shot lasers from their eyes or had claws that popped out of their knuckles, she felt a little out of her depth.

"It was before she ever met Magneto," Scott explained, his voice sounding far away. "It was shortly after Phoenix died on the moon. I was . . ." He paused for a moment, swallowing hard. "I needed to take some time away. I roamed around for a while, and eventually ended up down in Florida. Joined the crew of a fishing boat out of Shark Bay, and got to know her captain pretty well."

"And that was Lee?" Kitty asked.

"Sole owner and operator," Scott said, sounding more than a little proud. "She'd turned her back on a life of ease to work for a living, instead, and I don't think I've ever met a more resourceful, strong woman. Well, we got to be friends, and then maybe a little more than friends. One night Lee was washed overboard during a freak squall, and I dove in after her. We kept afloat, but only barely, and then we ended up washing ashore on a little atoll in the middle of the Bermuda Triangle."

"And then Mags entered the picture," Logan said, his voice low but level. "Yeah, I remember that day, alright."

Scott glanced back at Logan, but only nodded. Then he turned to Kitty and continued. "Magneto just . . . he just raised up this strange, deserted city from the bottom of the ocean, a mile off the shore of the atoll, and used it as his base for a while, trying to terrorize the nations of the world into recognizing his authority." He paused, then said, "You remember the city, don't you, Kitty? We stayed their briefly, a few years back."

"Oh," Kitty said sarcastically, "you mean *that* strange alien city in the middle of the Bermuda Triangle. I thought you were talking about some *other* alien city." She treated Scott to her most withering stare. "My mistake."

Scott smiled slightly, and shrugged. "That's right, of course," he said, apologetically. "You were with us on that mission, weren't you? I'm sorry, Kitty, I sometimes forget just how long you've been with us—" Scott paused, and then added quickly, "With the X-Men, I mean. I still think of you as the 'new kid,' but you've been around for years."

"And there's a lot more 'new kids,' these days," Kitty said. "One whole wing of the mansion is full of them."

"Heck," Logan put in, "feels like Rogue just got here yesterday, but she's an old campaigner by now."

"It must be some strange inverse of dog years or something," Kitty said. "Except that it's not seven for every one, but the other way around."

"Time flies when you're busy saving the world," Scott said.

In the passenger seats behind them, Logan began to chuckle loudly.

"What?" Kitty asked.

"Yes, Logan," Scott said, glancing back over his shoulder. "What's so funny?"

"You and Mags," Logan said, still chuckling. "The same woman took a liking to *both* of you?"

"Yeah?" Scott's eyes narrowed behind his ruby quartz glasses. "What about it?"

"Well," Logan said, pulling the brim of his hat down over his eyes and crossing his arms over his chest, "there's just no accounting for taste, now, is there?"

Scott was about to answer, his teeth bared, when a ping from the instrumentation caught Kitty's attention.

"Hey, you guys," Kitty said, leaning over and studying the digital readout. "I've located the GPS transponder of Lee's ship, the *Arcadia*. It's anchored about a mile off the shore of something called Julienne Cay."

"Cripes," muttered Logan under his breath.

"What?" Kitty said, looking from Scott to Logan and back.

"Remember that atoll I was telling you about?" Scott said, his hands tightening on the controls. "That's Julienne Cay."

"So that means . . ." Kitty said, realization dawning.

"That means that Lee's in that alien city."

"Her message said something about 'others,'" Kitty said. "But I thought the city was deserted."

Behind her, Logan said simply, "Not anymore."

4

They were only minutes away from their destination when the *Blackbird*'s proximity alarms went off, klaxons blaring.

"What the devil?" Scott glanced at the instrumentation, and saw the telltales of another craft coming in fast. He gritted his teeth, tightening his grip on the controls. "Hold on."

Kitty gasped as Scott sent the plane into a tight roll, veering off to port just as the other craft shot past them. And just in case there was any doubt as to the newcomer's intentions, tracer fire raked across the nose of the *Blackbird,* only narrowly missing puncturing the hull.

"We're under attack," Scott said, unlocking the *Blackbird*'s weapons systems.

"Gee, Cyke," Logan said with a sneer, "you think?"

"I didn't get a good look at it, but it must be that UFO Lee mentioned."

"I don't think so, Scott," Kitty said, holding a set of headphones to her ears, working the *Blackbird*'s communications controls. "I'm monitoring radio frequencies, and I'm pretty sure that bogey is local."

To illustrate her point, Kitty reached over and toggled on the plane's loudspeakers.

". . . repeat, this is Colonel Alysande Stuart, of Her Majesty's Royal Marines, to unidentified craft. You are entering British airspace without clearance, and should you proceed on your present heading you *will* be shot down."

"Um," Kitty said, setting down the headphones, and turning to Scott. "Correct me if I'm wrong, but isn't Britain quite a bit *that* way?" She jerked her thumb over her shoulder.

"The Brits used to have an empire the sun never set on, pun'kin," Logan said. "Don't be too surprised they hung onto one or two bits of it."

Scott kept one hand on the controls and used the other to set the headphones on his head, and switch the microphone on.

"This is Scott Summers, piloting private aircraft X-ray Alpha Victor out of Salem Center, New York, bound for Julienne Cay. This is a rescue operation. Over."

A moment's silence followed.

"Permission to approach denied. Proceed back along your previous course or you will be shot down."

Logan growled, rubbing his knuckles, but Kitty waved him quiet.

"On what authority?" Scott demanded, trying to retain his composure.

"On the authority of Her Majesty Queen Elizabeth II," came the answer. "These waters, and airspace, are part of the British Virgin Islands, and as such are under the jurisdiction of the British Crown. No unauthorized craft or personnel are permitted to approach."

In a voice barely above a whisper, Kitty said, "Just what are they *doing* down there, anyway?"

"Askin' for a world of hurt," Logan growled, teeth bared.

"Look, Colonel Whatever-your-name is," Scott said, his voice raising, "I've got friends down there who've called for help, and I'm landing this plane, whether you like it or not."

After a momentary pause, the reply came. "Then you leave me no choice. Lieutenant, prepare to . . ."

Without warning, the voice on the other end of the radio broke off.

Scott looked over at Kitty, confused. "Where'd they go?"

Kitty checked the radio instrumentation and shook her head. "They're still there, and we're still receiving."

Faintly, over the speakers, they could hear low voices muttering.

"Sounds like somebody had a dissenting opinion," Kitty said.

"Very well!" The voice on the radio returned, sounding exasperated. "Private aircraft X-ray Alpha Victor. You have permission to land. Our fighter jet will act as escort. Follow him on the approach vector. However, if you deviate from that course, or your people step one *inch* out of line once you're on the ground, I'll order my men to open fire."

Then the transmission ended, and the radio bled static.

"Well, you heard the lady," Logan said. "So land already?"

"Lady?" Kitty said, turning around in her seat. "You think that was a woman?"

Logan retracted his claws back into his forearms, and then reached up to tug at one earlobe. "I've got pretty good hearin', kiddo. That was a woman, no doubt about it."

"Oh," Kitty said, turning back around in her seat.

Scott watched as the British fighter jet approached on a heading parallel to theirs, the pilot giving him a thumbs-up.

"Don't let that relax you any, though," Logan said guardedly. "You know as well as me that a skirt can pull a trigger just as easy as anyone else."

5

Colonel Alysande Stuart stood on the sandy beach of the atoll, looking across the waters at the unknown. Only a mile or so of unbroken sea separated her from the strange alien city that grew from the calm waters of the Sargasso like some sort of nightmarish tumor. The towers and obelisks and other protuberances that marked the city's skyline were all of strange angles, of uncomfortably organic shapes and curves, and Alysande could not shake the sensation that as she was looking at them, they were looking *back*.

A short distance off, one of her men was on the radio with the fighter pilot, guiding the interloping aircraft down to an amphibious landing. When it had finished, the fighter would return to the carrier group, and to the HMS *Valiant*, her base of operations, only a few dozen miles away. If circumstances demanded, Alysande could have an aerial strike force overhead in a matter of moments. But what circumstances those might be, she hadn't a clue.

This isn't what I signed on for, she thought, regarding the alien city. *Not by half.*

A short distance off, the man in the plain black suit finished up his conversation with his distant masters, and shut his satellite phone down. Then, with the same unctuous smile that had been maddening Alysande all morning, he made his way back down the beach toward her.

"Downing Street is quite pleased with how you've handled matters so far, Colonel Stuart," the man said, still smiling. "I'll make sure your superiors get a full report."

"And what of your shadowy superiors, Mr. Raphael? What does the RCX have to say about all of this?"

"Oh, it's just Raphael, Colonel," he said, stopping just beyond arms reach, his hands tucked casually into his pants pockets. "And I'm obliged to remind you, of course, that I'm merely a simple servant of the crown. Even if such an organization as the RCX existed, there'd be no connection between it and myself."

Alysande pursed her lips, biting back the answer that suggested itself.

"Ri-ight," she said simply.

She understood full well that the rank and file weren't to know of the existence of the Resource Control Executive, but even any knowledge about the shadowy agency was on a strictly need-to-know basis, under the circumstances she herself surely *needed* to know.

"With any luck, Colonel," Raphael went on, "we'll have this mess sorted in no time, and you and your men can get back to your little launch, yes?"

Alysande bristled, holding her hands together behind her back to resist the temptation to throttle the little troll, and with a curt nod, said, "Yes, well . . ."

As though the most cutting-edge space plane yet designed, the result of billions of pounds and countless hours of effort on the part of the British Rocket Group, was nothing more than a "little launch."

It was dumb luck that led Alysande to be in charge here, so far from home. She'd just been in the wrong place at the wrong time, to her way of thinking.

Colonel Stuart had been sent to these waters to command a security detail, responsible for safeguarding the launch of an experimental spacecraft. The launch was to have taken place from a floating platform anchored off the coast of the tiny island of Tortola, and up until shortly before dawn that morning, everything had proceeded exactly according to plan.

Then an unidentified object had appeared on their radar screens, moving impossibly fast, and touching down less than a hundred miles away from the launch site.

Without hesitation, Alysande had ordered the launch scrubbed, and immediately notified her superiors, while the boffins in the British Rocket Group shouted their demands that her orders be contravened and the launch continue.

Following her superiors' orders to hold position and wait for further instruction, Alysande spent the morning organizing her men into a search-and-rescue operation, should the need arise. Then, midmorning, a supersonic jet had boomed out of the east, and set down on the deck of Alysande's command aircraft carrier. Besides the pilot, the jet had carried only one passenger, a squat little man, round and balding, wearing a black business suit. Wearing completely opaque wrap-around sunglasses, he'd hopped down to the deck, extended his hand to Alysande, and introduced himself simply as "Raphael."

Alysande recognized a spook when she saw one, as did most of her men, who eyed the stranger warily.

Raphael had presented his bona fides to Alysande when requested, a simple document printed on Downing Street stationery and bearing the personal signature of the prime minister and the head of the Ministry of Defense. However, though his paperwork practically granted him the latitude to buy and sell the whole carrier group at his whim, Raphael had insisted that he was present in a strictly advisory capacity, and that Colonel Stuart would retain operational authority in the area.

That was quickly put to the test, though, a short while later, as Alysande prepared to order an interloping aircraft shot out of the sky.

"Then you leave me no choice," Alysande had said, when the pilot of the private plane had refused to break away. She turned to the officer at her side, who was in communication with the fighter pilot. "Lieutenant, prepare to . . ."

"Colonel Stuart," Raphael had said in a stage whisper. "A moment of your time?"

Irritated, but knowing that the little troll had the authority to strip her of command if he so desired, Alysande had tossed the microphone to the lieutenant and stalked over to the man in black.

"Colonel . . ." Raphael began, and then tilted his head to one side. "May I call you Alysande?"

"I'd prefer you didn't," she answered coolly.

"Alysande," he went on with a smile, "I hate to interfere with your duties—and you're doing a superb job, let me state—but I feel compelled to point out that the gentleman to whom you've been speaking is not completely unknown to me."

"Yes?" Alysande raised an eyebrow, regarding the little man.

"Which is not to say that I know him personally, of course," Raphael continued, "but certain . . . elements . . . of Her Majesty's government have been aware of the activities of a Mr. Scott Summers, late of Salem Center, New York, for some time now."

"And what's this man done that's of interest to your lot?"

"Well, Alysande, have you ever heard . . . that is to say"—Raphael looked to either side, almost comically, as though checking for eavesdroppers—"have you ever heard of an organization calling itself the 'X-Men'?"

Alysande had merely sneered, an expression of distaste passing quickly across her features like a cloud drifting over the face of the moon. "Mutants."

Now, a short while later, Alysande stood on the beach, waiting for this Summers and his companions to arrive. She was curious to find out what their connection to all of this business was. So far as Her Majesty's government had been able to determine in recent hours, no one had ever sighted this strange alien city before this morning. It didn't appear on any maps, surveys, or satellite surveillance photos. For all that, it appeared, at the outset, to be unspeakably old, or it might just as well have been built overnight. What connection the city had with the impossibly fast flying object of the early morning hours, no one could say, but no one doubted for an instant that a connection existed.

So why was the leader of an international band of mutants—alternatively thought of as adventurers, heroes, or terrorists—flying here, and on *this* particular morning?

This Mr. Summers knew something about all of this, Alysande was convinced. And in short order, he'd share what he knew. Or Summers would, in turn, know Colonel Stuart's displeasure.

6

As Scott brought the *Blackbird* in for an amphibious landing, Logan tugged on a pair of leather gloves and settled his cowboy hat on his head. He glanced over at Kitty, who was perched nervously on the copilot's seat, her mask in her hands.

"Looks like we're doin' this one in civvies, darlin'," Logan said, checking to make sure the three parallel slits cut into the backs of his gloves were lined up. "No reason to go in masked."

"Yeah, I guess," Kitty said, a little uneasily. "I still cling hopefully to the notion of a 'secret identity,' you know. If it gets out that a kid from Deerfield is traipsing around the Atlantic with British marines, it's going to get a little difficult to explain to the folks."

"Don't worry, kid," Logan said with a smile. "I've had to wipe out all manner of records and such, covering our tracks before, and I can do it again, if need be."

Kitty replied with a halfhearted grin, and tucked her mask into the pocket of her blue jacket.

"I suppose," she said, shrugging. "At least my uniform passes as street clothes." She gestured to her blue jacket, light blue tights and leggings. "I'm not sure what street your usual brown-and-tan getup would pass on."

"Kid," Logan said, clamping a cigar butt between his teeth, "you obviously ain't been on all the streets I have."

Scott swiveled the pilot's chair around, having toggled the hatch open.

"Be ready for anything, you two," Scott said, stepping over to the slowly opening hatch. He wore a black sweater and jeans, his wide red glasses covering half his face. "We don't know what to expect from these people."

"Relax, Cyke," Logan said, coming to stand beside him. "Me and the Brits, we got a history. We won't have any trouble at all."

The hatch swung all the way open as Kitty came to stand between them.

"No sudden movements!" barked the marine standing just beyond the hatch, the barrel of his automatic rifle trained on them. Another half-dozen marines were at his side, their rifles likewise aimed and ready.

"Gee, Logan," Kitty said with a smirk. "The way you make friends, I don't know why I should have worried."

The way Logan saw it, he was on his best behavior.

Scott and Kitty probably didn't see it that way, but they always did tend to overreact. As for the marines? Well, it was pretty clear what *they* thought.

Logan had been the first to hit the ground, hopping down from the open hatch.

"Keep your hands where I can see them!" the young marine said.

"You mean *these* hands?" Logan answered, raising his fists.

"Lo-gan," Kitty said, an imploring tone in her voice.

"No talking," the marine barked. "We're to escort you to the colonel, but we've got orders to open fire if you refuse to follow our instructions."

"Look, bub," Logan answered, treating the soldier to a humorless smile, "I'll thank you not to wave that peashooter in my face, if you don't mind."

"Oi!" the marine answered, advancing, jabbing his rifle only inches from Logan's nose. "I said button it, you."

"Logan," Scott said warningly, reaching out to rest a hand on his shoulder.

"Just a second, Cyke," Logan said, and then exploded into motion.

With one hand he grabbed the marine's rifle, pulling it forward, yanking it from the marine's grip, and then he brought his other arm down elbow first, cracking it into the marine's neck and sending him sprawling onto the sand.

The other marines tightened their grips on their rifles, but Logan quickly tossed the rifle to the ground and raised his hands in a posture of surrender.

"Sorry about that, fellas," Logan said, smiling. "Reflex, I guess. Something about the way he was talking must have set me off. Now, take us to your leader, why don't you?"

The marines left standing glanced at one another, uncertain what to do next.

"You heard the man," Kitty said impatiently. "Let's go, already."

Logan glanced over at Scott, who scowled back at him.

"What?" Logan said innocently. "That was hardly even a love tap."

Without further incident, the marines led the three X-Men to the tent they'd set up as a makeshift command center. Inside, a statuesque woman in the uniform of a marine colonel waited with a short, unpresupposing man in a cheap black suit.

"Colonel Stuart?" said their marine escort, shouldering his rifle. "These are the individuals you wanted to see."

"Yes, yes," the woman said impatiently, waving them in. "We haven't got all day."

Scott moved to stand opposite the colonel, back straight as if he had something stuck up his backside, while Kitty found a folding chair to slump down into. Logan went over to lean against the tent's center pole, his arms crossed lightly over his chest.

The colonel took them in at a glance, and then looked to the small man in the black suit. "*These* are the infamous X-Men?"

Logan chuckled. "See, kiddo," he said to Kitty, "I told you not to worry about that whole secret identity business. Seems like someone already spoiled it for us, anyhow."

The colonel turned, and narrowed her gaze at Logan.

"So you'd be the Canadian operative Mr. Raphael was telling me about, then?"

"Could be," Logan said, fishing a toothpick out of his shirt pocket and clenching it between his teeth. "Depends on who Mr. Raphael is, I suppose."

"Ah, that would be me," said the man in the black suit, his voice as oily as the little hair he had left. "But it's just Raphael, if you please." He stepped forward, and extended a hand toward Logan.

Logan looked at the man's hand before him like it was a dead fish, his only movement to shift the toothpick from one side of his mouth to the other.

"Erm," Raphael said uneasily, trying to shift his attention to Scott, but Summers had his attention fixed on the colonel. Raphael then looked helplessly over at Kitty, who just shrugged in response. "Yes, well . . ." He backed away, stuffing his hands into his pants' pockets.

For his part, Logan was busy eyeing the colonel, as well.

She's a big one, and no doubt, he thought appreciatively. *She's got to be as tall as Petey, if she's an inch.*

Logan doubted she could turn into organic steel like Peter Rasputin, but she was an imposing figure, nonetheless. She hadn't moved since they'd walked in, her hands clasped at the small of her back, but Logan could tell by the way she stood that she was a trained fighter. She'd be something to see in a scrape, he was sure.

"In the interests of avoiding an international incident," the colonel now said, fixing the three X-Men with a hard stare, "I've been dissuaded from shooting you on the spot. But I'd very much like to know what a group of internationally infamous mutants are doing violating British airspace, and if I don't get the answers I'm after in short order, I might reconsider that decision."

"You know," Kitty said, sitting forward in her folding chair, "I'm not sure I like the way she said 'mutant.'" She glanced at Logan, who nodded.

"There's lots of bigots all over, kid," Logan said.

The colonel stiffened, lips curled, and Logan was glad to see that he'd gotten a reaction. So she *wasn't* made out of stone, after all.

"I'll have you know that I don't have a bigoted bone in my body," the colonel said hotly. "And if you don't believe me, I think you can ask your friend Mr. Cassidy, and he can set you right."

"Sean?" Scott said, taken aback.

"Yes," the colonel said. "Without going into unnecessary details"—she glanced over at the man called Raphael—"suffice it to say that there was a point at which I might have brought your 'Banshee' to account for a number of . . . legal questions . . . that plagued him, and I chose instead to put him at his liberty. Which is not to say that there wasn't unfounded prejudice against mutants involved in the incident, but that I was on the opposite side of that unfortunate line."

"Yeah, maybe," Kitty said, "but when was that? Years ago?"

The colonel's expression seemed to soften, but only for the briefest moment. "Years, and more."

"Well, what have you done for us lately?" Kitty said, crossing her arms over her chest. "I've been hearing rumors about the British rounding up mutant kids and putting them in special camps. Wouldn't know anything about *that,* would you, Colonel?"

"Now, see here," Raphael cut in haughtily. "The Warpies aren't mutants, regardless of what you might have read, and besides, any stories you might have heard were doubtless horrible, groundless exaggerations." He paused, and grinned, making an expansive gesture with his hands. "If anything," he went on, his tone conciliatory, "the British government has only the best interests of the children at heart."

"What?!" The colonel wheeled on Raphael, her mouth open in shock, and Logan could see that whatever the two Brits were to each other, they weren't friends. And if they were allies, they were uneasy ones, at best.

Raphael shifted uneasily under the colonel's hard gaze. "Colonel, perhaps we might discuss this at a later . . ."

"*Mister* Raphael," the colonel said sharply, cutting him off. "Is it true that the RCX is really rounding up *children*?"

"Well," Raphael said, suddenly the epitome of composure, "the issues aren't nearly as black-and-white as they might sound."

Logan realized that the slightly bumbling, stuttering act to which they'd been treated was just that—an act. This Raphael, whoever he might be, was a cool customer, in complete control of his reactions.

Before the colonel could do more than fume, Kitty interrupted.

"RCX?" she said, sitting up in her chair. She turned to Logan, then glanced at Scott. "Hey, I've heard Betsy talk about these guys. They're some kind of British spookshow, totally top secret."

"Ah," Raphael said. He took a small notebook from his jacket pocket, and scribbled in it briefly with a pencil stub. He looked up under his brows at Kitty. "That would be Betsy *Braddock,* would it?"

"Why?" Kitty said, jumping to her feet. "You planning on putting *her* in a camp, too?"

"Hold on, now," Scott said, placing a hand on Kitty's shoulder.

"No, you hold on, Cyke," Logan said, pushing off the tent pole and stepping forward. "I'm not too crazy about the idea of anybody put in a camp against their will. I've seen it before, just like I've seen friends turned into walking skeletons, and worse."

The colonel looked at Logan, her expression softening momentarily. "The war . . ."

"I've been in more wars than you can count, lady," Logan said, "but don't kid yourself it only happens in wartime."

"Look, everybody," Raphael said, raising his hands, "perhaps we've gotten off on the wrong foot here . . ."

Logan took a step forward, adamantium claws popped out of the backs of both fists.

"Bub, if you've got a wrong foot, I'd be happy to get rid of it for you."

"Logan!" Scott barked.

Before Logan could respond, a marine appeared at the open flap of the tent.

"Colonel Stuart," he said, snapping off a crisp salute. "I think there's something out here you should see."

The colonel treated Raphael to a cold glance, then turned to follow the marine out onto the beach.

Scott didn't waste a moment, but followed close on the colonel's heels.

Kitty hopped up and followed them, glancing back over her shoulder. "If you're going to kill that guy, Logan, hurry up and get it over with."

His gaze on her retreating back, Raphael chuckled, but the laughter stopped when he turned and saw Logan's hard expression.

"She was joking?" Raphael said, and Logan thought he might see genuine fear somewhere behind the spook's carefully cultivated facade. "Right?"

Logan glowered at the man in black for a long moment. "Another time, bub."

The claws retracting back into his forearms, he turned and followed the others out of the tent, leaving Raphael alone.

7

The marines were spread out in defensive positions up and down the beach, looking toward the alien city, unsure whether to shoot or start running, and waiting for orders one way or the other. Kitty couldn't blame them. Her own fight or flight instincts were currently duking it out in her gut.

There were a half dozen of the circular platforms, each about ten or fifteen feet across, skimming over the water toward them.

That they were moving without any noise, or any visible means of propulsion or support, came as no particular shock to Kitty. She'd seen more amazing things than *that* in the last few years. Heck, her best friends included a guy who could turn into solid metal and a girl whose skin could absorb memories and abilities on contact.

What *was* surprising, though, was to see what was riding on the platforms. Or rather, *who*.

People.

Just that. Not big bug-eyed monsters, or sentient robots, or humanoids with feathers instead of hair, not

squishy piles of goo, or colonies of space whales, or
giant insect things. Just people.

Sure, each of them had precisely as much hair on
their heads as Professor X—which was to say, none at
all—but that could be chalked up to simple fashion.
Faulty genetics, at best. But aside from that minor characteristic, not a one of them would be unable to walk
through the Salem Center mall without drawing comment or attention.

Well, their clothing might draw *some* comment or
attention, Kitty supposed. The bright colors and oddly
geometric patterns looked more like something out of
an arabesque fantasy than the typical attire of a
Westchester County shopper, but then it wasn't so
long ago that shoulder pads and *neon* colors were all
the rage, for god's sake, so it wasn't *that* out of the ordinary.

Of course, typical Westchester County shoppers
didn't arrive at the mall in high-speed UFOs, or skim
through the department stores on big floating platforms, so Kitty had to admit there was still *something* unusual about these people.

But still and all, they *were* people.

The nearest of the flying platforms stopped just
short of the atoll's beach, hovering in midair, and Kitty
was able to get a better look. Two men and three
women were standing on its featureless surface, each of
them looking to be somewhere between their mid-
twenties and their mid-thirties.

The other platforms behind them veered off to either side, as though to circle around the small island.

The lead platform's five riders regarded everyone on the beach, silently.

And then . . .

Nothing happened.

Kitty thought she was going to scream. The bald platform riders were silent; the marines were silent; the colonel and the balding spook were silent; even Scott and Logan were silent. Kitty was tempted to shout, but knew better. She'd learned long before that when entering an unknown situation it was far better to keep your eyes and ears open and your mouth shut. But what if everyone else had learned the same lesson? Would you just stand around forever, silently *looking* at each other?

The colonel motioned to one of her men. When he drew near, she said in a low voice, "Lieutenant, begin passive and active scans of those humanoids on all bandwidths and frequencies."

Before the marine could reply, a voice range out in Kitty's head.

"Oh, so you use *verbal* communications? How . . . quaint."

Kitty winced. The mind-call was easily twice as "loud" as the ones Professor Xavier used to send out. From the expressions on everyone around her on the beach, she could tell she wasn't the only one on the receiving end, either.

"Please," blasted the mind-voice again, "allow me a moment to scan your language centers . . ."

An instant later, one of the bald platform riders stepped forward, opened his mouth, and addressed everyone on the beach in clear, unaccented English.

"This one bears the name Vox Tertius, servitor unaugmented clade, of the House Nine-Mirror-Eclipse, preeminent among the Collective. This one bears greetings in the name of the Kh'thon, supreme masters of Earth."

Okay, Kitty though. *So maybe that's a little surprising . . .*

8

Colonel Stuart stepped forward to address the strange figure calling himself Vox Tertius, but before she could speak Scott pushed ahead of her.

"Where are our friends?" he demanded, stabbing a finger at the platform. "What have you done with Lee Forrester and her crew?"

"Summers," the colonel said warningly, in a low voice, but kept her eyes on Vox Tertius, waiting to see how he responded.

The figures on the platform exchanged confused glances, and then Vox Tertius's eyes widened, and he turned to look back down at Scott and the others on the beach.

"Oh, you refer to the individuals we seized," he said.

"Yes," Scott managed through clenched teeth, having to fight the urge to lift his ruby quartz glasses and give these guys the full brunt of one of his optic blasts.

Get it together, Summers, Scott thought. *Logan's supposed to be the one with the berserker rage, right? Not you. What is this reaction about, anyway? Lee's in your past, isn't she? Or she's supposed to be. You're with Jean now, aren't you?*

Scott's musings were cut short when Vox Tertius replied, nodding serenely.

"The individuals you mention have been taken in hand for entering areas restricted to all servitors who do not bear appropriate proof of their master's permissions." Vox paused for a moment, and glanced at one of his fellows before looking back to Scott. "Do you claim these individuals as your own?"

"Listen," Colonel Stuart said, "I'm here as a representative of Her Majesty's . . ."

"Yes," Scott said brusquely, interrupting. "They are our friends."

"Ah," Vox Tertius said, nodding. "Well, it would appear that the observance of protocols has lapsed somewhat in our absence, but such is to be expected." He smiled indulgently, as though addressing misbehaving children. Tilting his head to one side, he said, "To which house and clade do we address ourselves?"

Colonel Stuart and Scott both began to answer at the same time, but Stuart gave him a hard stare, conspicuously lowering her hand to the pistol holstered on her hip.

"Listen, Summers," she hissed quietly, "this is a potential first-contact scenario, and I am *not* about to let it be handled by amateurs. We'll get your people back, but we'll do it *my* way." Then, in a louder voice, she turned and answered Vox Tertius. "I'm afraid that I don't understand the question. Can you clarify?"

Vox Tertius sighed dramatically. "Which master-strain do you serve?"

"Master-strain?" Kitty said.

When Vox Tertius spoke again, his words were slow and deliberate, as though he were addressing an animal, or an imbecile. "To which House of the Kh'thon do you owe fealty?"

Colonel Stuart opened her mouth to speak, closed it again, and then turned to Raphael, who shrugged.

"What the flamin' heck is a Kh'thon?" Wolverine said, voicing the question foremost on Scott's mind.

Vox Tertius screwed his face up, looking perplexed and more than a little alarmed. As he stood silently regarding those gathered on the beach, one of the women behind him on the platform stepped forward, lightly touching his elbow.

"Vox Tertius," the woman said in the same unaccented English, "the servitors in the city of Dis report no sign of habitation, and considerable entropic damage to the city's systems and services. Further, we detect no Kh'thonic emanations from anywhere on the planet."

Vox Tertius looked from the woman to the people on the beach, shocked. When he spoke, he addressed her, but kept his eyes on them. "Then this world has been entrusted solely to the keeping of servitors?"

The other male platform rider stepped forward, and pointed a long, slender finger toward Logan. "And clearly, Vox Tertius, some of the servitors are augmented phenotypes, perhaps even Exemplar-class."

"This . . ." Vox Tertius began, shaking his head. "This won't do at all."

Without another word, he gave a brief sweeping motion with his hand, and the platform spun around and sped back toward the city. The other platforms followed close behind, skimming just above the waves.

"Well," Kitty said, stepping forward and draping an arm over Scott's shoulder. "For a first-contact situation, I think that could have gone a little better, don't you?"

9

Bloody cheek, Alysande Stuart thought, but didn't allow herself the luxury of responding. If these so-called X-Men hadn't interfered, she was convinced she'd have had this mess sorted by now. Instead, the situation was deteriorating quickly.

"Corporal!" Alysande barked. "Initiate airborne pursuit."

A few yards up the beach, a marine wearing a bulky metal pack on his back snapped off a crisp salute, and turned to two others, each wearing an identical pack.

"You heard the colonel," the corporal said. "Up and at 'em."

Without another word, the three marines unshipped their assault rifles, took three running steps toward the shoreline, and then *leapt* into the air. Gouts of blue flame blazed from the metal packs, and the three marines shot off, jetting after the retreating platforms.

"What the heck . . . ?" the American girl named Kitty said in amazement.

Clasping her hands behind her back, Alysande glanced over at the girl. "You'll find that Her Majesty's government is quite prepared for any eventuality, young lady. If you could content yourself with letting the professionals handle this, we'd have matters well in hand in short order."

"You think?" the man called Logan said, and pointed with the stub of his cigar toward the alien city.

As the platforms reached the city itself, having crossed the mile of open water separating it from the atoll, a shimmering energy field sprang up. In the afternoon light it flickered multicolored, like a frenetic rainbow.

The jetpack-wearing marine in the lead had very nearly reached the city himself, only lengths from the energy field.

"Colonel?" A lieutenant, in his hands a radio connecting him to the airborne marines, looked to Alysande questioningly.

Just then the marine slammed into the energy field, and was instantly engulfed in coruscating energy that danced over his body like lightning trapped in a bottle.

"Break away!" Alysande shouted, and spun around to the lieutenant with the radio. "Order them to break away, now!"

The lieutenant immediately began relaying the orders over the radio waves in breathless tones, but it was already too late.

The second jetpack-wearing marine had already flown too close, like Icarus brushing too near the sun, and as he attempted to veer away slammed bodily into the energy field, and was consumed by the same coruscating energy as his companion, like an insect caught in the blue light of a bug zapper.

The third marine, for his part, managed to change direction just before reaching the field, and jetted back toward the atoll at speed.

"Damn," Alysande swore under her breath, hands tightened into white-knuckled fists.

"Weren't your fault, Colonel," Logan said, in all sincerity. "There was no way of knowing they'd be able to throw up a defensive shield that quick."

"Perhaps," Alysande said through gritted teeth, "but my role is to anticipate and account for the unexpected, and I neither request nor desire your permission to fail in that obligation."

Logan shrugged, and blew out of a cloud of cigar smoke that hung around his head like a halo. "Suit yourself."

"Colonel Stuart," Scott Summers said, hurrying to her side. Alysande noticed that he'd replaced his red sunglasses with some sort of yellow wraparound visor, his eyes faint red glows behind a narrow red lens. "My people have experience dealing with these sorts of things, and with all due respect I think your men are out of their depth."

The third of the jetpack-wearing marines was now landing on the beach, looking shaken.

"We are *marines,* Mr. Summers," Alysande snapped back. "I think you'll find that, land, sea, or air, we are well trained to handle whatever depths we might encounter."

"Excuse me? Colonel?" Raphael was approaching,

coming from the direction of the helicopter transports that had carried Alysande and her men to the island. He carried in his hands a device the size of a portable computer. "I've just had a peek at the scanner readings your men did of the . . . individuals . . . we so recently encountered."

"Yes?" Alysande replied impatiently. "What of it?"

"Well," Raphael said, tilting his head to one side, "there's definitely some strange aspects of their physiology, no doubt about it, which at first guess I'd take to be surgical alterations. But in terms of genetics, well . . ."

The man in the black suit trailed off.

"Well, spit it out, man!" Alysande barked.

"Genetically," Raphael answered, "they're nothing more unusual than baseline *Homo sapiens.*" He glanced across the water at the alien city, now safely ensconced inside its dome of coruscating energy. "They're human."

Well, of course they are, Alysande thought. *They* looked *human, didn't they?* But then she reminded herself that humans, in her everyday experience, don't typically fly out of the sky from parts unknown in impossibly fast spacecraft, take up residence in previously unknown nightmarish cities in the middle of the Bermuda Triangle, and issue cryptic pronouncements while riding atop levitating metal platforms. Which, taken all together, suggested there might be something unusual about them being strictly human, after all.

"Look!" Kitty shouted, pointing at the sky.

Alysande looked up, shielding her eyes against the afternoon sun, and saw a glint of silver.

"Another craft," relayed the lieutenant with the radio gear, hand to his headphones. "The carrier group reports that it's on an approach vector, traveling at supersonic speeds but quickly decelerating." He listened carefully, and then added, "Trajectory suggests it just came in from high orbit."

Between one eyeblink and the next, the glint of silver became a large craft, easily the size of a troop carrier helicopter. Without making a sound, it stopped dead in midair directly over the city, just outside the reach of the defensive force field. Though constructed of some smooth, unmarked metal, its shape was almost organic in design, looking like an internal organ removed under dissection, or some microscopic bacterium.

Alysande turned to her second in command, standing nearby. "Major! Tell the men that I want all safeties off, all weapons hot, but that they are to fire only on my command."

"Yes, sir," the major snapped back, taking to his heels to relay the orders down the line.

"What's it doing up there, anyway?" Kitty asked, squinting up at the strangely shaped craft.

As if in answer, the craft rotated slightly in midair. Then, as Alysande and the others on the beach watched, it began to *unfold*—that was the only word for it—to unfold, sections opening up and curling back, looking more like the petals of a blossoming flower than anything man-made.

Without warning, from the top of the blossoming vessel, five figures emerged. They were all roughly human-shaped, but while each was as hairless as the platform riders had been, there the resemblance ended.

"Blimey," Alysande swore under her breath.

They were flying under their own power, for starters. That was the first thing one noticed. And they were coming straight for them.

As they drew nearer, more details emerged. All of them were dressed in strange, metallic formfitting clothing, but their appearances were anything but uniform. One had wings; another seemed to be covered in a sheath of green flame; another seemed to be made entirely of stone; still another had pointed ears and blue fur.

The lead figure, a massive, heavily muscled male whose skin appeared to be made of highly reflective metal—organic steel?—hovered in midair above the atoll, addressing Alysande and the others on the beach.

"I am Invictus Prime of the Exemplar, augmented clade, and you are hereby ordered to vacate this area."

"On what authority?" Alysande shouted back.

The steel-skinned figure regarded her coolly before answering.

"The Exemplar carry out the will of the Kh'thon Collective, former occupants and rightful owners of the planet Earth."

Before Alysande could voice a response, or give orders to her men, Raphael tapped her on the shoulder. He stuck the scanning device in front of her face. "Now *that's* interesting," he said, an unexpectedly jolly tone to his voice. "These new blokes? They're *mutants!*"

Scott knew the attack was coming an instant before the Exemplar exploded into motion. It came of fighting for his life on an weekly basis—if not more frequently—since he was a teenager. A life of facing down genocidal maniacs, alien invaders, evil mutants, and more had given him an almost preternatural danger sense, allowing him to anticipate an opponent's movements, and to have a counterattack ready at a moment's notice.

In most instances, that meant that Scott was able to win a fight almost before it had begun.

In this instance, it simply meant that he got to stay alive for another few moments.

The figure calling himself Invictus Prime, the sun glinting off his steel-like skin—*so much like Colossus,* Scott thought—simply motioned with his hand, and the five figures hovering in midair behind him rushed forward like a wave breaking on a rocky shore.

Scott didn't hesitate an instant, tapping the side of his visor and widening the aperture of the ruby-quartz lens.

His eyes exposed, a wide scarlet beam of concussive force lanced from the visor, catching the nearest of the

Exemplar in her midriff. She had wings sprouting from her back, gray and leathery like those of a bat, and long talons on her fingers.

Scott didn't waste time waiting to see the effects of his blast, but swung his head around and sent another beam lancing toward the male figure wreathed in a sheath of green flame. The impact of the optic blast sent the green torch tumbling backward, but before Scott could sight on another target, he was knocked off his feet by a beam of force that caught him in the chest.

The wind knocked out of him, he struggled into a sitting position, and looked up to see the steel-skinned figure of Invictus Prime regarding him, white energy dancing at the corner of his eyes.

"Your blasts are unfocused, your aim undisciplined," Invictus Prime said, his tone haughty. "Shall I demonstrate proper form?"

Beams of solid white light shot from the Exemplar's eyes, and Scott managed to roll to one side just before they blasted into the ground where he'd been, kicking up a huge cloud of sand.

Scott scrambled to his feet, parrying with an optic blast of his own that missed Invictus Prime only by inches, and began looking for cover. He hoped the others were faring better than he.

"Quickly now," Alysande shouted as the last of the marines raced toward the transport. "Pick up the pace or we'll leave you here with *that* lot."

The rotors had already been turning on the transport by the time Alysande had ordered a retreat, her marines laying down suppressing fire as they broke off in twos and threes and raced to the helicopter. Now, as the last of them climbed aboard, she motioned to the pilot, who gave a thumbs-up and prepared to take off.

"Discretion here," Raphael said, as Alysande strapped into the jump seat beside him, "being the better part of valor?"

"We'll be back," Alysande said, keeping her tone level, "and with reinforcements, and we'll see to this alien incursion, once and for all."

"If they *are* aliens." Raphael's tone was suggestive, insinuating, but Alysande refused to rise to the bait. "And what of the X-Men?"

Alysande glanced out the helicopter's windscreen as the transport lifted off the ground. Back on the beach, the two groups of mutants were in pitched battle, and seemed to have forgotten all about the *humans* formerly among them.

"The X-Men can bloody well look after themselves."

Logan hadn't forgotten about Alysande and her men. He had been busy keeping these Exemplar jokers busy while the marines beat a hasty retreat, and now that their transport was speeding away from the atoll, and the battle, he allowed himself a little grin, biting down hard on his cigar.

Now that the bystanders are out of the way, Logan thought, *I can cut loose and have a little bit of fun.*

Logan saw that Scott was busy swapping optic blasts with the big metal guy, and the flying chick and the green torch had both gone off somewhere, which left the other two for him. Both were female, at least as near as Logan could tell, and stood on the sandy beach a few short yards away from Logan's position.

One was built like a brick house—literally. She was maybe twice Logan's height, and looked to be made of gray stone, like living granite. She looked like the Thing's older sister.

The other was closer to Logan's height, but lithe, built like a dancer. She had pointed ears, yellow eyes, and blue fur, with long bony talons growing from her fingertips, and hopped from one foot to another like an acrobat.

Without preamble, the blue acrobat leaped toward Logan, talons raking the air.

Logan, with a minimum expenditure of energy and motion, sidestepped the acrobat's attack, grabbing hold of one of her forearms and using her own momentum to swing her around, hurling her through the air.

"Alley oop," Logan said casually.

The acrobat, though, yellow eyes flashing, twisted in midair, and landed effortlessly on her feet a short distance away, arms held out slightly to her sides for balance.

"Hey, darlin'." Logan smiled at the acrobat, and raised his hands in front of him. "You showed me yours. How 'bout I show you mine?"

From the back of his own fists popped adamantium claws, each like a tiny, unbreakable sword, capable of cutting through anything short of adamantium itself.

"Degenerate," the blue acrobat spat, and bared pointed teeth. "I see now I shouldn't have gone easy on you."

"Desist, sibling," the brick said, motioning with a hand the size of a shovel. "Allow me to deal with this mongrel."

Before Logan could react, the brick rushed forward.

Cripes, he thought in the split second allowed him, *how can something so big move so fast?!*

And then the brick plowed into him with the speed and force of a freight train.

Logan skidded into the sand a few yards away. It would take a bigger blow than that to break his near invulnerable adamantium-laced bones, but a couple more hits like that and his healing factor would be working overtime.

"Okay," he said in a low voice, rising to a crouch, claws out and ready, "so maybe this won't be quite as easy as I thought."

Scott was on the beach, and the winged woman, the green torch, and Invictus Prime were converging on him. His optic blasts were nearly spent, the most recent beams carrying little more impact than a rose-colored flashlight. It would be only a moment or two before his reserves of energy replenished themselves, provided he lived that long.

"To think," Invictus Prime said, looking down his nose at Scott, "that the once proud Earth has fallen into the clutching grasp of such as this."

"Oh, yeah?" came a voice blaring over a loudspeaker. "Well . . . suck it."

The three Exemplar turned in the direction of the voice and were caught completely unawares as the nose of a Lockheed RS-150 rammed into them at speed, knocking them for a loop.

The *Blackbird* stopped short, hovering in midair just above Scott, the sound dampeners on the engines acting at full capacity, with only a whisper of noise escaping.

"Well?" Kitty Pryde was visible through the windscreen at the controls, her voice reverberating over the plane's external loudspeakers.

"'Suck it'?" Scott asked, climbing to his feet and dusting off the legs of his jeans.

"Okay, so I choked under pressure," Kitty answered. "Now, will you guys come on, already? The meter's running here."

Without sparing a glance to see what had become of the Exemplar, Scott leapt up into the open hatch of the *Blackbird.* As he maneuvered into the copilot's seat, Logan lurched through the hatch behind him, his face and arms crisscrossed with deep cuts and scrapes.

"I'm not usually one for runnin' from a scrape, but I know when I'm outmatched. So what you waitin' for, kiddo?" Logan said impatiently. "Punch it!"

The hatch swung shut automatically, and Kitty gripped the controls as the plane shot up into the afternoon sky, steadily climbing toward Mach 4.

Invictus Prime hung motionless in midair, watching the little craft zipping away toward the horizon. The rest of his Exemplar cell gathered around him, taking up their accustomed positions.

"They were more powerful than we had been led to imagine," said the winged woman.

"And more skilled," said the one with the skin like gray granite.

"But still not a match for us," said the blue-furred acrobat, yellow eyes narrowed.

"Perhaps," said the green torch. "But they were few, and we do not know in what numbers they infest this world."

"We should have pursued them," the blue-furred acrobat said angrily. "We could have made short work of them."

"Enough!" The voice of Invictus Prime rang like a bell. "We have done as ordered. The time will come to attend to these degenerates. And soon."

Once upon a time, Magneto had made this room his bedchamber. Now, it was a prison cell.

Lee liked it better the old way.

Their captors, it seemed, were none too pleased that others had taken up residence in the city before their arrival. Before Lee and her crew had been locked away in this high tower room, the strange hairless beings who'd captured them had made a show of removing every tapestry and stick of furniture that Magneto had brought to these strange, unearthly buildings. From the high, narrow window of their cell, Lee could even now see the pillar of smoke rising from the courtyard far below, where their captors had set everything of Magneto's to the torch.

Lee had stayed in the city as well, a time or two, first with Scott, then with Magneto, and then on her own, after she'd lost touch with both of them. Lee had been fascinated with the city, and with the beings who'd originally built it, sometime in distant prehistory. Based on the statuary that covered the city, and the shape and dimensions of the doors and corridors, she'd had to conclude that whatever the original inhabitants of the city had been, they weren't people. At least not by any definition she was accustomed to using.

But now, all this time later, she found herself back again, and the prisoner of men and women who, though hairless, silent, and strange, were nonetheless inarguably *people*.

There were six of them locked in the otherwise empty chamber. Lee and Paolo sat in one corner, while Richie, Jose, and Merrick clustered around Frank in another.

Lee didn't have to possess the mutant ability to read minds to know precisely what Frank and the others were thinking.

This was all Lee's fault.

Lee couldn't find it within herself to disagree. It *was* her fault. Had she spent so much time rubbing elbows with men and women who had the ability to move mountains with a glance that she'd forgotten that she was just a regular human being? Just a person, with only the strengths—and weaknesses—that entailed.

Lee had been watching their captors carefully, though, both when they were captured in the courtyard and when they were escorted here to their makeshift cell, and Lee suspected that they, too, shared all those same strengths. And, more to the point, all the same weaknesses.

She tried to outline her plans for escape to the others, but they were having none of it.

"Look, *Cap'n*," Frank had said, managing to turn the syllables of the title into a curse, "we got this far followin' your suggestions, so maybe you'll excuse us if we don't hurry up and listen to the next brilliant idea to fall out of your head, m'kay?"

And that was that. Frank had sulked back to his corner, his little coterie of crewmen gathered tight around him, and fell to whispering plans of their own. Paolo, for his part, had just propped his chin on his hands, looking older and more tired than Lee had ever seen him. At one point, Frank raised his voice just loud enough and long enough for Lee to hear the word *rifle*, and beside her Paolo blanched, averting his gaze.

She knew the old man blamed himself for letting their captors get hold of their only weapon, but what choice had he had? One of the bald UFO people had pulled some sort of crystal rod out of his pocket, pointed it at the rifle, and the next thing anyone knew the shark gun had gone white hot. Paolo's hands were still blistered and burned from the heat of it, but Frank and his cronies hardly cared about that. Like Lee, Paolo made for a convenient scapegoat, a target toward which they could pour their anxieties and fear, redirected as aggression and blame.

Then, suddenly, they had another target, if only briefly.

The door to the chamber slid open, with a whisper of stone upon stone. The mechanism responsible completely eluded Lee, as it had in all her previous visits. One moment the door was closed, and the wall looked unbroken and smooth; the next moment part of the stone had collapsed back into itself, revealing an open doorway.

A slim, hairless figure stood in the opening, regarding them serenely. He looked to be about thirty, but there was something about his eyes that suggested a far greater age. He was dressed in a loose-fitting robe of deep purple, with scarlet bands around his wrists and ankles, his feet and hands bare. In his hand, he held a crystal rod that was all too familiar.

Wordlessly, the figure advanced into the room, seeming more to glide across the floor than walk, so graceful were his motions. As he approached, another figure was revealed behind him, staying in the corridor beyond the doorway. It appeared to be a woman, but Lee couldn't be sure; with large eyes in a round, wide face, no ears, and only two slits for a nose, the figure regarded them with an unreadable expression.

"Get 'im!" Frank yelled, without warning, and launched himself into the air and at the purple-robed figure.

"Wait!" Lee shouted.

With a somewhat disinterested air, the robed figure raised the crystal rod fractionally, pointing its end at Frank. But while the movement was slight, the results were dramatic.

Blinding white light leapt from the rod's tip, and Frank was sent tumbling head over heels, slamming into the far wall with a thud. He slid down to the ground, alive but only semiconscious, moaning softly.

"This one requires to know which of you is the leader," the robed figure said, speaking in soft, gentle tones.

Richie, Jose, and Merrick looked at Frank, moaning

insensate against the far wall, then turned to look back at Lee.

She began to rise, but Paolo spoke up first. "I am," he said, climbing unsteadily to his feet. "What of it?"

Lee wasn't sure whether to expect some kind of "I am Spartacus" moment, but the other crewmen averted their eyes and stayed resolutely on the ground, so it looked like the competition would be pretty light.

"No," Lee said, climbing to her feet and laying a hand on Paolo's shoulder. "I'm the captain."

Lee stepped forward, planting her hands on her hips, and narrowed her eyes at the robed figure.

"You are the leader, then?" he asked serenely.

"Yes. I'm responsible for bringing these men here." She planted her hands on her hips. "Now, just what do you want with us? Who are you people, anyway?"

"Please excuse this one," the robed figure said, bobbing his bald head slightly. "This one had only now been instilled with the ability to communicate in your tongue, and some of your conceptual structures are still problematic." He paused, and then added, "People, did you say?"

Lee raised an eyebrow. "Right. Who are you?"

"Ah," the robed figure said. "I am Vox Septimus, servitor unaugmented clade, of the House Nine-Mirror-Eclipse, preeminent among the Collective." In response to Lee's blank stare, he added, "Merely a humble servant of the masters of Earth, the Kh'thon."

"The who, now?" Paolo asked, stepping forward to stand beside Lee.

"The Kh'thon, of course," the man named Vox Septimus said, as though it were the simplest thing in the world. "The Kh'thon were the original sentient inhabitants of this planet, though there is some debate among their servitors whether they originated here or on some other world or plane. This city, called Dis, was once one of their strongholds."

"So you're one of these Kh'thon things, then?" Lee asked.

Vox Septimus's eyes opened wide, and he let out a short, loud bark of laughter. "*This one?* Oh, gracious no. This one is simply one such as you, an unaugmented servitor, descendant of those first raised up from among the other animals to serve the needs of the Kh'thon."

"Where in the what now?" Paolo said, brows knitted.

"The distant ancestors of us all were subsentient organisms native to this biosphere," Vox Septimus continued. "As they had need for such, the Kh'thon altered the genetics of a strain of subsentients, creating the first servitors. This one, and you as well, are made in that same phenotype."

Lee opened her mouth, then closed it again. She thought she understood what the strange man was saying, but if she *did,* she didn't like it.

"The Kh'thon are, of course, near immortal," Vox Septimus went on, "and aeons ago a contingent of them grew weary of their perhaps too comfortable existence on Earth, and decided to explore the distant reaches of the galaxy. Dozens of millennia passed, and at long last those Kh'thon explorers have decided to return home, to rejoin their earthbound brethren.

The journey has been long, but at last they have arrived. However, in the intervening millennia, it appears that the Kh'thon who remained on Earth have departed for other worlds themselves, or for other planes of existence, or perhaps migrated on to some more advanced form of being. Whatever the reason for their departure, they evidently left their servants behind, who have since multiplied uncontrollably, and now run rampant over the planet."

No, that clinched it. Lee *knew* she didn't like what the strange man was saying.

"But as though matters were not already bad enough," Vox Septimus continued, "it now appears that some of these errant servitors have been triggered, without the control of a Kh'thon master."

Lee regarded him through narrowed eyes. "Triggered?"

"Yes," Vox Septimus said, growing impatient. "The randomizing element in their genome activated, secondary and tertiary mutagenic characteristics allowed to come to the fore. Some are even . . . *Exemplar* class." An expression of extreme distaste twisted his lip, as though he'd just smelled something horrible. "To think of augmented servitors, running rampant." He shook all over, like someone had just walked over his grave. "It is anathema, the height of blasphemy."

Lee shook her head slowly.

"I don't buy any of this," she said, keeping her tone level. "I can't accept that humanity is little more than stray pets for inhuman aliens who moved out hundreds of thousands of years ago."

Vox Septimus shrugged. "Your opinions on the matter are of no special importance. It is the truth."

Lee thought for a moment. "So what do you want with us anyway?"

"Ah," Vox Septimus said, nodding slightly. "Yes. It has been given to this one and another"—he gestured to the large-eyed, earless woman still standing in the corridor beyond the doorway—"to discover how best to communicate to the current inhabitants of Earth a simple message."

Lee glanced at Paolo, who cast back a worried look.

"What sort of message?" Lee asked.

"Only this," Vox Septimus said. "That the Kh'thon have returned, and will now put their home in order."

12

Elizabeth Braddock wasn't at all sure what she'd gotten herself into. It had been only a few days since she'd accepted the invitation to come and live at the Xavier mansion, and while everyone had welcomed her with open arms, she couldn't help but feel like an outsider.

She'd accepted the invitation, in large part, because she didn't have anywhere else to turn. Betsy had possessed her psi talents for years, and even though she'd put them to use a time or two in the service of queen and country, she still felt like a novice. She had tremendous potential—or so she'd been told—but so far, Betsy herself had seen precious little evidence of it.

Betsy knew she was no hero, as much as she'd tried. Her brother, Brian? Now, *he* was a hero. True blue and courageous, no question about it. But for all her ability to peer into the minds of others, to peek momentarily into the future, Betsy had ended up too often a victim, someone to be rescued by others.

Most recently, she was rescued by students of the Xavier school.

It had been a year since Betsy was taken by the extradimensional slavemaster known only as Mojo and forced to cavort for his pleasure. Brian had searched for her for the better part of a year, and then managed to get himself captured, in the process. In the end, Doug Ramsey and a handful of other Xavier students had managed to rescue Betsy and her brother.

What little remained of her old life back in England had crumbled to dust in the long months she'd been away, and Betsy found herself with no compelling reason to return. When she'd been invited to come and live at the Xavier mansion, to study with the X-Men and learn how better to use her powers to protect herself and help others, she'd jumped at the task. She'd had visions of studies, and exercises, and careful training. Things like that Danger Room down in the sublevels, where she'd watched Kitty Pryde fight gangsters and giant holographic robots that morning.

What she hadn't foreseen, however, was that before she'd even unpacked her bags, she'd be sitting with the world-hopping X-Men in the tastefully appointed library, hearing the details of an alien encounter.

Scott Summers, Kitty Pryde, and Logan had left the mansion in a rush only a few hours before, flying off over the waters of Breakstone Lake in their sleek, jet-black spy plane. Now, they were back, more than a little worse for wear, with an unbelievable story to share.

"Unglaublich!" said the blue-skinned man named Kurt Wagner, code name Nightcrawler, who perched on the arm of the couch, his prehensile tail swaying slightly behind him like a charmed snake.

"You took the words right outta my mouth, sugah,"

said the woman known only as Rogue. She ran a gloved hand through her white-streaked hair.

Kitty was curled up in a big reading chair, her legs folded under her, a steaming cup of coffee in her hands. Logan was stretched out on the couch, his feet propped up on a low coffee table—which to Betsy's untrained eye looked to be a priceless antique, its value no doubt only slightly decreased by the scuff marks of Logan's sand-crusted boots. Scott, for his part, paced impatiently back and forth in front of the fireplace, his hands behind his back.

"Enough of this jawin' already," Logan said, taking a deep sip from his bottled beer. "The only reason to turn tail and run was to come back for reinforcements, and now that everybody's back from Scotland we oughta load up and head back there, already."

Scott opened his mouth to say something, but quickly shut it and continued his pacing.

Betsy had no desire to read anyone's mind without their permission, unless circumstances truly demanded, but whatever was going through Scott's head was so intense that stray thoughts bled off him like heat off a stove. Without even trying to peer into Scott's consciousness, Betsy knew that he was tempted to do just as Logan suggested, but that long years of training and experience demanded that he have a more complete picture of the situation before charging in half-cocked.

Even after a year as a mind-slave of an extradimensional impresario, Betsy felt more than a little out of her depth with all this discussion of aliens.

"Isn't it possible," she said, raising her hand tentatively, like the new kid in class asking the teacher a question, "that this all mightn't be some kind of misunderstanding? Couldn't we just *reason* with these aliens?"

"We got a mighty good taste of the aliens' reasoning style, darlin'," Logan said with a sneer. "It seems to come at the end of a fist, and punctuated by death rays. So really, thanks, but no thanks."

"Look," Kitty said, putting her coffee cup down on a side table and swinging her feet to the floor. "I think everyone is missing the point here. These *aren't* aliens. They're *Homo sapiens sapiens* and *Homo sapiens superior.*"

"What about these . . . Kh'thon?" Rogue asked.

"Whatever the flippin' heck *they* are." Logan finished off the last of his beer, and tossed the empty bottle into the corner.

Scott stopped his pacing, and regarded the others, his expression hard. "Focus, people. We've got a problem, and we need a solution."

"The problem being Captain Forrester and her crew, *nicht wahr?*" Kurt rubbed his chin with one of his oversize fingers, and Betsy tried hard not to stare. As many odd creatures and beings as she'd dealt with in recent years, she still found it difficult to get used to six fingers, six toes, a prehensile tail, and blue fur.

Which, come to that, reminded her of something.

"Um, if you don't mind?" Betsy raised her hand again, and Scott and the others turned to her. "From your description of these . . . Exemplar, it sounds as if they might be a little . . . familiar?"

Beside her on the couch, Logan narrowed his eyes, but nodded slightly.

"Like familiar, how, sugah?"

"Well, Rogue," Betsy said, and placed her hands on her knees. "It's a little untoward and out of the ordinary, I know, but if Scott, Kitty, and Logan wouldn't mind, I could show everyone what I mean by sharing their memories of the Exemplars telepathically."

Kitty merely shrugged. "Sure, take whatever you need." Betsy could tell that she had been around telepaths for a long time, and had never learned to fear them.

"Okay, Bets," Logan said guardedly, "but don't touch anything else in there, or else I might just forget my manners." Logan, too, clearly had long experience with telepaths, but Betsy could see that his experiences had perhaps not all been as positive as Kitty's.

Scott was the most reluctant to accede to her idea. A long silence ensued. "Okay," he said at length, "but make it quick."

Betsy nodded, a small, almost notional gesture, and closed her eyes. She reached out with her mind, looking for the minds of the others.

Kitty was easy to find. Her mind flared like a searchlight in the night, bright and optimistic. She'd seen darkness, that much was clear, but hadn't let it overwhelm her. Betsy found the memories of the day scattered haphazardly through Kitty's thoughts.

Betsy took only what she needed, sensory information specifically, and primarily the visual record. She brushed aside the lingering fears and anxieties about the day, Kitty's emotional and intellectual responses to the situation, her impressions of the tall British soldier

Colonel Stuart, even residual bleed-over of Kitty's feelings about and toward her companions, Logan and Scott. Betsy couldn't help noticing the way that Kitty looked at both men as older brothers, or as avuncular figures, even while she was aware that they were in many respects polar opposites. Each had served as a different kind of role model for Kitty since she first came to join the X-Men. Whenever Kitty faced danger, an unconscious part of her always seemed to ask "What would Scott do?", and then "What would Logan do?", and then puzzled out which of the responses best suited the situation.

Drawing back gracefully from her brief communion with Kitty's thoughts, Betsy turned her attention to Logan. While Kitty's memories had been scattered and haphazard, though intermingled with other impressions and recollections, the far-reaching skein of associative memory, Logan's thoughts were quite different. Here, it was like looking at an animal in a cage. But what surprised Betsy was not the animal, which one might have expected in the mind of such a fierce warrior, but the cage itself. It was an incredibly complex and sophisticated bit of mental architecture, and suggested a mind of considerable dimension and discipline. At first glance, Betsy was sure that this was a structure imposed on the man by someone else, perhaps the X-Men's founder and mentor, Charles Xavier. But on closer examination, it was apparent that, instead, this was a self-imposed structure. Through careful study, meditation, and self-examination, Logan had learned to keep his thoughts under careful control.

Which wasn't to say that the cage door couldn't be opened, on occasion, and the animal within allowed to run free. But when it did, it was Logan himself who opened that door, and closed it again when the need arose. Betsy shuddered to think what reserves of self-control that must require.

Betsy found Logan's memories of the day set in front of the cage door, wrapped up like a present, waiting for her. She was neither invited nor welcome to view anything else of Logan's mind. Gratefully, she accepted the memories, and withdrew.

Scott was next. In one sense, his mind was precisely as Betsy might have expected. The mental and emotional landscape of a complex man in the prime of life, with the fears and hopes, loves and hatreds of someone who has spent a lifetime in the service of others. What *was* surprising, however, was the tendril that ran from Scott's thoughts out into the ether, like a golden thread, unseen by any but a telepath allowed a brief and privileged view into his mind. Where the thread went, and to what it connected Scott, Betsy couldn't say, but she didn't have time to contemplate further. She found Scott's memories of the day. After dusting off Scott's anxieties about the safety of the captured crew, and his confusion over his unresolved feelings for Lee Forrester himself, Betsy folded the memories close to her, and withdrew.

For the briefest instant, she held the three sets of memory impressions in front of her, there on the astral plane—Kitty's, bright and hopeful, Logan's, strictly ordered and structured, and Scott's, sincere and conflicted. Then she pressed the three sets together, until only one remained. With a judicious bit of editing, she was able to shear away personal associations, emotional undercurrents, subconscious references, or any other mental or emotional baggage, leaving only the visual and auditory record. Then she patched over any discontinuities, and eliminated redundancies, until she was left with what amounted to little more than a psionic video recording.

Then she opened her eyes. Only a scant few seconds had passed.

"Well?" Rogue said. "You gonna get started, or what?"

"Already did, and done." Betsy gave a slight smile. "Now, I'll share with the rest of you, and perhaps you will see what I mean."

With a tiny telepathic "push," Betsy sent the little psionic recording she'd edited together to everyone in the room.

"That's them," Logan said simply, as everyone got an up-close, if perhaps impersonal, look at the five Exemplar.

Across the room, Betsy saw Scott's hands tighten into fists at his side, and could feel the waves of aggression and anxiety rolling off him.

"Now," Betsy said, "does anything about these people seem in the slightest . . . familiar?"

They looked at the woman with the blue fur and yellow eyes, the optic blasts shot by the leader, and the leader's own steel-like skin.

At just that moment, the tall Russian named Peter Rasputin ran into the room, eyes wide.

"What's the matter, *mein Freund*?" Kurt Wagner said, a concerned expression on his dark-blue features.

"We've just received a call from Dr. Corbeau," Peter answered grimly.

"Oh, no!" Kitty leaned forward, her hand flying to her mouth. "He's not down there near that island, is he?"

From Kitty's thoughts, Betsy caught the image of a stolid, resourceful man at the wheel of a yacht, deep intelligence glinting in his eyes.

"No," Peter answered, shaking his head. "He's still on Starcore. His people were the first to the vessel of the aliens you encountered."

"So what's the bad news, Petey?" Logan asked.

Peter took a deep breath before continuing, his expression hard. "The doctor reports that another dozen such ships are now approaching Earth orbit, with more following not far behind, the largest of them the size of a small moon."

"Oh, dear," Betsy said, gaping.

"You can say that again, sister," Logan said. "Aliens or not, this is a flamin' invasion."

13

The first of the landers touched down within an hour. Moments later, telecommunication systems worldwide were interrupted. Bandwidth was choked by a signal transmitted from high orbit. Worldwide, the message suddenly appeared on televisions, cellular phones, and computers, overriding all firewalls and protocols, the local dominant language or dialect automatically selected from more than a thousand alternate audio tracks. But the video feed remained unchanged, and countless billions of eyes around the world, in that moment, beheld the same image.

A man with silvery skin and white glowing eyes stood in the center of a vast amphitheater, while arrayed behind him were hundreds, even thousands of figures in all shapes and sizes, some crouched on the ground and some soaring overhead.

"People of Earth, attend. I am Invictus Prime of the Exemplar, first exarch of the Shining Fist Cohort. Even now, my siblings from among the serried ranks of the Exemplar are descending upon your world. We bring with us glad tidings. Your onetime and future masters, the rightful owners of this planet, have returned. No more will you wander alone, unguided, through the wilderness. With the Kh'thonic Collective once more resident on Earth, all will be as it should always have been.

"All unaugmented individuals, those you would class as 'baseline human,' should submit themselves to the will of the Kh'thon immediately. Depots will be established near centers of population for you to gather, for future examination by your superior servitors. All augmented individuals, whether mutant by birth or mutant by accident or design should surrender themselves immediately to the nearest Exemplar, who will determine on the spot if their talents may be of use to the Kh'thon.

"Those who are of no use, whether augmented or unaugmented, will be disposed of in an appropriate and humane fashion. Those who refuse to submit, or who resist the will of the Collective, will be dealt with in a far harsher manner.

"Thank you for your attention, and welcome back to the loving grace of your masters, the Kh'thon."

14

As the image faded from the television set in the far wall, Kurt Wagner could feel a strange pang somewhere deep within him. Was it hunger? Or something else?

Before he could puzzle it out, Logan had leapt to his feet, adamantium blades slicing out from the backs of his hands.

"What are we doin' waitin' around for?" In this moment, teeth bared, Wolverine seemed more like the animal whose name he shared than a human being. But then, Kurt reflected, he himself was named for a worm and looked like a demon, so labels and appearances could not always be trusted. He knew that somewhere inside his friend Logan lurked a gentle man; at the moment, though, that gentle man appeared to be hidden beside an unstoppable engine of fury. "We gonna bust your lady friend out of that alien city or not?"

Scott stiffened, and turned his attention to the television without answering.

"Oh, you guys . . ." Kitty said, her voice sounding distant and small.

Kitty was sitting on the edge of her seat, mouth open

and eyes wide, using the remote to flash from one station to another. Since the Exemplar signal had ceased, the airwaves had been filled with news of the armada overhead, and of the ships now landing in cities all over the world.

"Hang on, Kitty," Scott said, stepping over and placing a hand on her shoulder. "Go back one."

"Aw, heck," Rogue said, whistling low.

The image on the screen was of Manhattan, Times Square to be precise.

"By the white wolf . . ." Peter said softly.

One of the alien landing craft had set down in the middle of Broadway, and was only now blossoming open like an enormous, cruel metal flower, just as the others had described the craft in the Bermuda Triangle doing earlier that day. It was now approaching sunset, and as the last rays of the sun reddened the sky, the figures that emerged from the craft into the neon-lit always-daylight of Times Square seemed to glow with a strange, unearthly illumination of their own, like will-o'-the-wisp, like corpse light.

There were a half-dozen of them, or so it seemed. They climbed from their blossoming metal flower, took to the air, and hovered over the heads of the close-packed crowds of tourists and commuters.

Kurt, who had traveled to the stars and visited other dimensions, fought aliens and demons and monsters, could not help being impressed by the bravery and presence of mind of the news camera operator on the ground. He was clearly having some difficulty keeping the Exemplar in focus, but even so the camera operator had held his ground, even when the crowds began to realize that standing around and looking up with gaping wonder at the alien invaders floating just overhead was not perhaps the safest course of action.

The television picture began to shake, as the camera operator was bumped on either side by pedestrians struggling to get out and away from the Exemplar overhead, and the audio was filled with shouts of alarm and warning.

Just then, the camera swung around, finally coming to rest on one of the Exemplar, who had raised his arms, commanding attention. Well-muscled from the waist up, from the waist down he was completely encased in some sort of silver device, sleek and aerodynamic like a lift body.

"Something's happening," said an unseen person, and Kurt realized it was the camera operator. It was a woman, by the sounds of it, brave but frightened.

"Attend," the seated Exemplar said in English, his voice echoing off the buildings, distorted and buzzing through the television speakers. "I am the Capo of the Judgment's Watch Cohort, and it is given to us to secure this region of the continent. All unaugmented individuals should gather immediately in this place for processing. Interruptions and delays will not be tolerated."

Without warning, another of the Exemplar, a young male with bright green skin, transformed into some sort of vicious flying animal, like a cross between a bat and a shark, and swooped down over the crowd.

"You heard Nilus," roared the strange flying creature with the voice of a teenage boy. "Gather!"

Kurt and the others watched in helpless horror as the strange bat-shark creature flew directly into the path of the camera operator. In the blink of an eye, the video signal was gone, replaced by static.

"Mein Gott!" Kurt swore, yellow eyes squinting briefly shut in empathy, as he tried desperately not to imagine what might just have befallen that brave woman.

"We've got to get *down* there," Kitty said breathlessly.

"Agreed," Scott said, and pulled his sweater over his head. Underneath he was wearing the plain blue tunic of his uniform. He reached into a pocket and took out a pair of reinforced yellow gloves, and tugged them on. "But we need to do this smart. We've got these landers coming down all over the planet."

"Da," Peter Rasputin said. "But it is not as if we did not have friends, Scott."

Squinting his eyes shut, Scott pulled on a blue cowl, and then settled his battle visor over his eyes. "True. But we need some way to coordinate with them. We could use Cerebro, but it'd take a pretty powerful telepath to reach as far as we need to reach, and with the professor gone . . ."

"Excuse me," interrupted Betsy Braddock, sitting demurely at the far end of the couch. "I believe I can be of assistance there. Though I'll need to know who I'm to contact."

"Leave that to me," said a new voice from behind them, and Kurt turned to see Doug Ramsey standing in the doorway. He was one of the newer students, one Kurt had had precious little opportunity to get to know. Was he sufficient to the task?

"I don't know . . ." Scott said, shucking off his pants, unselfconsciously, revealing the uniform he was already wearing beneath.

"Cripes, Cyke, do you wear that thing *everywhere*?" Logan muttered under his breath. "What's the matter, couldn't find a phone booth to use?"

Scott ignored him. "Perhaps Kitty would be a better choice to assist Betsy . . ."

"No way," Kitty said, slipping her mask over her eyes and jumping up from her seat. "I'm more help out in the field. But Doug can do it, Scott. He's got more brains than the rest of us put together."

"That's good enough for me, *Katzchen*," Kurt said, and disappeared, a puff of brimstone and a tiny *bamf* noise the only sign of his passing. For the briefest, imperceptible instant he was *elsewhere,* and then he was standing by the open doorway. "If Kitty trusts him, so do I."

"Great," Doug said, waving a hand in front of his face, nose wrinkled, an expression of distaste curling his lip. "I appreciate"—he sputtered, coughing slightly on the strong smell of the brimstone residue of Kurt's teleportation—"the vote of confidence."

Kurt touched a small device at his belt. No larger than a pocket watch, it was an image inducer, which allowed the wearer to display any outward appearance he chose at will. An instant later, Kurt was no longer wearing a loose-fitting white shirt and black slacks, but was clad in his black, white, and red uniform. Kurt seldom wore casual clothes, preferring the unstable molecules of the uniform, which moved and glided effortlessly with his acrobatics, preferring to use holographics when he wanted to affect a more relaxed appearance.

"Then what are we waitin' for?" Logan said, shouldering past. "There's people out there gettin' their backsides handed to 'em, and we've got to stop it."

As he watched Logan go, Kurt thought of what Scott and the others had said about the power levels of the invaders they'd encountered down in that alien city, and about the images he himself had just seen on the television screen. As Peter, Kitty, and Scott followed Logan out the door and down the corridor, Kurt felt again the strange pang deep inside. But he realized now that it wasn't hunger, but a sensation he hadn't experienced in quite some time.

It was fear.

15

A sliver of moon was visible through the high, narrow window of the cell. Lee Forrester sat against the wall, her knees tucked up to her chest, her arms wrapped around her legs.

Night had fallen only a short while before, which meant it had been something on the order of fifteen or sixteen hours since they first spotted the UFO blazing across the sky, little more than twelve hours since they'd been captured. Only half a day, and it felt like a lifetime.

But then, Lee thought ruefully, life ended at death, so unless they were very lucky, half a day might end up being a lifetime, after all. Or what was left of one, at any rate.

Frank had regained consciousness sometime after being thrown into the far wall, and now sat apart from the others, gingerly prodding his bruises from time to time. Richie, Jose, and Merrick, while still clearly blaming Lee for their troubles, had lost confidence in Frank's ability to lead them to freedom, and so they sat dispirited in the corner, muttering occasionally to one another. Paolo kept his place at Lee's side, as always.

The wall had been unbroken stone, ever since the strange little man in the purple robes had left, sometime that afternoon. Now, without warning, the stone flowed once more, and in the newly open doorway again stood the purple-robed man who'd called himself Vox Septimus.

He still carried the crystal rod, and the sight of it was enough to keep the others from attempting to duplicate Frank's earlier plan.

Lee, though, had some learning yet to do. Maybe they wouldn't get out due to brute force, but she was convinced there was still a chance to find some angle, some advantage.

"What do you want?" Paolo said sharply, before Lee could speak.

"This one merely comes to offer humble thanks, for your leader's contributions to the objectives of our masters, the Kh'thonic Collective."

"Contributions?" Lee said the word like a curse, sliding her feet out in front of her and putting her hands palm-down on either side. "And just what did I *contribute*?"

When Vox Septimus had come to them a few hours before, asking about how best to deliver their ultimatum or whatever it was to the people of Earth, Lee had refused to answer. She'd kept her mouth shut, even after the purple-robed man asked a whole string of questions. But rather than the angry response she'd anticipated, and instead of zapping her with the rod or turning and questioning the others, Vox Septimus had merely smiled, nodded, and left the cell. He'd rejoined the strange, large-eyed, ear- and noseless woman in the corridor, and the door had flowed shut.

So what, precisely, was Lee supposed to have done that helped Vox Septimus and his masters?

"Simply put," Vox Septimus said with a smile, "the knowledge that this one's associate was able to glean from your surface thoughts was invaluable in preparing a broadcast signal that transmitted to his world's population our masters' message."

Lee looked at the hairless figure, her eyes narrowed. "So you're telepathic, then? Or your friend is, at least?"

Vox Septimus's eyes widened a fraction, and his mouth opened in a "o" of surprise that quickly melted into a broad smile. "This one? An *augmented*? Ha. Ha ha."

It sounded as though he were mocking Lee, but when she realized the spasmodic gestures that shook his shoulders were *laughter,* she came to understood that the expression was sincere.

"Oh, dear, no," Vox Septimus said, and reached up to wipe the corners of his eyes. "This one is a humble unaugmented only. But the other who was likewise sent on this errand was indeed a low-ranking augmented servitor."

Lee nodded slowly, mulling it over. "You mean the woman with no ears or nose?" A sudden, inappropriate thought hit Lee, and she resisted the temptation to ask how a woman with no nose might smell. "So *she's* a telepath."

"Yes." Vox Septimus nodded, regaining his composure. "Though her psionic talents are an extremely low order. Not so powerful to pull the information from your brains unbidden, this one is afraid, but more than sufficient to pull the errant thoughts that drift through your consciousness upon hearing a question."

"Even those I didn't answer." Lee's lips pressed together, and she felt like smacking her head into the wall. She'd been so smug, so sure that she'd given nothing up to their captors, only to discover she'd been giving them everything they were after, all along. No wonder they didn't repeat any question twice, or torture the answers from her. There simply wasn't any need.

"So you sent your message," Paolo snapped. "Now what? You gonna let us go?"

"Oh, dear, no." Vox Septimus tucked his chin in, eyebrows raised, as though the question took him completely by surprise. As though he couldn't imagine *why* they would want to be released. "In fact, you'll be happy to know that, in short order, the rest of your world's population will be likewise detained."

"What?" Frank said, lifting his head and glaring at the purple-robed figure.

"Here," Vox Septimus said helpfully, and raised the crystal rod. "Allow me to show you."

On seeing the rod once more, Frank flinched and covered his face with his hands, but rather than lashing out as it had done before, this time the crystal rod merely shone a beam of light on the blank wall opposite Lee.

"What the . . . ?" Merrick said, and Lee thought he'd taken the words right out of her mouth.

In the empty air between the rod's tip and the blank wall, there now danced a fully three-dimensional image of a city. It glimmered slightly, and when Lee squinted she could just barely make out the texture of the wall on the far side, seen dimly through the image itself. It was some kind of holographic technology, Lee assumed, perhaps using the far wall to bounce light back, the interference between the first wave and its reflection creating the solid-seeming images.

As Lee and the others watched, the image shifted, and the perspective zoomed crazily, until finally it resolved itself. They were looking at a city square, which from the Spanish words on the street signs and the varied skin colors of the passersby must have been somewhere in Central or South America. There was some sort of carnival or street fair in progress, and everyone looked to be having a ball.

"What are we lookin' at, Cap'n?" Jose asked.

Lee shrugged. From what she could see, this was just an unremarkable city scene, which from the angle of the shadows and the color of the sky appeared to be just before sunset.

"Ah, this one offers apologies," Vox Septimus said. "The relevant element of this visual record is some short remove into the future. Allow this one to address."

Suddenly, the crowds, which moments before had been drifting leisurely across the miniature scene, shifted into high motion, blurring across the streets, and Lee realized that Vox Septimus had put the moving image into fast-forward.

"Here we are," Vox Septimus said with satisfaction.

The image slowed to a normal rate once more, but where before the scene had been of happy people at a street festival, now things had taken a darker turn. Both literally, in that the sun had set in the sky, and figuratively, in that now the happy revelers of the earlier scene had been replaced by men and women in terror for their lives.

A handful of hairless men and women, all dressed in strange clothing, were in the air and on the ground, rounding the festivalgoers into large metal pens, like cattle being led to the slaughter. Lasers shot from eyes, bone spears flew from palms, lightning crackled from fingertips, and the helpless people were powerless before them.

Beside her, Paolo's hands tightened into fists, and Lee saw a killing rage rising in the old man's eyes. She reached out and laid a hand on his elbow. "Not now," she whispered, though her instincts to injury were the same as his.

Lee turned her attention back to the purple-robed figure. Perhaps this was an opportunity after all.

"I can't help but notice, Vox, that you don't seem to have the same powers as so many of the rest of your kind. That you're . . . how did you put it? Unaugmented?"

Vox Septimus turned to her, and the image projected by the crystal rod vanished.

"Of course," he said, as though it were the most natural thing in the world. "And what of it?"

"You must have been pretty unlucky to be born

without any powers, I guess." Lee spoke as casually as possible, as though discussing the possibility of rain in the distant future.

Vox Septimus straightened, his head tilted to one side, quizzically. "Unlucky? This one was born for a task, as were all augments and unaugments alike. We are bred with the characteristics that our masters require, no more and no less."

"Ah," Lee said, nodding slowly. "So your people have your powers from birth? They aren't something that they get from some kind of machine?"

Lee wasn't sure what to expect, but if her experiences with powers in the past were any indication, strange abilities could sometimes be turned on and off, at will and otherwise.

"Machine?" Vox Septimus repeated, and then began to chuckle, once more with that strange, unnatural laugh. "Machine? Ha. As though the gifts of the Kh'thon were some mere mechanical contrivance? Ha ha. This one's talents derive from the genome, foolish individual, just as do those of every servitor from the lowliest unaugmented to the loftiest Exemplar. Ha ha."

Genetic engineering? Lee tried to stifle a frown. That wasn't exactly what she'd been fishing for. She was hoping that maybe all of this vaunted ability and power was something that came with a convenient "off" switch, preferably labeled with foot-tall letters. Something that was hidden in the genome? Perhaps a little trickier.

"So they're . . ." Lee felt her enthusiasm for this line of questioning quickly fading. "They're just *born* with their powers?"

"Some," Vox Septimus said. "But some are triggered in later life. The randomizing element in the genome allows the Kh'thon to engender whatever trait or ability they require in a servitor. The augmented, the most powerful of which are the Exemplar, serve an endless number of functions for the Kh'thon, everything from navigating through hyperspace with enhanced sensory organs to serving as the defensive capacities for Kh'thon who venture planetside. The Fathership and the other ships in the Kh'thonic flotilla are well armed and fortified, of course, but in situations where more precise means are required, the Exemplar are deployed."

"More precise means?" Something about the way he'd said that sent chills down Lee's spine.

"Such as removing native populations from the planets the Kh'thon wish temporarily to inhabit," Vox Septimus said simply. Then he treated Lee to a smile, and added, "Such populations are usually exterminated, but surely the Kh'thon will find a use for *some* of you, at least."

16

"It's right through here, Betsy," Doug Ramsey said. He pulled the chain on the desk lamp, and the headmaster's study was suffused with warm light. He was hyperconscious of the presence of the woman behind him, and did his best to keep his tone level and confident-sounding. His best, though, just didn't seem to be good enough, since every time he opened his mouth to speak he sounded just like a chipmunk. Or at least, that's what *he* thought.

Doug was no hero. Sure, he had the black-and-yellow uniform of a student of the Xavier School for Gifted Youngsters hanging in his closet, unstable molecules and all, but that's where it stayed, most of the time: hanging in his closet. Sure, he put it on whenever the rest of the gang got together to train in the Danger Room, but really, what good was he in those operations? All he really managed was to add another moving target to the team, another bystander to protect.

But an innocent bystander? Doug almost blushed. If measured by his actions, particularly with the fairer sex, then yes, he was as innocent as they come, as pure as the driven snow. But if judged by his thoughts, by his *ambitions*? He chanced a glance at the vision behind him, and suppressed a shudder. Well, if *thoughts* were enough to damn him, then he was as far from innocent as they came.

Up until a few short months ago, Doug just figured he was smart. Heck, if he was honest with himself, he thought he was a genius. No, he *knew* he was a genius. It was really the only answer for it. He'd always been a clever kid, getting high marks in school, and never having to work that hard on his assignments, but there'd always been one or two other kids as smart or smarter than him in class. But then a few years ago, he'd hit puberty, and *all* bets were off.

It was in Spanish class that he first realized he was a genius. He showed up, the first day, knowing no Spanish beyond *taco* and *burrito,* and by the end of that first class period he was correcting the teacher's improper use of intransitive verbs. The next day, he was watching soap operas on Spanish-language television, and the day after that he was finishing up Cervantes's *Don Quixote de la Mancha* in the original.

And that was the *longest* it had taken him to learn a language, ever since.

The computers came a short time later. He'd always played video games as a kid, but it wasn't until he glanced through a book on computer programming that he understood that computers were simply, at their base, language. The software code which underlay everything that a computer did was nothing more than another grammar and vocabulary to learn, and it took Doug no time to pick them up.

That was when he'd first met Kitty Pryde. They'd met at Stevie Hunter's dance class in Salem Center—which Doug's parents had insisted he take, so that he could get off his backside and *move* now and again—and had quickly hit it off. He'd initially thought that Kitty was some boarding school wannabe hacker, and had gone along with all her talk of hacking into government databases and the like because he thought she was cute. Having the ability to learn any language in short order, or to make any computer do whatever he wanted, strangely hadn't helped Doug one iota when it came to meeting girls. When Kitty wanted to talk to *him,* he was happy to talk about whatever she wanted.

Then, long story short, Kitty had revealed that she was a mutant. And more than that, her boarding school was a kind of training ground for mutants. And, the icing on the cake, the mutants trained at the boarding school were the *X-Men!*

Doug's mind was officially blown, however, when Kitty revealed to him that he was a mutant, too. *Him!*

It was at this point that Doug decided that he'd somehow been given someone else's life by mistake—someone much cooler than he was—but he wasn't about to complain.

In no time, Doug was palling around with Kitty and her mutant friends—and *his* mutant friends. Then the headmaster somehow convinced Doug's parents to let him come and be a student at the school, and then Doug was a bona fide *superhero.* Costume, code name, and all.

Except he wasn't, really. Oh, he was a mutant, and a member of a team of mutants, and he had a costume and a code name, but a super-hero? Doug didn't think so. He couldn't shoot lasers from his eyes, or teleport, or turn into steel, or pass through solid walls. What could he do? Well, he could *read*.

Did no one on the team realize that his code name, Cypher, didn't just connote the ability to *transcipher* or *decypher*, but meant, literally, *nothing*? Cypher meant "zero," but worse than that, according to the *Oxford English Dictionary*, it also meant "A person who fills a place, but is of no importance or worth, a nonentity, a 'mere nothing.'"

Gee, thanks, Professor X, Doug thought ruefully, *way to address any lingering insecurities I might have had.*

At the moment, while Kitty and the rest of the graduate team went off to save lives, Doug was left behind to man the home fires, and act as the yellow pages for Betsy Braddock. Which meant firing up Cerebro, which meant coming into the headmaster's office and opening the secret panel beside the bookshelf that swung open to reveal the hidden chamber behind the wall.

Sure, Doug wasn't a hero. But he knew languages, and he knew computers. And because of that, he'd gotten to go places, and experience things, that he'd never in a million years dreamed might have been possible. He'd put his life on the line, time and again, and done it happily, because it meant that maybe, just maybe, he wasn't so much of a "mere nothing" after all.

Doug knew that, as Milton said, "They also serve

who only stand and wait." Now, it was his turn to serve in his own particular fashion again, and stand beside Betsy. He hoped that she wasn't picking up any of his thoughts, hoped against hope that she hadn't seen any of the images that popped unbidden into his mind whenever he looked at her. But who could blame him? She used to be a *fashion model,* for cripes sake, and now she was living under the same roof? And maybe Doug was just kidding himself, but he couldn't help but think there was a chance that maybe she might like him, too. And not just like him, but *like* him.

Doug couldn't wait any longer. He steeled himself, taking a deep breath, and turned around.

"There it is, Betsy," he said, trying to think pure, innocent thoughts. "That's Cerebro."

He needn't have worried. Betsy had eyes only for the machine.

17

From Salem Center in Westchester County to Times Square in New York was a distance of just a bit more than fifty-four miles. Barring traffic, it could take just over an hour. With traffic, it could take forever.

At a top speed at sea level of Mach 2.3, the *Blackbird* could travel 1,770 miles per hour. Factoring in acceleration and deceleration, that meant that the X-Men's plane could get from the Xavier mansion to downtown Manhattan in a handful of minutes.

Even so, Peter Rasputin couldn't help but feel impatient as the lights of Times Square hove into view below them, and wished that there wasn't some *quicker* way to go. He was strapped into his accustomed seat on the *Blackbird,* his hands folded in his lap, eager to get to work.

"Everybody ready?" called Scott Summers from the pilot's chair.

Before Peter could answer, Rogue unbuckled her seat belts and moved over to the hatch. "I'll see y'all down there, 'kay?" With that, she flung open the hatch and jumped out.

Peter turned and peered out the window, and watched as Rogue flew by, her white-streaked brown hair rustling in the high wind. She turned, and gave him a broad wink before diving out of sight in a blur of black and green.

"Aw, cripes," Kitty said, looking out the window on the plane's opposite side.

"What is it, Katya?" Peter loosened his seat belts, and leaned over to see.

"That," Kitty said flatly, "is one big-boned gal."

Peter looked over Kitty's shoulder, and his mouth opened wide. Just below them was Times Square, and through the plane's side window could be seen a woman standing on the pavement, dressed in a strangely cut suit of green and white, lifting one foot off the ground, as though preparing to squash a bug underfoot.

Except that the woman stood at least one hundred feet tall, and the "bugs" she was preparing to squash underfoot were regular men and women, scrambling to escape from Times Square.

"Isn't this about the time you normally invoke that white wolf of yours, Pete?" Kitty glanced over at him and treated him to a tight smile.

"Perhaps later, Katya." Peter slapped the buckles on his seat belts and climbed out of his seat. He moved toward the open hatch, marveling as always at the Shi'ar force fields that maintained the internal cabin pressure. Even with the hatch wide open, one could barely hear the whistle of wind rushing by outside.

"Preparing to touch down, folks," Scott said at the controls.

The *Blackbird* stopped its forward motion and, hovering, began to descend straight down on the intersection of 42nd Street and Broadway.

"I believe this is my stop," Peter said, and with a quick smile, lunged out of the window.

For a brief, exhilarating moment, Peter luxuriated in the sense of motion, in the high whistle of the air whipping past his ears, the fluttering of butterflies in his belly as his senses tried desperately to reorient themselves.

Then, he triggered the transformation.

The briefest smell of ozone filled his nostrils, as it always did, some faint residual energy left over from the transformation of flesh to metal. And the rest of his senses, particularly sight and hearing, shifted further down their registers, the world becoming suddenly a slightly grayer, slightly quieter place, as it always seemed to him in his armored form. Professor Xavier had tried to explain it to him once, how rods and cones of metal were less sensitive to photons than those of organic cells, how the bones of the inner ear had a lower range of motion when made of steel than of calcium. But Peter, for all his fearsome mien and imposing stature, had the heart of the poet, and all that he needed to know was that when his body was armored, so too was his soul. He sometimes felt that was the only way he was able to live with the violent, often terrifying things he experienced as an X-Man: with his senses blunted, the experiences were always kept at a slight distance, so when he was once more a regular man, living in a world of rich sounds and vibrant colors, he could look upon those memories as though they'd happened to another person entirely.

Such as now, as he whistled through the air at terminal velocity, an organic steel bullet falling directly toward the towering giant of a woman, prepared any second to end the lives of innocents with a stamping foot.

Somewhere deep inside, the poet's heart hid inside a suit of solid armor, while the man of steel did what he had to do.

As Peter jumped from the open hatch, Kurt Wagner decided it was time for him to go as well. He glanced out the window to get his bearings.

"Auf wiedersehen," he said, with a jaunty salute, then disappeared with a *bamf* and a puff of brimstone.

Kurt reappeared a hundred feet to the west of the *Blackbird*. Since his momentum was always retained through teleportation, at first he and the plane were moving in the same direction, and at the same speed. But where the *Blackbird* had its powerful Shi'ar engines to act against the force of gravity, Kurt was out in the empty air, and so after hanging briefly in midair, he began to fall, slowly accelerating at thirty-two feet per second per second.

Kurt spread his arms and legs wide, drawing on his years of experience as a trapeze artist with Der Jahrmarkt to slow his fall, and then scanned the swiftly approaching ground below.

To one side, Peter was plowing into the shoulder of the giant woman, knocking her off balance and preventing her from squashing a crowd of innocents underfoot. The woman fell against a building, sending a rain of dust and small debris on the crowd below, which meant the worst of their injuries would be minor cuts and bruises, not liquefaction.

Below, Rogue was setting to with a large figure, whose golden skin glinted brightly in the neon lights. That he was taking and giving blows with Rogue by turns suggested he was even stronger, and tougher, than he looked.

Kurt was just a few hundred feet above the ground by now and would have to choose a target quickly. Then he saw his man. With pale white skin and glowing green eyes, the hairless figure looked almost like an animated corpse, but he was all too lively, shooting beams of crackling black energy from the palms of his hands, using it to herd the panic-stricken humans into the metal pens set up by his fellows.

Kurt grinned, and did some quick calculations in his head. Fixing the image of his destination in mind, he concentrated, and disappeared once more.

Bamf.

Making a vertical jump was always harder than making a horizontal one, though it was far easier to jump down than up. And, for that matter, it was far easier to 'port north-to-south than it was east-to-west. Professor X had always suspected that it had something to do with the Earth's magnetic field, which seemed reasonable enough to Kurt. It wasn't as if it mattered, though. That was simply the terrain through which he moved. Just like a mountain climber rarely has to worry about the *cause* of gravitation, whether curved space-time or the presence of theoretical gravitons or what-have-you; all that mattered to him was that if he let go of a mountain side he would *fall*. So too did Kurt care little *how* his teleportation actually worked, so long as it *did*.

As before, Kurt emerged from his almost-instantaneous teleport with the same momentum with which he'd gone in. And considering that he was now only three feet off the ground, that should have meant a very short trip and a very painful end to a long and distinguished career of adventuring. However, while Kurt had retained his inertia, he had reoriented his *direction,* so that on completing the teleport he was now moving horizontally, parallel to the ground. And, more important, directly toward the back of the pale-skinned, green-eyed man shooting black energy from his palms.

"Heads up, Black Light," Kurt quipped.

Straightening his legs out, his knees slightly bent, Kurt slammed feetfirst into the back of the Exemplar. Kurt's legs collapsed like a spring, cushioning the blow for him, but still imparting the majority of his momentum to the black-energy wielder.

The black-energy wielder stumbled forward, falling face-first on the pavement, while Kurt tucked his legs, rolled in midair, and then landed gracefully on his feet, his tail outstretched for balance.

"You are quite accomplished at harassing innocents, *mein Freund,*" Kurt said, his smile revealing wickedly pointed canine teeth. "Let's see how you do against someone who fights back, shall we?"

• • •

The golden behemoth threw a punch, lightning fast, his huge fist catching Rogue in the abdomen. The momentum of the blow carried her backward, folded in half, soaring up in the air.

Oof, Rogue thought. *I'm nigh invulnerable, but even so, danged if that didn't hurt!*

She straightened out in midair, hanging motionless above the gold mountain for a moment.

"Not bad, sugah," Rogue said, rubbing her chin with a gloved hand. "Now how's about *I* take the next shot?"

Without hesitating, she dove, pouring on speed, both arms straight out before her, hands curled into tight fists. By the time she connected with the Exemplar, she was moving just a hair slower than the speed of sound. That, coupled with her super-strength, meant that the impact really packed a punch.

The golden behemoth, though, barely even flinched.

"Automa isn't sure, little one," the Exemplar said, his voice rumbling like distant thunder. "Was that meant as an expression of affection, or were you intending to *hurt* me?"

"Trash talk?" Rogue said, curling her lip. "Nice." She landed on the cracked pavement a dozen yards away, taking stock of the situation.

"Come, little one." He motioned her forward with hands large as shovel blades. "Now let Automa give you a love tap in return."

"Why don't Automa just stick it," Rogue replied.

In response, the Exemplar who called himself Automa rushed forward, impossibly fast, and it was all Rogue could do to dance out of the reach of his next attack.

This ain't goin' nowhere good, Rogue thought ruefully. *Try as I like, him and me look to be too evenly classed.*

There was another way, of course. A quicker path to victory. But it carried with it a kind of defeat, and Rogue wasn't willing to surrender on that front just yet.

Automa rushed again, and Rogue instinctively countered, sweeping her foot out in a whip kick, which connected with the back of his golden legs, and then following up with a bent armed hook and a jab.

The kicks and punches raining on the Exemplar's metal skin seemed to have a momentary effect, sending him staggering slightly back.

I suppose it's just like Mikey always used to say, Rogue thought. *Precision and speed win out over brute strength every time.*

She nodded, mulling over the truth of that, before realizing that the memory and the sentiment weren't hers.

The kick-and-punch combination, she realized, were a *savate* technique, French kickboxing that a woman named Carol Danvers had studied a lifetime ago. The advice, and the instruction, had come from Colonel Michael Rossi, who was with Air Force Intelligence.

But Rogue had met Mike Rossi only once, and he'd not been forthcoming with advice. It was because she'd met Carol Danvers once upon a time on a bridge in San Francisco that she now shared her memories.

Rogue's mutant power was the ability to absorb memories and abilities through physical contact. If she came skin-to-skin with another organism, for a brief time she'd know what they knew, and be able to do what they did. The exchange left the other person drained—literally—usually lapsed into unconsciousness for some length of time, but it wasn't much easier on Rogue. She had trouble keeping her own memory, her own identity, distinct from the flood of new experiences.

The transfer was typically temporary, lasting only about sixty times longer than the initial contact, so that for every second she was skin-to-skin, she retained the memories and abilities for a single minute. But there was the possibility, however slight, that if she remained in direct contact for too long, the transfer might be permanent.

That's what had happened with Carol Danvers, all those years ago. She'd been a super-heroine, once upon a time, superstrong, nigh invulnerable, and able to fly. And she'd tussled with Rogue, who at the time was a mixed-up kid who'd fallen in with a bad crowd. For all intents and purposes, that was the end of Carol Danvers. When she'd woken up, she'd become a blank slate, with no memories of her former life, and no powers.

Of course, in the days and weeks to come, when Rogue woke up in the middle of the night, she sometimes thought that *she* was Carol Danvers. She had the woman's powers, and all her memories, a lifetime of experiences, just as vivid and real as anything Rogue had experienced in her young life.

Rogue had sought out help, going to the home of the X-Men, asking for the help of Professor Charles Xavier. And he and the X-Men had guided her back, step by step, from the brink.

Even now, though, while she was able better to control the transfer of powers and memories from another, and to keep the contact just long enough to get what she needed, from time to time Rogue found herself thinking another woman's thoughts, remembering another woman's life.

Every time she touched her skin to another person, every time she initiated contact and transfer, there was a part of Rogue who worried that this might be the last time, that in the transfer what remained of the girl who called herself Rogue would be lost, swallowed forever in a flood of alien thoughts and memories. And when the other was actually *alien*, as this Automa seemed to be, the fear of losing herself was even greater.

That's why she preferred to solve problems with her gloved fists these days whenever she could. Better to err on the side of caution, she figured.

So I'll take my licks, Rogue thought, as she and Automa closed for another round. *But what he don't know is, if push comes to shove, then the gloves are* off.

Kitty, Scott, and Logan leapt to the ground, as the *Blackbird* slowly rose back into the air. Its autopilot would steer it over the city, parking it out on the waters of the Hudson until the X-Men needed it once more.

"Looks like Rogue, Petey, and the elf have already picked dance partners," Logan said with a smile. "I'm thinking the green kid is about my speed."

He gestured toward the green-skinned shape-shifter, who even now was transforming from a bat-shark thing to some sort of oversize, taloned ape-creature, menacing a family of tourists who stood petrified on the spot.

"Be my guest," Kitty said, stepping aside and motioning him forward.

"Much obliged, squirt." Logan bared his teeth, and from the backs of his hands adamantium blades popped out with an audible *snikt*. "Hey, green genes! Why don't you pick on someone your own size?"

A short distance off, a woman dressed in black and yellow with a purple headdress was evidently using telekinesis to harass a bus full of schoolkids, levitating it off the ground and slowly rotating it end over end.

"I guess I'll take the telekine," Kitty said with a shrug. "Scott, you got the half-man/half-sled over there?" She pointed at the Exemplar who'd identified himself as the Capo on the televised broadcast.

"Yes, Kitty," Scott said, his jaw set. "I've got him alright."

"Sounds good," Kitty said, and set off on a jog toward the telekine. "Give a shout if you need a hand."

Scott turned to watch her go and marveled. Still in her teens, she'd seen and done such things that facing an invading army wasn't enough to knock her off balance. She might be afraid, somewhere deep down, and was wise enough to be cautious, but clearly wasn't going to let that stand in the way of doing her job.

"Okay, jokers," Scott said to the empty air, turning toward the Exemplar in the floating silver sled. "You picked the *wrong* planet to invade."

18

Betsy held the silver headpiece in her hands. It was like a giant's skull and seemed to reverberate with mental echoes, old dreams and hollow memories.

"It's a psionic amplifier," Doug Ramsey explained. "Anybody can use Cerebro to pinpoint the location of nearby mutants, but a telepath like you can use it to communicate with specific mutants anywhere on the planet."

Cerebro itself was fairly unimposing—a bank of controls and electronics in a casing of brushed steel, with leads going from the casing to the wide helmetlike headpiece. In the empty space in front of the machinery was a simple office chair on casters. Betsy wondered why such an incongruously normal chair, and not a more permanent fixture, until she remembered that the machine's designer had wheeled his own chair with him, wherever he went.

Betsy settled into the chair, the upholstery squeaking slightly under her legs. She swiveled around, facing the machine.

"So I just . . . put this on?" she asked, sounding uneasy, feeling the heft of the silver helmet in her hands.

"Erm, I haven't actually ever *used* it myself," Doug said bashfully. "But if you can figure out how to use it to place a telepathic call, I can help you out with *who* to call. I've memorized the X-Men's Rolodex . . ." He paused, and glanced over at Betsy, as though he'd said something he shouldn't have. "Oh. I guess that sounds insufferably geeky, doesn't it? The kind of guy who reads dictionaries and memorizes other people's phone books for fun?"

Betsy treated him to a slight smile, and laid a hand on his elbow.

"No," she said gently. "I think it's perfectly charming."

She drew her hand back and, taking a deep breath and steeling herself, carefully set the headpiece on her head.

"Hmm," she hummed thoughtfully. "Nothing's happening. Oh, wait . . ."

And then, the world opened up before her.

Betsy Braddock had been a telepath for some years, and had been "intuitive" far longer than that. She'd read countless minds, both intentionally and by accident; learned to project her consciousness onto the astral plane for brief periods of time; and caught quick glimpses of the near future, though maddeningly without any real degree of control.

This was the first time, though, that she'd experienced anything like *this*.

It was as though another world were overlaid on the

one she saw with her eyes. It was something like the astral plane she'd visited psionically, but denser, more vivid, more *real*. She was seeing the world through her mind's eye, but her mental "vision" extended far further than she ever might have imagined possible.

It was an amazing experience, and Betsy was sorry that it took an alien invasion to make such a thing possible. If the news was to be believed, there were alien landers touching down all over the planet, and soon no corner of the world would be safe.

A thought occurred to her unbidden—*I wonder what Brian's doing in all this?*—and before she'd had time to think again, she felt the sudden sensation of motion without acceleration, and suddenly she was looking at another place entirely.

She'd wondered about her brother, Brian, and here he was. In the white, blue, and red armor of Captain Britain, he was standing in the middle of Piccadilly Circus, facing off against a quartet of Exemplar invaders, their metal-flower landing craft perched a short distance away. At Brian's side was his fey companion, Meggan, her feet floating a few inches off the ground.

The four Exemplar they faced looked formidable. A woman and three men, they were hovering in midair, miniature stars dancing around them, lightning flashing in their eyes. But as imposing as the quartet might have been, it was clear that Brian and Meggan were holding their own.

It took the briefest moment for the reality of her situation to process through Betsy's thoughts. Here she was, sitting in a quiet room in a mansion in New York

State, peering with ease through the astral plane to see events unfolding thousands of miles away.

Okay, then, Betsy thought. *Now I've got work to do.*

Before she withdrew, though, she reached out with her thoughts, butterfly wings that brushed the edge of Brian's mind.

Take care of yourself, brother.

Suddenly, Brian smiled, and straightened slightly, as though drawing on some inner reserves of strength, and Betsy knew he'd heard her.

Time to go.

Then she lifted the silver helmet off her head and the world shrank to just the space in front of her and the young man standing at her side.

"Wow," Betsy said breathlessly.

"It works, I take it?" Doug said.

"Yes, I believe you can say that." Betsy blinked a few times and shook her head. "That was simply . . . wow."

Doug leaned against the brushed-steel cabinet that housed the Cerebro mechanism itself, crossing his arms over his chest. "Okay, I guess it's time to start making some telepathic calls, then. You up to it?"

Betsy thought for a moment and nodded. "Yes, absolutely. Where shall we begin?"

Doug rubbed his lower lip thoughtfully. "Probably best to start with the other New Mutants, make sure they're doing okay out there. We haven't heard from them since Illyana 'ported them all out to Colorado yesterday to visit Dani's parents."

Betsy nodded, lips pursed. "Very well, that seems simple enough."

She'd met Doug's fellow Xavier students only a few days before, but had mind-touched each of them briefly, and had solid mental images of each in mind. She had only the vaguest of notions of how far and in which direction Colorado could be found, but if her experience with Brian had been any indication, she had only to think of the person she wanted to reach, and Cerebro did the rest.

Settling the headpiece back over her head, Betsy closed her eyes.

A brief sensation of rushing forward, and she was in Denver, Colorado. A trio of Exemplar, two them as tall as buildings and the other moving so fast he was almost invisible, were harrying pedestrians and drivers alike, while water shot up from a broken main and rained down on their heads like a summer torrent.

Arrayed against them were more than half a dozen young men and women, each of them wearing the yellow-and-black uniform of a Xavier's student.

Can you hear me? Besty mind-called. *It's me, Elizabeth Braddock.*

"Betsy?" said the determined-looking Native American girl with the belt of turquoise and silver.

Yes, Danielle, it's me. I'm using Cerebro to communicate with you all.

"How're things back at the homestead, Ms. Braddock?" said the tall, lank young man with the short-cropped blond hair, his ears sticking out slightly on either side.

As well as can be expected under the circumstances, Sam. Doug is here with me, and the others have gone to Manhattan to repel the invaders.

"We've got our hands full with a few o' the cursed spaleens ourselves, ma'am," growled the werewolf with the voice of a young girl.

As I see. Will you be needing any assistance, then?

"It would seem not, mam'selle," answered the young Asian woman with the shoulder-length hair.

"Have no fear on our account, dear lady," said the angry young Brazilian. "We'll soon bring these demons to account for their actions today."

Fair enough. Try to contact us right away if you should need help. If I'm using Cerebro, there's a good chance I'd hear a mind-call, but if I don't answer, use the telephone, I suppose.

"You got it," said the young blonde woman, the faintest hint of a Russian accent beneath her American teenage bravado. She gave a thumbs-up, then pulled a sword out of thin air, eldritch armor appearing on her torso, arms, and legs, and she threw herself at the nearest of the towering Exemplars.

Take care, friends, Betsy thought, and then removed the helmet once more.

"Okay, that's them sorted," Betsy said. She briefly brought Doug up to speed on the situation in Colorado, and she could tell by the expression that flitted across his face that part of him wished he was out there with them, while part was grateful to be safely here inside the mansion. Betsy could see, without having to peer inside his thoughts, how conflicted Doug was about his powers. He often viewed his life with the Xavier students as one big adventure, but at the same time was plagued by the suspicion that he was terribly out of place, and that the team would be better served to be rid of him.

"Come on, then, Doug," Betsy said, and reached out a hand to him. "Let's get to work."

19

Even though he appeared to be completely immobile inside his sled, the Exemplar who called himself the Capo of the Judgment's Watch was proving to be far more nimble than his motionlessness might suggest. For Scott, this was more than a little frustrating.

"You degenerates are no match for the Judgment's Watch Cohort," boomed the voice of the Exemplar. With his lower extremities completely encased inside a sleek sled of some silvery metal, he looked almost as though he were seated in a motorcycle's sidecar. If, that is, a sidecar could fly and had somehow managed to lose track of its motorcycle. "Stand down, and submit to the will of the Kh'thonic Collective."

Scott didn't respond, but opened the aperture on his visor, sending a wide beam of scarlet energy lancing toward the Exemplar.

In the split second before the beam connected, the Exemplar suddenly blurred into motion, moving blindingly fast for the briefest of instants, and then stopping again only a few yards away.

"What the blazes?"

"This resistance is pointless, and is an insult to our shared masters. Desist!"

Scott gritted his teeth. His first instinct was that the Capo had teleported the short distance, but there'd been no sound of inrushing air, no flash of energy discharged. It was only on reflection that Scott realized that the sled had simply *moved,* albeit extremely quickly.

"Just what is your talent, anyway, Capo?" Scott taunted, darting to one side, looking for an opening. "Boring your opponents to death?"

"Mine is the power of mentation, degenerate."

Scott opened the visor again, and another scarlet beam lanced out. Again, though, the sled moved at lightning speed, so that when the beam arrived the space in which the sled had been was now empty.

"A futile effort," the Capo said.

"Maybe," Scott said, and scarlet beam after scarlet beam shot from the visor, one after another after another. "But I'm not done trying."

Scott's powers flowed through his eyes, so that to look at a thing and to aim a beam at it were the same action. And yet, though he had only to glance at the Capo to send a beam of concussive force lancing toward him, still the beams always failed to connect.

The Capo made a sound something like laughter. "Fool. My cognition is so far advanced above your own that I stand in relation to you as you yourself do to a lowly amoeba."

"Stop thinking, Scott!" came a voice from behind him.

Scott turned to see a man hanging from the side of a

lamppost a short distance away, suit disheveled, tie askew, huge feet bare.

"Don't think!" the man repeated. "Just keep shooting at random in his general direction."

Scott nodded, then turned back toward the Capo, opened the visor, and let fly, one beam after another, not bothering to line his gaze up with the Capo, but simply loosing blast after blast in the Exemplar's direction.

For a few seconds, it seemed as though this new strategy would be no more successful than Scott's had been, when suddenly one of the beams struck home.

Scott stopped, and held his breath.

The Exemplar made a sound like a groan, as his sled listed slightly to one side.

"Quickly, Scott, hit him again!"

Scott didn't waste time replying, but poured it on, his visor opened all the way, his eyes as wide as he could make them. For several seconds, scarlet force lanced out, and the sled-riding Exemplar was buffeted back, like a car slowly pushed across the pavement by the force of a fire-hose blast.

Finally, Scott could feel his power reserves begin to wane, the beam gradually reduced to little more than a red light, and he closed the visor's aperture.

The blasts ceased, the Capo briefly surged forward, his resistance no longer finding anything against which to push. Then he hung motionless in midair for a moment.

"I am . . . the superior . . ." the Capo said, his voice faint and distant, and then his eyes closed, and he listed far over to one side.

As the Exemplar drifted high overhead like an errant

balloon, Scott turned to the barefoot, suit-wearing gentleman who'd come to his aid at such a crucial moment.

"Good to see you, Hank," Scott said, extending his hand and treating his old friend to his broadest smile. "What kept you?"

"Ah, well," the man named Hank McCoy said, pushing his glasses up on his nose. "I was down at the Coffee A-Go-Go in Greenwich Village, enjoying the pulchritudinous prose of Bernard the Poet, when his epic 'Amorphous Ode to the Bebop Bonobos' was interrupted by the sounds of invasion. I've been working my way uptown ever since, but traffic, as I'm sure you can imagine, has been a beast."

Scott grinned a bit wider, if such a thing were possible. "Have you heard from the others?"

Hank shook his head. "Bobby was down in Texas, as I understand, while Warren and Jean were answering a call in Detroit."

A cloud passed over Scott features, if only momentarily. "They're big enough to take care of themselves," he said, his tone strained.

Hank reached out a massive hand, and laid it on Scott's shoulder. "She'll be fine, Scott. We've faced worse and gotten through it unscathed."

Scott looked at the confusion of Times Square, the pitched battle still going on here and there.

"Have we? This was all done by six extraterrestrial mutants, Hank. How many do you suppose they're keeping in reserve up there?"

The two men looked skyward, where only the brightest stars were visible through the city's light pollution. Neither of them had an answer to that.

20

All around the world, battles broke out and fires raged, as more and more of the landers touched down, each disgorging a cadre of the super-powered Exemplar. By now, there was not a man, woman, or child on Earth who had not heard the news of the invasion. In many areas, where the combined might of the police and military were insufficient to combat the invaders, and where no powered individuals stood in the breach, the populations had already been herded into hastily erected containment centers, just hours after the first of the alien landers touched ground.

But in other places, where the local authorities were sufficiently well armed and organized, or where superheroes or other powered adventurers were on hand, resistance was still being mounted.

On the astral plane, Doug Ramsey stood, holding hands with an angel.

Well, he wasn't really *standing,* as such. This was some sort of idealized self-image, projected telepathically from his mind, that only *seemed* to be standing. If

Doug had a greater degree of self-control, he was sure, then his body could take on any shape he imagined, could fly, crawl, or swim. But Doug imagined himself standing, just as he always did, and so that's what he appeared to be doing.

But it *was* an angel at his side, that much was certain. An angel, strangely, with a butterfly over her eyes.

"What?" Betsy had asked when he'd pointed out the butterfly. He'd just noticed it, as they materialized side by side here on the astral plane, and couldn't help but mention it.

"It's almost like a domino mask," Doug explained, "but it seems to be made out of light, and is glowing. Orange, pink, and other colors I can't even describe."

"How strange . . ." Betsy reached up and touched her face, and again Doug remembered that this was not her body, but merely a memory of it. "Let me see, if you don't mind."

Doug felt something brush against his mind, like butterfly's wings, and he realized that Betsy had just reached out and touched his thoughts, briefly.

"Very strange, indeed," Betsy mused. "But a mystery for another time, I think. Now, though our bodies are still in that little room off the headmaster's study, so long as my powers are amplified by Cerebro and you remain in contact with me, our astral forms are free to travel whatever distance we like, to whatever destination we wish."

"Understood." Doug nodded, marveling at the sensation of moving a body that wasn't there.

"Very well," Betsy said, clapping her hands together.

"I was able to make contact with my brother in England, and the New Mutants in Colorado, because I have an image of them in my mind. Cerebro appears to work on a system of sympathies, somehow checking that image against all of the minds on the planet, like a fingerprint matched against all the entries in a database, until it finds the one it's searching for. In order for us to contact the X-Men's allies around the world, you need only imagine them, one at a time, and via our psychic connection I'll be able to do the rest."

Doug thought for a moment, and then nodded again. "Seems simple enough. So where do you want to start?"

Betsy shrugged. "Distance is no object, and any place is as good as another."

"Fair enough," Doug answered. "How about we start close to home, then?"

In Boston, a group of young mutants wearing uniforms of red and black stood in Quincy Market. Doug identified them as the Hellions, students at the Massachusetts Academy, and rivals to the students at the Xavier School. There'd been bad blood between them and the New Mutants, and bad blood between their headmistress the White Queen and the X-Men, but now that the Earth was under threat of invasion from forces beyond the stars, such grudges and jealousies could be put aside, at least temporarily. Against a common foe, mutant stood with mutant, to protect the world itself.

If they survived, perhaps, then they could return to their old war. For the moment, they were allies, of a sort.

∙ ∙ ∙

In Ottawa, in the Canadian province of Ontario, a group of heroes gathered in the shadow of the Parliament Buildings. Led by a woman wearing a power suit emblazoned with the red and white of the maple leaf flag, they numbered a pair of mutant speedsters, a goddess, a shaman and his daughter, a man of metal and a master of metal, and a feisty little person. Together, they were Alpha Flight. In their time, they had been allies, then enemies, and then allies again of the X-Men, and while the mutants of Xavier's school ranged all over the world and beyond, the men and women of Alpha Flight were dedicated to securing the borders of their native land. But threats to the world at large were threats to their homeland, as well, and in the face of an alien invasion the Alphans would not consider surrender.

They stood, shoulder to shoulder, as a phalanx of invading Exemplar approached, prepared to raze the house of Canadian governance to the ground. Alpha Flight had no intention of allowing that to happen.

Across the Atlantic, in Glasgow, Scotland, a motley assemblage of scientists and civilians, human and mutant alike, had gathered together, armed with weapons, powers, and determination. At their head were a human woman, Moira MacTaggert, and the man she loved, Sean Cassidy. Once a mutant, his abilities stripped from him years before, Cassidy had been a tearaway, a policeman, an unwitting criminal, an adventurer, and a hero. For a time, he'd even been an X-Man. But now, he was simply a man, looking to protect what was his, in which count he included the woman at his side. The head of the Muir Island research facility, Dr. MacTaggert had long been a friend of the X-Men, and longer a friend to their founder, Charles Xavier.

With them was an army, but an army of one man. Numbering in the dozens, and growing by the moment, the bodies of Jamie Madrox, the Multiple Man, spilled out into the surrounding streets. Any impact, any kinetic energy, was transformed by Madrox's unique mutant makeup, creating a complete and autonomous duplicate of Madrox himself. These duplicates could be reabsorbed by Madrox's body at will, but if he chose, he could let them continue their independent existence indefinitely. Each body, on its own, was unremarkable; no stronger than the average man, nor faster, nor smarter. But taken together, in their dozens, or even hundreds, the army of Madroxes could be formidable, indeed.

Two lovers and an army of one. They stood together, Scotland's last line of defense against the invaders.

In Tokyo, in the middle of the normally crowded Ginza Strip, two mutants stood back-to-back. Cousins and sometimes enemies, the two now shared a common enemy, their feud momentarily forgotten. Both were scions of the Clan Yoshida, both born with abilities that set them apart from their families and their fellow Japanese. Sunfire, for a brief moment a member of the X-Men, controlled the nuclear fire that burns at the heart of the sun itself. Silver Samurai, frequent foe to Wolverine and his teammates, could direct strange energies into the sword he wielded, making it capable of cutting through virtually any substance short of adamantium.

In the shadows, far from the bright neon lights of the Ginza, a woman named Yukio, with no particular powers or abilities beyond an aptitude with knives, the ability to pick locks, and a complete lack of fear, eyed the advance of the Exemplar, wondering how to turn the situation to her advantage, and considering, for perhaps the first time, if this might not be the time to do something selfless. To try, for once, to be a hero.

Into the small hours of the morning, Doug and Betsy moved hand in hand through the astral plane, touching first one mind and then another. Coordinating the efforts of the X-Men's allies around the world, sharing strategies as to the best ways to defeat the alien invaders, the two persevered, hoping against hope that this might not be mankind's final stand.

21

So the kid can change into any kind of animal, looks like.

Logan faced off against the green-skinned Exemplar. In those rare moments when his body reverted to a humanoid shape, while transforming from one animal shape to another, he looked like the Hulk's scrawny kid brother. Couldn't weigh more than one hundred and fifty pounds, tops, standing only a couple of inches taller than Logan himself. Where all the extra mass was coming from for each of the transformations, Logan couldn't say, but it didn't seem to matter much. All that mattered was that the kid was proving to be more difficult an opponent than Logan would have guessed.

That's alright, Logan thought with a tight grin. *I've got some animal in me, too.*

For the last few minutes, Logan had been tussling with an oversize apelike creature with talons for fingers, and big scalloped ears like batwings. With a bellowing roar of rage, the green ape-thing lunged at Logan, but the X-Man danced easily out of the way.

Thing is, it isn't the animal that counts, most of the time. It's the man.

Evidently deciding it was time to try a different strategy, the Exemplar retreated, and transformed, first into a skinny, green-skinned kid, and then into some sort of green-furred bear. Its snout open wide, revealing double rows of vicious teeth. It was even taller than the ape-creature had been, taller than Logan and Peter Rasputin put together. And on the end of its powerful arms were long, razor-sharp claws.

Logan smiled. He'd faced bears once or twice in his time.

Bears, I know how to handle.

Before the newly transformed Exemplar could move in to attack, Logan surged forward, and swiped his adamantium claws downward in a wide arc, connecting with the bear-creature's right arm.

The unbreakable adamantium blades cut through the green-furred arm like a hot knife through warm butter, and as Logan's swing continued its downward arc, the severed limb flopped onto the pavement at his feet.

This'll be easier'n I thought.

But then, as Logan watched, the severed arm skittered across the pavement, like some sort of strange, fur-colored crab. When it touched the bear-thing's foot, it suddenly flowed like mercury, reabsorbed back into the body.

For a brief instant, the Exemplar reverted back to human shape, a momentary expression of discomfort flashing across his features, and then he treated Logan to a wicked smile. Without preamble, he transformed again, this time into a giant scorpion, as big as a Cadillac, its tail raised and poised to strike.

Or maybe not.

• • •

Kurt Wagner crouched low, legs compressed like springs, and then leapt high in the air, just as the beams of black light blasted chunks of asphalt out of the pavement where he'd stood.

"You're getting closer, *mein Freund*," Kurt laughed. He dangled from a traffic light, suspended by his prehensile tail. "Keep trying, you're bound to hit me sooner or later."

The pale-skinned, green-eyed Exemplar replied with a wordless moan.

"What's the matter? Wake up on the wrong side of the sarcophagus this morning, mummy?"

The Exemplar raised his hands, palms first, and black light leapt out, lancing directly at the spot where Kurt dangled.

Bamf.

Kurt displaced a few dozen yards to the north, appearing in a buff of brimstone and smoke on top of an abandoned yellow cab.

"Missed . . . again . . ." Kurt said, out of breath.

For all his cocksure bravado, this constant 'porting and acrobatics was taking its toll. He'd so far managed to keep a step ahead of the pale-skinned Exemplar, providing a distraction while giving the civilians who'd previously crowded the street a chance to get to safety. But now that the streets were almost empty, Kurt wasn't sure how much longer he'd be able to keep it up.

Then, like clockwork, the Exemplar swung around, and fired another pair of black light beams in Kurt's direction. He teleported out of harm's way, but when he appeared halfway up the block, he had to hold his side, doubled over, like a marathon runner reaching the end of the race.

Okay, Kurt thought, ruefully. *This is growing tiresome. . . .*

Peter Rasputin, meanwhile, had problems of his own.

At the moment, he clung to the shoulder of the giant woman like a tick, as the Exemplar batted at him with her massive hands, trying to knock him loose. When they'd first set to, he'd been worried about her treading on innocents underfoot, but in the time that he'd been occupying her, most of the pedestrians had fled to the safety of the surrounding buildings, or down into the subway tunnels, beyond the Exemplars' immediate reach.

Now, of course, Peter had to work out what to do next. Sadly, his strategy had not extended much beyond harassing the giant, and he wasn't quite sure what his next course of action should be.

The woman had grown to such a size that Peter was no taller than one of her fingers was long. He'd contented himself with tugging at her earlobe and delivering punches to her neck and jaw, but they'd proven little more than irritants. If he was going to end this skirmish, he'd have to find a way to do a bit more damage.

And then he saw it.

It hung on the side of a theater, above the marquee. The giant's struggles had carried them farther up Broadway, away from Times Square, so that now they were in the theater district.

A giant metal lightning bolt, it was a promotion for

the new *Arkon: The Musical*. It was easily twenty-five feet long, made out of a skin of aluminum over a skeleton of steel.

Da, Peter thought. *That should do.*

Peter grabbed the giant woman's earlobe, steering her like a horse on a lead. As he'd hoped, she pulled to one side, coming closer to the theater and the giant lightning bolt. When they were only a short distance away, Peter leapt off, jumping as far and as fast as his legs would propel him, launching like a missile at the theater.

He landed with a shower of sparks on the top of the marquee. The lightning bolt was just within reach, and with little effort he was able to wrest it from its moorings.

"Over here!" he called out, and the giant woman spun around.

Before the Exemplar could react, Peter swung the lightning bolt like a baseball bat, its end connecting with her chin.

As the giant fell to Earth, insensate, Peter felt a pang of guilt. It somehow didn't seem right, doing violence to any woman, however dangerous she might be.

Muttering a brief apology to the unconscious giant, he carefully returned the now-mangled lightning bolt prop to its moorings. From his vantage point atop the marquee, he was unable to see the street directly below, but it appeared that all pedestrians had cleared the area, and so, shouting down for anyone below to stand clear, he leapt to the ground.

He landed, still armored, with a deafening thud.

From behind him came a slight moaning sound.

"Bozhe moi!" Peter shouted, alarmed. "Have I hurt someone?"

He spun around, and behind him, only a half-dozen feet away, stood a pale-skinned, green-eyed Exemplar, who held his hands out before him, palms forward.

Before Peter could react, twin beams of black light lanced from the Exemplar's palms, striking him point blank. And then the world went black.

Knocked unconscious, Peter was unable to maintain the levels of concentration needed to sustain his armored form, so that by the time his body struck the pavement, he was merely flesh and bone.

The pale-skinned Exemplar slowly stepped closer, raising his hands to finish the task.

"Comin' through!"

The Exemplar glanced over, mouth opened lightly in the barest hint of confusion, and before he could respond Logan barreled into him like a freight train, knocking the Exemplar off balance and sending the black light beams shooting harmlessly off into the night sky.

"Nightcrawler!" Logan shouted, wheeling around and facing the giant green scorpion lumbering close behind him. "Front and center!"

Kurt teleported in, appearing just a couple of feet from Peter's side.

"Get Petey out of here, will ya?" Logan said, and scrammed himself, just in time to avoid being impaled by the scorpion's tale. Behind him, the pale-skinned

Exemplar regained his footing, and raised his hands, palms first, menacingly.

"What about you?" Kurt said, kneeling down beside Peter.

"Don't worry about me, elf," Logan said with a smile, turning to the pair of Exemplar advancing on him. "These two'll keep me entertained for a little while, at least."

22

Kitty Pryde wasn't sure what time it was. Sometime in the early morning hours, she guessed. She felt like they'd been at it all night and really, she supposed, they had. It had been right at sunset that the *Blackbird* had brought them from the Xavier mansion, and Kitty wouldn't be surprised to see the sun pinking the eastern sky any minute now.

Oh, boy, is tomorrow going to be a heck of a day, she thought ruefully.

This was going on all over the world, whatever the hour, whatever the time of day. A while back, Betsy Braddock had checked in with the team, telepathically, with Doug Ramsey riding shotgun, psionically speaking. Betsy had been busy coordinating the resistance to the Exemplar invasion, redirecting the X-Men's allies from places where they weren't as needed to places where they were. The only problem was, as the night wore on—or day, on the opposite side of the planet, if you wanted to get technical about it—there were fewer and fewer places where the defenders *weren't* needed, and more and more places where they were.

Kitty wasn't one to use pessimism as a first resort. Heck, her outlook was so sunny she could practically have starred in her own animated musical, complete with cute little anthropomorphized animal sidekicks and a dreamy Prince Charming to win over. But she was beginning to suspect that this might be a fight they couldn't win.

At least, the fight she was in was one *she* couldn't win.

It must have been hours that she and the Exemplar telekine in the yellow-and-black getup and purple headdress had been going at it, but to Kitty it felt only like days.

I'm beat, she thought, as she phased through an airborne motorcycle, flying riderless and end over end through the air. *I wonder if this chick will agree to a temporary cease fire, potty break, and snack time?*

The motorcycle crashed into a city bus, and burst into flames.

I'm guessing not.

Kitty had been fighting a mostly defensive battle so far. Her strategy had been to get the civilians out of harm's way first, and then see if there was any way of neutralizing the threat posed by the telekine. That meant that, for the first few hours, she'd been grabbing hold of hapless tourists and pedestrians, phasing them down through the city streets, and depositing them safely on the subway platforms below. Then she'd swum up through the stone and soil and concrete once more, and done the whole thing over again.

There'd not been hide nor hair of a civilian above

ground in close to thirty minutes, and Kitty hoped that the last of them had cleared off to safety. Of course, that meant that, as a result, *she* was the sole remaining focus of the telekine's attention, and target of her displeasure.

Delightful.

A short while before, their battle had carried them into and through the Port Authority Bus Terminal. Kitty had felt her strength begin to flag, her body weak and weary, but there was nothing to perk up your spirits like dodging a city bus thrown at you at high speed. Adrenaline rushing, Kitty had led the telekine on a merry chase, back out of the Port Authority—and away from the civilians Kitty herself had phased into the underground passage beneath it—and down toward the docks.

Now, the Hudson River was just a block or two away, and Kitty could feel the slight drop in temperature as they approached.

The temperature started to rise again, unexpectedly, and Kitty turned to see the fiery twist of wreckage that had moments ago been the motorcycle and the bus, slowly drag across the pavement toward her.

She glanced over at the telekine, who hovered a few feet off the ground, advancing from a hundred or so yards away.

"Are you kidding me with this?" Kitty said, hands on her hips. "Not just a bus, but a bus on *fire*?!"

"Surrender, degenerate," the telekine said, her voice flat and affectless. "Resistance is pointless."

"Bite me," Kitty snapped back.

In response, the bus-and-motorcycle flaming wreck

picked up speed, sending up showers of sparks as the metal scraped cruelly across the pavement.

Kitty barely had the energy to phase, too tired to move left or right, and as the flaming wreckage passed through her body, she could feel the heat prickling the flesh of her cheeks and hands.

"Cripes," Kitty said under her breath. "Does this chick *ever* get tired?"

Kitty turned and looked at the telekine, her shoulders slumped. The telekine raised her arms, and Kitty knew that she was going in for a killing blow.

Just then, a streak of black and green blurred in from one side, stopping just behind the Exemplar.

"Hey, Kitty, mind if we switch partners for a sec?" Rogue said.

Before Kitty could answer, Rogue reached around and covered the Exemplar's eyes with her bare hands.

"Guess who," Rogue said, as the telekine suddenly went limp, like a marionette whose strings had been cut.

Rogue let go, and the Exemplar collapsed to the ground.

"Hey, good job with . . ." Kitty began to call out.

Rogue looked up, and casually interrupted. "Hey, watch out there, Kitty."

Kitty felt a breeze on her cheek, and phased just as a towering figure with huge muscles and golden skin barreled through her.

"Thanks for the heads-up," Kitty said mirthlessly.

The golden behemoth was clearly confused, stopping short and looking underfoot for the girl he was sure he'd just plowed under. That hesitation was all the advantage Kitty needed. Drawing on some unknown reserves of strength, she took three running steps forward, and then vaulted into the air, just like she'd practiced in Stevie Hunter's dance class.

She was pretty sure, though, that Stevie hadn't had anything like this in mind for the dance step.

Landing gracelessly on the golden behemoth's back, Kitty wrapped both arms around his thick, golden neck, and then phased both of them.

"Giddy up," Kitty said, and hung on for dear life.

It was a tricky proposition, of course. Even though Kitty and the Exemplar were both phased, and so could pass harmlessly through people and objects alike, so long as they remained in physical contact they could still touch each other, which meant he could still do her some serious damage. It was all Kitty could do to keep from getting swatted off his back, while keeping him phased so that he couldn't hurt anyone else.

It was just like riding a bucking bronco, Kitty guessed. She'd never ridden a bronco, but she'd seen it on TV a time or two. Of course, she didn't have a rodeo clown there to help her, should she fall of the Exemplar's back.

What she *did* have, though, was a superstrong friend, which was almost as good.

"Thanks, Kitty," Rogue said, hovering in midair just in front of them. "I think we can switch back, now."

Kitty sighed with relief. "He's all yours!"

Still phased, Kitty pushed off the metal man's back. The instant they broke contact, the Exemplar was solid once more, while Kitty gently airwalked back down to earth, slow as a falling leaf.

Rogue, who now possessed the abilities of the telekine, crossed her arms over her chest.

"No point'n getting my hands dirtied," she said with a sly grin.

As though in the grip of an invisible hand, the golden behemoth suddenly lifted up off the ground, and before he could do more than bellow wordlessly, was sent flipping end over end, high in the air, finally splashing down far out in the Hudson River.

Kitty slumped to the ground, exhausted.

"This has been fun, Rogue," she said wearily. "We should do it *every* night."

"Rogue, Shadowcat!" shouted a voice from somewhere nearby. "Let's go!"

Kitty rolled her head around, looking in the direction of the voice.

It was Scott Summers, running at a healthy clip toward them, a barefoot Hank McCoy following close behind.

"Hey, look," Rogue said, pointing languidly, "Scott's found hisself a Beast."

Scott skidded to a halt just before them, breathing heavily. Hank joined him a moment later.

"Good evening, Rogue," Hank said mannerly, sounding scarcely out of breath. He turned, and nodded in Kitty's direction. "Ms. Pryde."

"So," Kitty said, "how's *your* evenin' been, boys?"

Scott gave her a sharp look, his expression taut.

"This isn't working," he said. "We're managing to

fight a holding action, and nothing more. We've occupied the invaders long enough for most of the civilians in the area to get to shelter, but the longer we stay and fight, the more collateral damage there will be, and the greater the risk of the deaths of innocents."

"It would seem," Hank put in thoughtfully, "that a different approach is in order."

"You took the words out of my mouth," Kitty said.

A faint whine sounded from out over the Hudson, and Kitty leapt to her feet, wheeling around, expecting to see the return of the golden Exemplar or one of his fellow invaders.

Instead, the *Blackbird* hove into view.

At the controls sat Kurt, wearing a pilot's cap on his dark curls, a white scarf wrapped around his neck.

"Did anyone call for a taxi?" his voice boomed over the spy plane's external loudspeakers.

"Okay, everyone," Scott said. "Pile in." He pointed to the unconscious telekine laying a short distance off. "Let's bring her with us. We might just be able to get some answers from her."

"What kind'a answers, Scott?" Rogue asked, using her temporary powers of telekinesis to lift the unmoving Exemplar into the air.

"Just how to defeat these Kh'thon, one imagines," Hank said.

"Yes," Scott said seriously. "For starters."

23

The sun was rising over the waters of the Sargasso Sea, and within the high tower cell, signs of life were beginning to stir.

Lee had slept fitfully on the cold stone floor, if at all, but if their snores were any indication, Paolo and the others hadn't had that problem. She'd finally fallen asleep, sometime shortly before dawn, only to be awaken in short order by a babble of voices from outside the high, narrow window.

A babble of voices?

Lee sat bolt upright. She *was* hearing voices.

Normally I'd expect that to be a sign of madness, Lee couldn't help thinking, smiling slightly. *I suppose it depends on what they tell me to do.*

But it was clear that these voices had nothing to do with Lee. At least, not directly. And judging by the annoyed and worried expressions of her crew, the others were hearing them, too.

Lee stood and moved closer to the window. From her vantage point, all she could see beyond was clear blue sky, but if she titled her head and strained her hearing, she could make out individual voices, sounding as though they were coming from below. She picked out a few words of English from one, a smattering of German from another.

"That there's Portuguese," Paolo said, raising up on his elbows, eyes squinting sleepily.

"Come on over here, old man," Lee whispered impatiently. "Give me a leg up."

It had taken some maneuvering, and more than a little complaining on the part of the old man, but in short order Lee was standing on Paolo's shoulders, stretching her legs, neck, and back as far as she was able.

"Almost . . . got it . . ."

With the final fraction of an inch her neck was able to extend, her pulse roaring in her ear, Lee was able to peer out the window. She could see only a small segment of the courtyard below, but that was enough. Down there, in some kind of enclosure, were men, women, and children of all races and nations. Individually or in small clusters and groups, they moved randomly around their small enclosure, desperate to find a way out, and failing.

Lee couldn't make out much of what they were saying, but the expressions on their faces were plain enough. They were terrified.

"Ah, you waken," said a voice from behind her. "This one is pleased."

Startled, Lee barely managed to avoid falling flat on her back, which starting out five and half feet up in the air, would have been none too comfortable. As it was, she was scarcely able to maintain her balance, and she lurched gracelessly to the ground, landing with a sickening thud on her left leg, her foot twisted at a wrong angle.

She stifled the bloodcurdling scream that rushed to her throat, but tears stung the corners of her eyes. Lee was sure that she'd sprained her ankle, if she was lucky, perhaps even broken it, if she weren't.

Hobbling painfully, she collapsed into something like a sitting position against the wall, just beneath the high window, and looked up into the smiling face of Vox Septimus. He had brought with him a tray, on which were arranged bowls of some sort of greenish sludge. He set the tray on the ground, and when he backed away, his crystal rod held casually before him, Richie crawled over and grabbed the bowls, sliding one to each of the crew.

"Mornin', Vox," she managed, not a trace of warmth in her voice. She picked up the bowl that Richie had slid over her way and sniffed. It smelled profoundly unpleasant, but Lee was hungry enough not to mind too much. She took a bite, and discovered the stuff tasted even worse. It was, at least, filling. Around bites, she continued. "Something . . . we can do for you?"

Vox Septimus tilted his head to one side, and turned his ear toward the high window.

"Ah, so you have heard the sounds of the new arrivals. Splendid."

"Just what you doin' with all them people, anyway?" Merrick asked, his tone a mixture of fear and anger.

"These are those in whom the randomizing element is present but not yet expressed," Vox Septimus said simply. He turned from the window to face Lee. She noticed that no matter who spoke, he always addressed his answers to her. It was the product of living in a deeply hierarchical society, she assumed. "They have been culled from those population centers the Exemplar cohorts have pacified since yesterday, and brought here to the city of Dis for closer examination."

The pain of her injured ankle throbbing in her head like a kettle drum, Lee tried not to think about all that the word "cull" suggested. She tried to puzzle out the servitor's circuitous, obfuscated meaning instead. He had said "randomizing element." Lee had established in earlier conversation that the servitors used the phrase to mean the X-gene.

"You mean . . ." she began, then paused, weighing the implications for a moment before continuing. "These are all mutants?"

Vox Septimus glanced at the ceiling, considering his reply. "Whether these are 'mutants' as you term them— congenitally modified—or 'mutates'—modified in later life through accident or design, each of these specimens is in some way gifted, when compared to unaugmented individuals such as this one. Some of them may even have capabilities that they don't yet know themselves. Living feral, as you have, your people have bred without any limitations or controls. There is no way of telling what characteristics these may have. But there is a chance that they could be of use to the Kh'thon."

There was that suggestion again, implicit in the servitor's words, but never said outright.

"And what about those that *don't* prove to be of use?" Lee asked, eyes narrowed.

"Oh," Vox Septimus said with a casual shrug, "their remains will be disposed of quickly." He paused, and then gestured to the bowls of green sludge they were all eating, helpfully adding, "Possibly even reconstituted into nutritional supplements."

Lee looked down at the half-finished bowl of gunk in horror.

24

Betsy Braddock was stretched out on a couch in the day room, as the first light of dawn pinked the sky in the east. Here in the west wing of the Xavier mansion, it was still dark, the only illumination from a green-shaded floor lamp, and the lights leaking in from the kitchen, where Doug Ramsey was fixing them a fresh pot of coffee.

They had spent the night with their bodies in the Cerebro chamber, their minds roaming the astral plane. For the moment, Betsy had decided, both body and mind could use a break.

Betsy had always considered herself well traveled. She'd been all over the UK and Ireland, and spent a summer in France, and vacationed once on the island of Malta. Now that she'd come to the States—with a horizon-expanding side trip into another dimension along the way—she felt that she'd hit the highlights. And yet, in the last hours, her astral projection had roamed the four corners of the globe, seeing through the eyes of others places Betsy had never imagined she'd see for herself.

And now, all that Betsy wanted to see was darkness. In the low light, she lay with her eyes squeezed shut, seeing only a red-lidded darkness, one arm thrown over her face, the other across her belly. She realized that she'd been wearing the same clothes for the last twenty-four hours, and that her hair must look a state. Not that it mattered, really. Not here at the end of the world.

She heard the X-Men with her mind before the sound of their approach reached her ears. Their thoughts, as weary and disordered as her own, wafted through the ether like distant shouts echoing in a vast, dark cave.

"Better get some more mugs, Doug," she said without opening her eyes.

When the others barreled through the door, Peter Rasputin in the lead carrying the unconscious form of an Exemplar invader, Betsy was standing near the front window, a steaming cup of coffee in hand, watching as the light of the rising sun slowly swept across the Xavier estate from east to west, the long shadows slowly emerging from the gloom as the light brightened sufficient to give them definition. Betsy mused as to whether the shadows had been there all along, hidden in the gloaming, or if the light had created them in the first place.

Don't be daft, girl, Betsy said, and took a long sip of her scalding hot coffee to wake herself. *Of* course *the light makes the shadows. That's what lights* do.

It came of being up all night, and taxing body, mind, and spirit to the limits, thinking such foolish thoughts when there was more important work to be done. Determining just what the X-Men intended with their prisoner, for one.

"Put her there," Scott Summer said, all business, pointing toward the couch where Betsy had been only a short while before.

As Peter deposited his burden on the cushions, surprisingly gentle, taking great care not to jostle the Exemplar unnecessarily, Scott strode right up to Betsy, his expression set.

"I need you to read her mind," he said simply, without so much as a by-your-leave.

"And good morning to you, as well, Mr. Summers," Betsy said, eyeing him over the lip of her coffee mug. "I trust the day finds you passing well?"

Twin lights flared behind the ruby-quartz visor, and Scott's hands stiffened at his sides. "Look, we don't have time for games . . ."

"No, Scott, we don't," Betsy shot back, cutting him off with a wave of her hand. "And while I appreciate that you and yours have been busy safeguarding lives all night, it's been none too pleasant or easy for me and Doug here at home base, I can assure you. Now," she set her coffee cup down, harder than planned, some of it jostling over onto the polished wood of the side table. "I'm perfectly willing to do as you ask, but I'd remind you that I'm not formally a member of your little merry band yet, and respond much better to requests than to command. And come to that, so far as I'm aware, you're not exactly a member in good standing at the moment, are you? So if it's all the same to you, Scott, I'd ask that you keep things civil, and I'm sure the end of the world will just go swimmingly."

"I like her, Cyke," the man called Logan said, collapsing into an upholstered chair and propping his feet on a Louis Quatorze table, taking a long pull on the beer he'd already fetched from the kitchen. "She reminds me of me, at that age."

"Oh, ick," Kitty said, coming around the hallway from the foyer. "A beer? This early? Really, Logan?"

"Heck, pun'kin, it ain't early," Logan said with a wan smile. "It's just really, really late."

Kitty scowled at him, but then caught sight of the coffee service out of the corner of her eye, and her scowl turned into a hungry smile. "Java!" she said, and pounced on the cart.

With a puff of brimstone and an almost imperceptible *bamf,* Kurt teleported into the room, and perched on the mantel over the fireplace. Doug came in from the kitchen, and then Rogue entered from the foyer, with a man in a disheveled business suit and tie askew following close behind. Betsy was not sure which fact was most remarkable, that his feet were bare, or that each was easily twice the size of a normal foot.

Kitty gulped her coffee, and then winced as the scalding liquid hit the back of her throat, but quickly went back for another sip. Swallowing it loudly, she glanced over at the newcomer, then to Betsy.

"Betsy Braddock, Hank McCoy. Hank McCoy, Betsy Braddock."

"Charmed, my dear Ms. Braddock," the gentleman said, stepping across the rug in a couple of long strides and taking Betsy's hand in his. "I'm sorry we weren't able to meet under better circumstances."

"Dr. McCoy was one of the founding X-Men, along with Mr. Summers," Doug put in, helpfully, and Betsy couldn't help but detect a note of jealousy hidden in his tone. "His code name is Beast."

Betsy glanced at Doug, nodding, and then back to Hank. She smiled, shaking his hand. "What a desperately inappropriate name for such a refined gentleman."

Hank beamed. "Ah, a lady of exacting tastes, that much is obvious. You'll have to excuse my cognomen, dear lady. It was chosen for me by our teacher, Professor Charles Xavier, and I'm afraid that tact was never one of his strong suits."

From across the room, Betsy could hear Doug mutter, "You can say *that* again."

Scott cleared his throat *loudly,* and got everyone's attention.

"Okay, so now everyone knows everyone, and we've all been reminded to be on our best behavior. Now, seeing that we're staring down the barrel of Armageddon here, would anyone mind if we got on with the business at hand?"

"Nah, sugah," Rogue said, sitting cross-legged on the floor, her clothes and hair disheveled. "You go right on ahead."

Scott sighed, and then turned to look at the unconscious Exemplar stretched out on the couch.

"Rogue, you touched minds with this woman when you absorbed her powers, didn't you? What can you tell us about her masters, the Kh'thon?"

"Well," Rogue said, rubbing her chin thoughtfully with a gloved hand. "Most of what I absorbed's already gone, I'm afraid, but little impressions remain."

"What kind of impressions?" Hank said, holding a coffee cup in a dainty grip, his pinky extended.

"Bad ones," Rogue said, brows lowered. "Whatever these Kh'thon yahoos are, it ain't good."

Scott turned back to Betsy. "So," he said wearily. "Can you read her mind or not?"

"Well," Betsy said, her lips pursed, "all you had to do was *ask*."

Doug wanted to do something, wanted to help, but all he could do was watch. Even though he'd spent the whole night at Betsy's side, guiding her when necessary, lending her his strength when possible, now that the X-Men had reentered the picture, he was shoved back into the background again, just another article of furniture.

Betsy sat at the end of the couch, the head of the unconscious Exemplar cradled in her lap. She had her hands on either side of the strange woman's smooth, hairless head, one on each temple, and her eyes were closed in concentration.

"She's not going to wake up during this, is she?" Betsy said uneasily, opening her eyes a fraction and glancing around the room.

"We're right here if she does, darlin'," Logan said, giving a little salute with his half-empty bottle of beer.

"Hmph." Betsy gave a little smirk. "I must say, that simply *fills* me with confidence."

With a final glance and a quick wink at Doug, she closed her eyes again.

Then, nothing.

Betsy sat still as a statue, her hands frozen in place, her mouth hanging slightly open but immobile. The only sign of life that came from her was the slight rising and falling of her chest.

"Betsy," Scott said, gently. "Can you hear . . ."

Suddenly, Betsy sat bolt upright, her eyes wide and white. Her mouth opened in a wide "o" of surprise, and she gasped.

However, Doug noticed that at no time did her hands break contact with the Exemplar's temples.

"See . . ." Betsy said, her voice rough and ragged. "Feel . . ."

She threw her head from one side to the other, eyes darting, as though trying to escape from something, but finding herself unable to move.

"I don't like this, Cyke," Logan said guardedly.

"Neither do I," Doug said louder than he'd intended.

"Just hang on a second, everybody," Kitty said, keeping her eyes on Betsy. "Give her a chance to . . ."

"I see it!" Betsy shouted, looking straight forward, her eyes opened so wide that white showed all around.

"See what, Ms. Braddock?" Hank asked gently.

"The fleet. The Kh'thon. The fleet of the Kh'thon. Oh dear, oh dear. It's bigger, bigger, so much bigger than I'd imagined. Ships as large as moons, and without count. And more, and more, and more of them. Coming, coming, coming."

"What about the Kh'thon?" Scott said, his tone level but insistent. "What about the Kh'thon themselves?"

"I can . . . I can't . . . I can . . ." Betsy shook her head again, and closed her eyes tight. "Hard to see. There are . . . 'fingerprints' . . . telepathic traces of their presence, of their passage, all over this woman's mind. And even these small traces are . . . inhuman. Unhuman. Not just alien, but utterly alien, incomprehensibly alien. We've never experienced anything like these before."

"I don't *like* this," Doug repeated, lips drawn and white.

"Show us," Scott insisted, reaching forward a hand, gently touching Betsy's shoulder. "Can you share with us what you're feeling, what you're seeing?"

"Hey, now," Rogue said, sitting upright. "I don't know about all this."

"Yes," Betsy said before anyone could respond. "Here. See."

Suddenly, Doug's mind opened up, and pure evil poured in.

Betsy had been right. They had never experienced anything like these creatures before. No one had, in living memory. Except for the Exemplar and the other servitors of the Kh'thon, of course, but they had been so fundamentally altered by the exposure, so deeply changed, that they weren't really human anymore, at least not at their core. Genetically, to be sure, and biologically, but their minds, their *minds,* had been twisted into shapes that no human should have to endure.

These were brief glimpses which Betsy had caught,

and which she was now sharing with the others. Little more than fingerprints, glancing traces, but even brushing up against them made one feel an unease that seeped down to the core of their being. These were not natural things, these beings who claimed to come from Earth's unimaginably distant past. They were monsters, fiends far stranger than anything dreamt by H. P. Lovecraft, the truth behind humanity's darkest nightmares.

And they were coming to Earth.

Betsy broke contact, pulling her hands away from the woman's temples, looking at her fingertips as if she'd never seen them before.

"Mein Gott," Kurt said, his hand over his eyes.

"Flamin' heck," Logan agreed, nodding.

Hank rubbed his lower lip with one of his massive fingers, his expression thoughtful. "Well, it was certainly . . . instructive."

"Yeah?" Kitty said, her mouth a moue of distaste. "How do you figure?"

"Well," Hank answered, "if at least part of the Kh'thon's claim is true, and they *were* present on Earth at some time in prehistory, then we could be looking at the roots of some of mankind's oldest mythologies. It may well be that the legends of demons and devils in all the world's cultures might devolve from dim racial memories of the Kh'thonic beings from humanity's distant past."

"Which is flamin' fascinatin', I'm sure," Logan scoffed, "but that don't get us any closer to stavin' off doomsday, now does it?"

"Actually," Betsy said, her voice sounding strained, "I *was* able to glean something useful, I think."

All eyes turned on her, and no one spoke.

"There is a flaw in the defenses of the Kh'thonic Collective, it seems," Betsy went on, labored. "This Exemplar was aware of the problem, though she knew it was heresy ever to voice it to her superiors."

"What is it?" Peter asked, wide eyed.

"The ships of the Kh'thonic fleet are heavily shielded and armed," Betsy answered, "and individually would be far beyond Earth's ability to defeat. But the systems on each are slaved to a master control within the Kh'thonic Fathership. It seems that the Kh'thon themselves, who all ride in the master vessel, prefer to retain a final control over their slaves, in the rare chance that a group of them might prefer freedom to servitude and rise up against them."

"And this helps us how, exactly?" Rogue asked.

"Well," Hank said, before Betsy could answer, "I would have thought that much to be obvious."

Everyone looked at him expectantly.

Hank sighed. "Simply put, if we were to find a way to disable the ships' defenses from within the Fathership itself, then the fleet would be vulnerable to attack."

Peter shook his head, the thought clearly overwhelming him.

"And just what kind of attack would *that* be?" Logan asked.

Hank gave a sly smile. "I have a suggestion," he said. "Which, while suitably ironic, is something I suspect that none of you is going to like very much."

25

"Sentinels?!"

Everyone looked at Hank McCoy as though he'd just sprouted horns from his head.

"I told you that you wouldn't like it," he said.

They were gathered in the kitchen, eating a hastily prepared breakfast, and making plans. Betsy had managed to telepathically switch their Exemplar prisoner "off," rendering her unconscious until such time as Betsy delivered a psionic wake-up call, and they'd installed the prisoner in a secured room down in the medical facilities in sub-basement one.

"Okay, Hank," Scott said, warily, fork poised over a half-eaten plate of eggs. "I think you're going to need to sell us on this one."

Hank smiled. Always the cautious one, was Scott. He had been, ever since they were kids. Not that Scott was ever a kid, not really. They'd been teenagers when they'd met, years ago, but Scott had already thought and acted like an old man. Oh, he had the insecurities of childhood lingering about him like a fog, to be sure; Hank thought it possible that Scott would never leave those completely behind. But in his manner, his style of dress, in his attitudes, Scott always seemed as old as Professor Xavier, if not even older.

At least the professor could manage a smile, now and again. Not so dour old Scott. Hank felt as close to him as a brother, closer than anyone in his biological family, but in many ways they couldn't have been more different. Hank, who since childhood had looked like a shaved ape but had the brain of an Einstein, and who spent years at a time as blue and furry as a Muppet, couldn't help but see the humor in any situation. For him, being a mutant wasn't some kind of curse, or burden. As far as Hank was concerned, being a mutant was *fun*. If he'd been a regular guy, a workaday joe like his father had been, would he have been an X-Man, or an Avenger, would he have been able to travel through space and time, to other worlds and other dimensions, having adventures all the while? Not hardly . . .

Hank dragged himself back to the present moment as he noticed the incredulous stares of the other X-Men gathered around the long table.

"Look," he said at length, his tone jaunty, "based on the images that Betsy shared telepathically"—he spared a nod toward the British telepath at the table's far end, who looked a bit worse for wear—"I've made some back-of-a-napkin calculations regarding the size and capacities of the Kh'thonic Collective's flotilla. And I've come to the inescapable conclusion that the ships are simply too large for any conventional weapons to do much damage, assuming on the one hand that we were able to get the weapons into orbit in the first place, and on the other that we were somehow able to disable the flotilla's defense systems on the Kh'thonic Fathership."

Hank paused for a moment to let that sink in. Even if they were to do the impossible, and render the ships vulnerable, their chances of actually doing the ships any harm with conventional weapons were virtually nil.

"That said," he continued, "there *are* large, adaptable weapons on Earth, capable of reaching escape velocity under their own power, with sufficient armament to make a considerable dent in the Kh'thonic fleet."

He glanced around the table. It was Kitty who said what everyone was thinking.

"The Sentinels."

"Precisely, Kitty," Hank said, like a teacher commending a promising student.

He could tell from the expressions around the table that none of the X-Men were very pleased at the idea of using Sentinels, giant robots designed to hunt and kill mutants. Each of them had faced the metallic menaces at one time or another and barely survived to tell the tale.

"Now," Hank said, "I concede that the prospects are unsavory, to say nothing of aesthetically disharmonious, but I am quick to point out that there are, scattered around the globe in varying states of disrepair, any number of decommissioned and partially demolished Sentinels. If we were somehow able to get them up and running in short order, I believe we'd increase our chances of defeating that fleet exponentially."

"Even if such a thing were possible," Peter Rasputin said, rubbing the back of his neck, "how would we activate so many Sentinels?"

"And how are we meant to control them if we do?" Kurt put in, balanced on the back of a wooden chair.

"Yeah," Kitty said, setting her glass down on the table, "when they're up and running, aren't they usually pretty busy with that whole kill-all-mutants thing?"

"Ordinarily, I'd agree with all three of you, heartily," Hank said. "But as some of you may be aware, I sometimes do freelance consulting for SHIELD and other government agencies. They often call on me to provide a new perspective on nettlesome questions, or to draw upon my rather, shall we say, unique experience. Just last week, I was asked to give an opinion on some satellite surveillance photos. SHIELD was monitoring counterinsurgency forces in the South American republic of Santo Marco when their satellites picked up something strange a short distance away in Ecuador. It had been there for years, evidently, but until now no one had bothered to look in that direction."

"What was it?" Doug asked.

For a brief moment, the humor left Hank's voice, and his smile faded. "An abandoned Master Mold facility."

Across the table, Kitty blanched, and Logan's claws popped from between his knuckles.

"Excuse me, a what?" Betsy said, raising her hand like a schoolchild asking a question.

"The birthplace of the Sentinels," Scott answered, setting his silverware down on the table with a clatter.

"Precisely." Hank gave a curt nod. "Or one of them, at any rate." Hank turned to Betsy and continued. "The X-Men have been responsible—or at least involved—in the destruction of a number of such facilities in the past. Simply put, a Master Mold is an autonomous, semi-sentient factory for robots."

"Mutant-killing robots," Kitty corrected.

"*Giant* mutant-killing robots," Doug added.

"Yes," Hank said reluctantly. "Giant, mutant-killing, robots. Any one of which, if left to its own devices, could claim the lives of countless innocents. But one doesn't question the morality of a bullet. One simply pulls the trigger."

"What are you saying, McCoy?" Logan sneered, barring his teeth. "Guns don't kill people, *you* do?"

Hank bristled but kept his temper. "No, Logan. I'm saying that we can use the Master Mold to activate the decommissioned Sentinels, repair those that are broken, and control all of them once reactivated. And then we save the Earth."

26

"Okay," Scott said, raising his voice over the din. A wide-ranging debate had broken out around the table when Hank finished outlining his plan, and tempers were beginning to flare. "This isn't getting us anywhere."

"I just don't much like the idea of activating a whole army of mutant-killers," Kitty shot back, nostrils flaring. "Would you let Nazis out of jail to help you fight a war?"

"Who has Nazis in jail?" Kurt scratched his head. "And how many Nazis are left around, anyway? Baron Strucker is still at large, I suppose, but . . ."

"You know what I mean," Kitty snapped. "If it was after the war, and you had put Nazis in jail, and you were fighting *another* war . . ."

"With someone else . . . ?" Doug put in, trying to be helpful.

"Look, it's a hypothetical, okay! Like one of those killing-Hitler-as-a-baby questions. The point is, there are some lines you don't cross, and some stinks you can't wash out."

"I don't know, sugah," Rogue said thoughtfully. "If

lettin' a bunch of blamed Nazis out on the battlefield meant that me and mine would survive, I guess I'd be okay with that."

"Yes, but . . ." Kitty opened and shut her mouth. She looked around the table for support, found none. "But . . ." She crossed her arms across her chest, and dropped her chin, sulking. "Okay, then. But I still don't like it."

"Look," Scott said, playing the peacemaker, as he'd done since he was a kid at the orphanage. "We're all tired. But lots of lives are depending on us, so I expect we'll be a great deal more tired before we're through. Now, as I see it, we have three main objectives. First, we have to gain access to the alien city in Bermuda, to free Lee Forrester and her crew . . ."

"And the other prisoners," Betsy put in. "I saw it in the Exemplar's thoughts. They're rounding up X-gene-positives from around the world and transferring them there for 'examination.'"

"Delightful," Scott said dryly. "Okay, so we've got even more prisoners to rescue than I thought. In any event, we'll need to send in a strike team—assuming, of course, that we work out a way to penetrate the island's shielding."

"I may have some thoughts in that direction," Hank said.

"Good." Scott nodded. "We could use them. Now, I propose a three-man team—me, Kurt, and Peter. Assuming that Hank works out a way through the shield, we storm the city and free the prisoners."

"*Da,*" Peter said simply.

"Sounds like fun," Kurt said, though his tone suggested otherwise.

"Second, we need to get a team to Ecuador, to get the Sentinels up and running."

"I should be on that assignment." Hank raised his hand. "I've had experience in a Master Mold, as Scott will well recall, and I believe I know enough about the general layout to navigate inside. My only concern is that I'm not as familiar with the Sentinels' programming code as I could be, and may run into snags in that arena."

"So why not take someone who can talk to the computer in its own language?" Kitty asked.

"Did you have someone in mind?" Scott replied.

"Well, duh." Kitty pointed across the table at Doug. "It may have escaped your notice, Scott, but Doug's mutant ability is *language*. He can get that Master Mold to sit up and beg, if anyone can."

Scott glanced at Doug, and inclined his head slightly. A blush rose in Doug's cheek, and he looked away.

"Fair enough." Scott turned back to Hank. "Well, Hank, who else do you want on your team?"

Hank reached over and laid an enormous hand on Doug's thin shoulder. Smiling, he said, "I think the two of us should have the computational aspects of the mission well in hand." He paused, and then added, "But the need for pure strength may still arise."

"I ain't got nothin' planned," Rogue said sleepily. "I'll ride shotgun and take care a' any heavy lifting."

"Okay, then we've got only one objective left." Scott glanced around the table, his jaw set. "And it's a doozy."

"Let me guess," Kitty said, making a grand gesture with her arms. "Insurmountable odds, life-threatening menace, and a goal almost impossible to achieve that will, if left undone, doom the rest of the plan?"

Scott allowed the slightest hint of a smile to tug at the corners of his mouth. "Something like that."

"Figures," Kitty said, and slumped in her chair. "Count me in, I guess."

"I already had," Scott answered, his tone making clear that Kitty's abilities had never been in question. "You, Logan, and Betsy will need to go to the Kh'thonic Fathership, to disable the fleet's defenses."

"What?!" Betsy's mouth dropped open, her eyes wide.

"We need you." Scott's tone was gentle, but firm. "There simply isn't any other way. I'm guessing that locked in our Exemplar prisoner's head is the key for gaining entry to the Fathership. If you go along, you should be able to control her telepathically like a puppet, and get yourself and the others aboard."

"And me?" Logan asked.

"You?" Scott said, sparing him the briefest glance. "You just need to do what you do best."

Logan pursed his lips, and nodded appreciatively. "Good plan, Cyke. But there's one problem. I don't remember seeing a rocket ship parked in the hanger, last time I looked. How you plannin' to get us up into the black?"

Scott's mouth drew into a tight line, and he glanced from Logan to Hank and back.

"I've got an idea, but I don't think you're going to like this one, either."

27

"Okay, I gotta give this one to Cyke," Logan snarled. "I *don't* like it."

"Chin up, chappie," replied Colonel Alysande Stuart, glancing over her shoulder. "It's no days of wine and roses for me, either, I can assure you."

The diminutive Canadian sat behind Alysande in the high-g acceleration chairs, Betsy on one side and Kitty on the other, all three of them crammed into pressure suits and strapped securely in place.

Alysande, at the controls of the experimental space plane, lifted the clear, nearly indestructible helmet over her head and secured it to the neck seals of her pressure suit. She toggled her suit's radio to network with the craft's internal communications system, and spoke into the helmet mic. "How's our other guest doing back there?"

"Settling in nicely, I think, Colonel," came the voice of the RCX operative known only as Raphael. Alysande reached a gloved finger over to work the suit controls set on her left forearm, and reduced the volume of the helmet speakers. "If Ms. Braddock can assure us that

she'll be able to keep the . . . specimen . . . in an unconscious state until needed, I should think we're in good
shape."

"Don't worry on my account," Betsy said, shifting
uncomfortably in her seat. "The Exemplar won't regain
consciousness until I give her the trigger word, and
then she'll see and hear only what I choose."

"Charming," Alysande said softly, temporarily mut-
ing her helmet mic. Considering how a considerable
percentage of the world's population regarded mutants,
this Braddock woman was incredibly forthcoming with
details about how she could so easily enslave the mind
of another. Wasn't that precisely what crackpots like Bolivar Trask and Robert Kelly were always nattering on
about? That with their unimaginable powers, mutants
posed a threat that normal humans could scarcely com-
prehend?

Now, while a group of extraterrestrials that were, for
all intents and purposes, mutants themselves threatened
to conquer the world, and do God-knew-what with the
subjected peoples of Earth, here a terrestrial mutant ad-
mitted quite casually that she could use her powers of
the mind to subdue and confuse another sentient being
to her heart's content. How easily could Braddock or
another like her do the very same to her fellow Earth-
lings? Or, heaven forfend, her fellow subjects of the
British Crown?!

"You say something, Sandy?" the man called Logan
said, hefting his helmet in his hands like a rugby ball.

Alysande's expression soured, and not just because
of Logan's unwelcome use of the overly familiar nick-

name. Even with her helmet mic muted, he'd been able
to hear her muttered whisper. She'd read up on the
mutant abilities of Logan and his friends in the classified files of Her Majesty's government, and then
Raphael had provided a tidbit or two that were too top-
secret even to be recorded there—Alysande shuddered
to think how he might have come by them. Alysande
would have to be careful. With his enhanced senses,
Logan would be able to detect things normally safely
hidden. It was even conjectured that his enhanced auditory and olfactory capabilities would make it possible
for him to act as a walking polygraph of sorts, able to
hear when one's pulse quickened, or the surface temperature of their skin changed. Which was, of course, to
say nothing of his berserker rages and unbreakable
skeleton and claws.

Delightful. Just the sort of man to have on a maiden voyage.

When the notion of a collaboration between the international rogues—the X-Men—and Her Majesty's
government had first been mooted, only hours before,
Alysande had been against it from the start. From the
expression of Logan and his companion Kitty Pryde,
the young American, it was clear that they were no happier having to ask for Alysande's help than she was
happy to be obliged to give it. But, as she'd explained
when they'd reached the launch platform off the coast
of Tortola, her job was to safeguard the United King-
dom at any cost, and she didn't care whom she had to
get into bed with to get the job done. Had there been
any alternative, Alysande would have taken it, and
gladly; but so far, the plan proposed by the X-Men was

the only feasible strategy so far advanced, however out-landish or difficult a prospect it might be.

Key to the X-Men's plan was the need to deliver a small number of them to the flagship of the invading armada, the immense vessel they called the Kh'thonic Flagship. Fortunate for them, then, that the British had a bleeding-edge space plane already fueled and ready on the waters of the Sargasso Sea. The arrival of the Kh'thon had thrown a wrench into the plans of the British Rocket Group, so there was some justice, if not even some irony, in the idea of its virgin launch being the linchpin in a plan that might spell the end of the Kh'thonic threat.

Raphael maneuvered around the rear acceleration chairs, smiling unctuously at their passengers, Ms. Braddock in particular, and then settled himself into the copilot's seat. The RCX operative's presence was the only variable in the plan for which Alysande could not account. When she'd relayed the X-Men's request to her superiors, she'd volunteered her name as a potential pilot for the mission. There was every chance that they would not be returning alive, and that they might face violent resistance when they reached the Fathership; it was clear, then, that none of the space plane's planned crew could be sent along. They were scientists, to a man, none of them with any combat experience. Alysande, who'd overseen security for the space plane project since its early days, knew more about the craft and its controls than virtually anyone but the men and women who built it, and certainly knew how to handle herself in a firefight.

When the word had come down that the space plane would be put at the X-Men's disposal, then, Alysande was hardly surprised to hear her own name mentioned as captaining the vessel. However, when Raphael was listed as her second-in-command, she'd been taken somewhat aback.

It shouldn't have puzzled her at all, really. She realized that only in retrospect, while watching the secret agent oversee the installation of the unconscious Exemplar prisoner in the rear of the craft's passenger section. Seeing the care with which Raphael maneuvered the sleeping body into place, the almost naked hunger writ on his face, Alysande had first taken his interest in the woman to be one of a prurient nature. It quickly occurred to her, however, that the virtually sexless Raphael was not likely interested in the strange, unearthly woman's body. No, Raphael was interested in her *mind*.

Specifically, the ability of her mind to move objects. She could lift a car, bus, or boat, or so Alysande had been told, but it occurred to her that the telekine might also be able to manipulate objects on a smaller scale— say, something the size of a capillary in the brain? It didn't take much imagination to see what a backroom, black-ops type like Raphael wouldn't do with the ability to literally squeeze the life from a target, but from across the room. And when Alysande saw the way he hungrily looked at Ms. Braddock as he passed by suggested that he would not refuse the ability to pluck secrets from the minds of his enemies from great distances, either.

Despite Raphael's protestations to the contrary, Alysande knew that the RCX viewed this mission, in large part, as a shopping trip. In addition to helping to safeguard the safety of humanity and of the Earth itself, Alysande was sure that Raphael was under orders to secure and bring back any bits of technology, weaponry, or otherwise that he might come across and determine what might be of use to the British crown.

Which, Alysande realized with only a slight measure of distaste, was perfectly fine with her.

As Raphael strapped into the copilot's seat, Alysande patched her helmet mic into the ship's inboard communications.

"Everybody buckled in? Best you do, as I expect this might be something of a bumpy ride."

Out on the launch pad, the countdown had begun.

28

"So you used to be an Avenger, right, Mr. McCoy?"

"Still a reserve member in good standing, Doug. But remember, call me Hank. Why, you think they loan a Quinjet to just anybody that asks?"

"No . . . Hank. I was just wondering. What's Captain America really like?"

Hank sighed, and turned his attention back to the quinjet's controls.

The five-person, supersonic VTOL was now racing over the waters of the Gulf of Mexico, cruising at just over Mach 2. At this speed, they would reach Ecuador in just over an hour. Hank McCoy and Doug Ramsey were strapped into the two flight crew seats, while Rogue was sacked out in the back, stretched across three jump seats. She snored from time to time and the sound was so high and whistling that Hank couldn't help finding it irresistibly charming.

Yes, Hank chided himself. *If not for the fact that the barest touch of her skin knocks people unconscious, but only after depriving them of their powers and memories, then maybe you'd make a play for her, no? If, that is, she were able to get over the fact that you look like a shaved ape crammed unconvincingly into a human suit.*

For all that he approached the world, and its perils, with a light heart and a smile on his face, still there were times when darker moods struck Hank. Now, evidently, was one of those times.

He scowled.

"Mr. McCoy?" said the boy at his side, tentatively. "Erm, Hank? Is everything alright?"

"Hmm? Oh, yes, Doug. I'm sorry. Was a million miles away for a moment, there. You were asking about Captain America, were you?"

Doug nodded, wide-eyed and eager.

"Well, keep yourself in the game, young man, and you just might meet him yourself."

Provided, that is, Hank thought, *that any of us lives that long.*

Doug managed to keep a smile on his face, but just barely. He was grateful when Hank turned his attention back to the controls, giving him the opportunity to turn around and look out the cockpit's side window. Really, though, he was just trying to hide his expression from the former X-Man.

Even those that knew what his mutant power was, even those who'd seen him use it time and again, still didn't really understand what having a mastery of language really *meant.* Sure, Doug could learn to speak any dialect, or read any written form, in no time at all. Yes, he could familiarize himself with any programming code in a matter of minutes, if he applied himself. But it wasn't just words or numbers that he could understand; no, his power extended to *all* language.

What even Kitty failed to realize, Doug was sure, was that a language was any system for representing data. That data could be anything from thoughts, feelings, wants, quantities, qualities, you name it. And the system could be encoded using words, numbers, hand signs, arrangements of flowers, strings of beads, even unconscious gestures. It was this last that everyone seemed to forget, even though they had all doubtless heard of *body language.*

It wasn't unerring, to be sure, Doug's ability to read unconscious gestures. When he was in situations in which he was personally nervous, for example, he found it difficult to concentrate on the subtle cues, the slight movements that expressed another's unspoken thoughts. When he was with Betsy, for instance, he always felt the same way he did when first peering into a text written in Linear B: *I can't possibly understand* this! Around her he fumbled, tongue-tied, and was sure he misread every sign and gesture.

On occasions like this, though, in relatively calm, relaxed environments, Doug's comprehension of body language was much more complete. At times, it seemed to him, it almost approached the ability to read surface thoughts, at least when dealing with someone whose movements were undisciplined. (There were some, whether dancers like Stevie Hunter or fighters like Logan, who never betrayed *anything,* so measured and careful was their every move.)

So when Hank gave him the verbal equivalent of a pat on the back, figuratively tousling his hair like one would a child, Doug was scarcely reassured, since Hank's unconscious gestures were clear, practically shouting, *We're all going to die.*

29

At that moment, fifteen hundred miles to the east, another supersonic plane blazed across the sky. Scott was at the controls of the *Blackbird,* piloting the spy plane to the Sargasso Sea for the second time in as many days.

In the copilot's seat beside him was the imposing Russian, Peter Rasputin, while the blue-furred German, Kurt Wagner, crouched in the space between them, an arm draped over the back of each of their seats.

"What are you working on today, *mein Freund,*" Kurt said, glancing at the sketchpad propped on Peter's knee.

Peter blushed, his cheeks going a deep red, and Kurt for the millionth time was forced to resist the urge to mock his stalwart Russian friend. Even with all that they had seen and done these past years, the places they'd been and the foes they faced, still and all did Peter Rasputin so often seem like a little boy stuck in a man's body. A towering, well-muscled man's body, to be sure, but a little boy, for all of that.

So it came as no surprise that, having been caught sketching a devastatingly attractive woman with a Mohawk hairdo, in a state of casual undress, Peter would stammer like a school boy caught out by a scolding teacher.

"Who is she, then?" Kurt said. "The heroine from one of Katzchen's fantasy novels? A fierce warrior princess or a maiden to be rescued?"

His hands still on the controls, Scott glanced over casually. "Those are Fall People markings, aren't they?"

Peter blushed deeper, the red of his cheeks intensifying, and nodded. "She is Nereel."

"Ah," Kurt said, understanding dawning. He reached over and, gesturing for permission, took the sketchbook from Peter's hands. "That girl in the Savage Land. I remember her now." He looked up at Peter, a lascivious grin on his lips, sharp canines exposed. "Am I mistaken, Herr Rasputin, or did you not spend some . . . *quality* time with this attractive young lady?"

Peter averted his eyes, suddenly finding something of great interest in the featureless waves passing beneath them. "Perhaps," he finally replied.

Kurt's grin widened, and he regarded the sketch admiringly. Then, casually, he flipped to the previous page. It was a drawing of the same woman, with the same Mohawk and lax dress code, only this time she was carrying a small child in her arms, its hair and eyes dark, little more than an infant, really.

"A Savage Land Pietà," Kurt said, nodding appreciatively. "A primordial Madonna and child. Peter, I believe you missed your calling when you chose world-saving as a vocation, and not the pursuit of art. But tell me . . ." He handed the sketchbook back to Peter, open to the picture of Nereel and the child. "Why portray Nereel with a child? I don't recall her being a mother."

Peter accepted the proffered sketchbook, and gazed at the drawing for a long moment, as though seeing something in it he recognized, but being unable to say precisely what. "I'm not sure," he answered at length. "It just . . . felt right."

"Okay, gentlemen," Scott said, his tone pure business. "We're coming up on our destination. We're approaching from opposite Julienne Cay, and coming in so low they shouldn't be able to spot us, but if they do, this could be a very short trip."

Kurt returned to his seat, buckling the safety straps around him.

"There already?" he said. "But I was given to understand there would be beverage service on this flight, and I've yet to be given a drink."

Scott didn't answer, but kept his gaze focused as straight ahead as a laser, but Kurt was gratified to see that Peter smiled, if slightly, before returning his attention to his sketching.

30

It was midmorning when Vox Septimus and three other servitors, all wearing similar robes of varying shades and hues, all carrying identical crystal rods, came for Lee and the others.

"This one offers apologies," Vox Septimus said as he stepped through the newly opened door. "But there are other uses to which this space will be put. Besides, now that the other specimens have been relocated here to Dis, it is simplest to relocate you and your companions to the general population."

For a brief, futile moment, Merrick put up something resembling resistance, but it took only a minute gesture with one of the crystal rods for him to fall in line, with a guilty glance at Frank. For his part, Frank kept his eyes on the ground, and did everything he was told.

Vox Septimus walked in the lead, Lee and her crewmen following, and the other three servitors bringing up the rear.

"Where are you taking us?" Lee asked as they were ushered down a twisting corridor to a wide, sloping

ramp that spiraled from the tower's base to its crown.
Lee and the others had been brought this way the day
before—had it really only been a single day?—but in
the excitement and fear of the moment, very little of
their surroundings had registered with her. Now, more
composed and aware, she took careful note of everything they passed, of all of the branching corridors, of
the doorways and passages.

"As this one indicated," Vox Septimus answered casually. "You are being relocated to the general population."

They passed a broad landing, about halfway down
the ramp, where a trio of strangely dressed individuals
lingered. Silent, their mouths unmoving, they gestured
dramatically with their hands, pulling broad expressions. Compared to Vox Septimus and his fellows, this
trio were uniformly larger, more muscled, and the fab-
rics of their exotically cut clothing were of brighter hues.

Lee noted with interest that, as she and her crew
were led by, the trio regarded them with something like
disgust, laced with an almost naked hostility. This was
hardly surprising, given their circumstance. However,
what *was* surprising was the thinly veiled contempt
with which they regarded Vox Septimus and the other
three servitors.

As they drew near, Lee saw that Vox Septimus kept
his eyes averted, not looking at the three. When their
course brought them the closest they would come, only
a few yards away, one of the trio pointed at Lee, scowling. In response, another pointed at Vox, whereupon
the other two laughed out loud. Hearing their laughter

was unsettling, after so long a silence, and Lee realized that they must have been communicating telepathically all along.

Without warning, the trio leapt into the air. Zipping past Vox Septimus, coming only inches from him, they jetted out to the empty space at the middle of the tower, and with a dark glance back in her direction—or in Vox's?—they flew up toward the tower's crown at speed.

Vox, startled by their close passage, faltered, almost stumbling and falling. So near the edge of the broad, rail-less ramp were they that he might any second tumble over the side, no doubt falling to his death, hundreds of feet below.

Lee acted without thinking, and reached out and grabbed hold of Vox Septimus's elbow, righting him and preventing his fall.

"You will return to the line!" shouted one of the servitors at the rear of their train, waving his crystal rod menacingly.

"All is well," Vox Septimus said, raising his hand. He seemed shaken, out of breath. His fellow servitor returned to the end of the line, and then Vox Septimus regarded Lee, a strange expression on his face. Finally, he said, his voice somewhat strained, "You have this one's thanks."

Lee shrugged, not failing to see the tight grip Vox Septimus retained on his crystal rod. "Don't mention it."

Vox Septimus nodded slowly, and then turned and continued on their course down the ramp. Lee followed behind, trying to work out the implications of what she'd just seen.

They reached the ground level, where she and the others had entered the tower the day before, and continued downward. Lee knew from her previous visits to the city that beneath its foundations were massive spaces, akin to giant natural caverns, but lined on all sides with strange shapes of metal and crystal, punctuated here and there with enormous statuary, the same massive, inhuman grotesqueries that decorated the city above.

The ramp on which they now trod continued down a sloped spiral toward one of those massive spaces. When they emerged into this cavernous space beneath the ground, the walls fell away on either side. The lights were somewhat dim, but even though Lee could see before and behind her with little trouble, she could not see a wall or barrier in any direction, no matter how hard she strained. The vast, empty spaces swallowed the sound of their footsteps, and it seemed to Lee for a moment that she must have gone deaf.

Finally, they reached another landing from which projected a narrow bridge or walkway. At Vox Septimus's insistence, Lee and the others were marched across this narrow bridge, which could not have been more than three or four feet wide. Risking a quick glance over the side, Lee could not see any ground or floor below, only a crazed network of other ramps, landings, and walkways, with strange, bulbous structures here and there at the intersections. It was to one of these bulbous structures that they were being led. It resembled nothing so much as a human organ—a liver, say, or a kidney—constructed of steel and crystal and enlarged to an immense size. It was a huge structure, capable of fitting the trawler *Arcadia* a dozen times over.

At what appeared to be the structures' entrance, three walkways met at a wide platform. As they drew near, Lee saw that another group of prisoners was being marched to the left, with crystal rod–wielding servitors before and after. But these were not the ordinary men and women she'd glimpsed down in the courtyard, just a short while before. These were *super-heroes*.

Their uniforms, though ripped, scorched, and dirtied, were those of costumed crime-fighters. Lee could see that at a glance, even if their stature and muscular profiles weren't a give away, in and of themselves. At a distance, Lee didn't recognize any of them, but as both their party and hers drew nearer the platform, and the bulbous structure beyond, one or two of them grew more familiar to her. One was dressed in red, white, and gold, and Lee recognized him as Sunfire. Two wore identical uniforms of red and black, a triangle emblem on their chests, and Lee remembered Magneto once describing uniforms matching that description, and saying that they belonged to students of the Massachusetts Academy. Finally, there were three wearing uniforms of yellow and black, and not only did Lee recognize the design, but also their faces; she remembered having seen pictures of them during a brief visit to see Magneto in New York, before she'd broken off their relationship. They were students at Xavier's school, Scott Summers's old alma mater.

For the briefest instant, Lee allowed herself to hope. She entertained the fleeting thought that, if students of the Xavier School were here, then that meant that Scott, and a rescue, could not be far behind. But then she saw the dispirited way that the Xavier students shuffled along the walkway—the same, listless gait adopted by Sunfire and all the others—and she recognized the way in which each of their uniforms differed from those she had seen before, or had described to her.

All of them, without exception, were wearing broad silver collars around their necks.

It didn't take long to make the guess that the dispirited expressions and slow movements of the super-heroes—to say nothing of the fact that they willingly allowed themselves to be herded along like regular people, like *her*—had something to do with these strange, oversize silver collars. There was some property of the collars, Lee supposed, that was serving to dampen, if not completely nullify, the heroes' powers.

All of which suggested several factors in rapid succession.

First, that the Kh'thon *did* possess the ability to nullify a mutant's abilities.

Second, that things in the outside world were going worse than Lee might have imagined.

And lastly, that their chances for escape from the city of Dis had just grown much, much more complicated.

31

Kitty wasn't sure at what point traveling into outer space had become so routine for her, much less what that said about her lifestyle. Most girls her age were worrying about what college they'd go to, or obsessing over some boy in their class, or anxious about whether they'd pass their midterm exams.

Not Kitty. She was strapped into a bleeding-edge space plane, rocketing into cislunar space, and finding the whole thing just a little *boring*. It was when she realized that she'd just as soon get the whole saving-the-world thing done and over with so she could get home and catch up on some much needed sleep that Kitty realized that her standards had shifted somewhat these last few years.

It wasn't all that long ago that she'd been a regular suburban kid in Deerfield, Illinois. In the years since, she'd traveled in time, gone into space a time or two, adopted a dragon, kissed a boy, become a ninja, and saved the world more times than she could count. After a while, it all just got to be old hat. Kitty imagined this was how child stars must feel about Hollywood when they grow up; what seems magical and glamorous to outsiders is just another job to a kid who grew up doing it.

Of course, Kitty liked to hope that she'd be a little luckier when she grew up than most child stars. Assuming she grew up at all, that is. If she survived the next few hours, and the world didn't get blown up in the process, she had no intention of ending up on the news, a few years down the line, having gotten arrested trying to knock over a Quick Stop.

But then, Kitty ruminated, if she put her mind to robbing a convenience store, she'd do it *right*.

"Approaching the alien fleet," said Colonel Alysande Stuart over the ship's communication system, interrupting Kitty's reverie. "If you lot have a secret plan for keeping us from getting blown out of the sky as soon as these buggers notice we're here, you might want to get it into motion."

"Ah," Betsy said, raising a gloved finger, like someone placing a bid at an auction. "That would be me."

Betsy struggled to unbuckle the straps that kept her secured to the acceleration chair.

"Today would be nice, I think," said Raphael, his tone oily.

"Blasted . . ." Betsy wrenched at the buckles and straps unsuccessfully. "I can't . . ." She threw down her hands, and looked up, her expression through the helmet one of exasperation. Then, in a small voice, she said, "I'm stuck."

"Hmph." Logan, who'd been sitting with his eyes closed, his head lolled to the side of his helmet, made a noise somewhere between a grunt of annoyance and a bark of laughter. He raised his left hand, and a single adamantium blade slid out from the special pressurized seal Kitty had rigged in the glove of his suit shortly before take off. He reached over, bringing the razor-sharp tip of the claw near Betsy's straps. "Lemme fix it . . ."

"Logan!" Kitty batted Logan's hand away, like a mother scolding a child for sampling a cake's icing before it was time for dessert. "I'm sure there's an *easier* way."

Kitty reached over and took hold of the strap, wrapping her hand around the buckle. Then, without any visible effort, she phased her hand, the buckle, and the straps to which it was attached. With the straps intangible, Betsy was able to climb out of the acceleration chair without difficulty.

Kitty solidified again, and when she released the buckle, it floated back toward the seat, moving with an unexpected grace in the cabin's microgravity.

"See, Logan," Kitty reproached. "Not everything has to be hack and slash, you know."

"Hey, kiddo," Logan grinned. "I'm gonna be making some cuts before this caper is over and done, so might as well get used to it now."

Kitty blew Logan a raspberry, fogging up the inside of her helmet, while Betsy maneuvered with surprising elegance to the rear of the cabin. There, their Exemplar prisoner was secured by straps to a kind of gurney, in a pressure suit of her own.

"If what I was able to extract from our guest's memories this morning was correct," Betsy explained, her voice buzzing over the speaker's in Kitty's helmet, "then virtually all ship-to-ship communication in the

Kh'thonic fleet is done telepathically. The profile of our vessel matters, if it matters at all, far less than whether or not we respond with the appropriate telepathic call signs when contacted. If our guest's identity is confirmed, and the call signs are accepted, then we'll be able to approach the fleet without incident."

"And if they aren't?" Colonel Stuart asked.

"In that case," Raphael responded, "then I believe an *incident* would be in the offing, wouldn't you say?"

As it happened, they needn't have worried. Using the Exemplar as a kind of telepathic hand puppet, Betsy was able to interact with the fleet's security protocols, and seemingly without ever raising suspicion. Betsy had managed to cloud the Exemplar's perceptions, so that as far as the Exemplar knew, she was sitting aboard one of the Kh'thonic landers; and since Betsy had judiciously "edited" the Exemplar's memories of the events of the day, the Exemplar had no recollection of ever being defeated in battle by the X-Men, or of being taken prisoner. So far as the Exemplar knew, following on the hypnotic suggestion implanted by Betsy, she was returning to the Kh'thonic fleet for minor medical attention, and to bring supplies back down to the Kh'thonic forces on the ground.

Alysande's hands tightened on the controls, white-knuckled inside her heavy pressurized gloves. Not for the first time she wished that she'd been able to talk Bernard into incorporating weapons into the space plane's design, but the head of the British Rocket Group had insisted that this was principally a vessel of science and exploration, and in the end he'd managed to convince the British authorities that his was the correct view.

Which was all well and good, if one lived on a plane of pure abstraction, in the selfless pursuit of *knowledge*, but Alysande lived in the real world, a place of conflict, danger, and menace. And right now, she'd have traded all the pure abstraction and hidden knowledge in the world for a few guided missiles with nuclear warheads. Oh, she knew that there was little chance of even nukes doing any damage to the shielded Kh'thon vessels, but still, she'd have felt better having the option.

Just when things looked their tensest, though, and Alysande and the others waited in an excruciating silence while the mind-fogged Exemplar communicated telepathically with Kh'thonic flight control, Betsy gave the others the high sign, all smiles.

"It worked," Betsy said. "We've been given the green light to approach the Fathership."

"Well," Raphael said, forcing a smile. "That wasn't so bad, was it?"

Alysande looked over and saw the sweat glistening on the spy's forehead. She suspected he'd been the most nervous of any of them.

"Bub," said Logan from his acceleration chair. "That was the *easy* part. It's all uphill from here."

Even though Betsy had said they'd been given the all clear, Logan was sure they'd be looking at a fight as soon as they landed. But after Colonel Stuart had brought the space plane in, touching down in the Fathership itself, they'd stepped through the hatch to find the landing bay almost completely deserted.

From the outside, the Fathership had looked like something out of a nightmare, all jagged angles, spires, and spikes, blacker still than the dark of space around it. On the inside, though, it was even stranger, more resembling the inside of a living being than something constructed by hand. Or more resembling a corpse, rather, since there was no way that anything living could survive, as twisted and wrong as the Fathership was. Even the light had a strange, unsettling quality to it, and the air, though breathable, carried with it the faintest hint of putrefaction and decay. This was like a grave, a corpse ship built from the rotting remains of some impossibly large, impossibly *wrong* monstrosity beyond human imagination.

Logan stripped off his pressure suit, revealing the brown-and-tan uniform of unstable molecules worn beneath. He tossed his suit back through the open hatch, and slid his claws in and out, experimentally. Then he hopped up in the air, a tiny movement, but one that allowed him to judge the gravity in the ship. He read it as being just a hair over one g, almost exactly standard Earth gravity. *Good,* Logan thought, nodding appreciably. *That means we won't be at a disadvantage.* If it had been extremely high gravity, their muscles might not have been able to acclimate to the extra weight, and they might have been slowed down as a result. *Of course, it ain't doin' us any favors, either.*

"I was expecting some kind of welcome wagon, at least," Logan said, glancing around the cavernous landing bay. There were one or two figures moving in the far distance, but otherwise the enormous space was entirely empty.

"I don't know." Kitty smirked. "This lack of attention may just hurt my feelings."

"The Kh'thon maintain close controls on the population levels of their slaves," Betsy explained, sounding more like a schoolmarm every time she opened her mouth. Ever since she mind-melded with the telekine prisoner, Betsy had been the resident expert on all things Kth'thon. "There are humans here on the Fathership—and mutants, too—but most of them are busy servicing the needs of the Kh'thon. If we were really the minor functionary our prisoner purported to be, we'd just be another slave, no matter how powerful. And no one's going to be pulled off their duties to see to the arrival of more slaves. We'd have been trained to know what we were doing, and where we were going, and if we got lost, it'd be *our* problem."

"Lucky for us we have an informed guide, yes?" Colonel Stuart checked the action on her automatic pistol. She had changed out of her pressure suit, and now wore standard Royal Marine fatigues of khaki and green, with a dark beret pulled down over her head.

"Well," said Raphael, dressed incongruously in a black business suit and tie, carrying a brief case. He looked like a bank manager who'd gotten lost on the way to the office and ended up by accident on the flagship of an invading armada. "Shall we be off, then?"

"Yes, let's," Logan growled. "The sooner we're done and out of here the better."

So they set off, Logan in lead, Betsy and the others following close behind, moving ever deeper into the strange, unearthly ship.

32

As the Quinjet flew over the border with Santo Marco, and entered Ecuadorian airspace, the automated Avengers call sign broadcast on all frequencies immediately granted them the clearances they'd need to approach and land. From there, it was a matter of minutes before they'd reach the point in the jungle indicated on Hank's surveillance photos.

Rogue tried to stifle a yawn, and failed. She'd caught a quick nap, but it had done little more than serve to remind her how tired she was, rather than making her feel any more rested. She stretched her arms to either side, and rolled her head around in slow circles, trying to work the kinks out of her neck.

That's the problem with being invulnerable on the one hand, with power-sucking skin on t'other, Rogue mused. *Nobody's linin' up to give you a neck rub or back massage. Heck, I don't even know if I could feel it, if they did.*

Rogue blinked sleepily, yawned again, and leaned forward, sticking her head and shoulders between Hank and Doug. "We there yet?"

"Oh, I'm sorry," Hank said with a friendly smile. "Is

the end of the world interfering with your beauty sleep?"

"Well, now that you mention it . . ." Rogue grinned, and punched Hank lightly on the upper arm. "Though I do seem to recall puttin' in for a wake-up call at a quarter till Apocalypse."

"In that case," Doug said, "I think you're right on time."

Rogue looked in the direction that Doug was pointing, and Hank obliged by bringing up an enhanced telescopic view on the Quinjet's monitors, set in the control panel just before them.

"What the . . ." Rogue shook her head in amazement.

From this distance, it looked like nothing more mysterious than a man sitting in a chair. Or a statue of a man in a chair, perhaps, his legs out straight before him, knees bent at precisely ninety degrees, his arms lying on the chair's armrests.

But the scale was all wrong. Even without distance cues, it would be impossible to miss the fact that the statue towered over the lush greenery around it. So perhaps it was something like the statue of Abraham Lincoln in the Lincoln Memorial.

Except no, it was bigger even than that. The greenery on all sides was not shrubs and bushes. No, they were the towering trees of the rain forest. One hundred copies of the Lincoln Memorial statue, stacked one atop the other, would not be quite so tall.

And there was, of course, the fact that Abraham Lincoln was not sculpted in hues of purple and gray, with a strange, imposing helmet sculpted around his face.

But then, no one had ever been freed on the word of the Master Mold, either, so it should have come as no surprise.

The Master Mold was so large it would simply not fit into Doug Ramsey's mind. It was as though the sight of it hit his eyeballs and bounced right back, without registering on the rods and cones. His mind refused to accept that it could be real.

In the open space before the seated statue there was a clearing, beyond which was a steep drop-off, where a waterfall plunged to the jungle floor far below.

Rogue was the first out of the Quinjet door, and Doug wasn't about to complain. Virtually invulnerable, super-strong, and blindingly fast, there was little doubt that she'd be the best suited to handle any unforeseen difficulties. But, as Beast climbed to the ground, and Doug followed, it seemed that the biggest danger facing them at the moment came in the form of mosquitoes.

"Yeesh," Rogue said, wrinkling her nose. "What is that *smell*?"

Hank smiled. "That, my dear, is the bouquet of nature, the humble aroma of the jungle, the scent of the cycle of life inexorably turning and turning . . ."

"Crap," Doug said.

"Exactly," Hank answered with a broad smile.

"No." Doug shook his head, and pointed.

Hank turned, and looked in the direction Doug indicated. "Oh, crap, indeed."

Rogue smiled. "Finally," she said, cracking her knuckles. "And here I was worried this trip would be boring."

• • •

They looked, and moved, like chickens, but chickens made out of old motorcycle parts, and toasters, and refrigerator coils. Most chickens, naturally, did not come equipped with rapid-fire automatic weaponry, but then allowances had to be made for form and function.

Even as he worried that they might extinguish his life at any moment, Hank could not help admiring the genius of the mechanisms design. These were Sentinels, that much was clear, but Sentinels unlike any he had encountered before. These seemed more like wild creatures than the giant, stoic behemoths he and the other X-Men had faced time and again. These diminutive things were feral Sentinels, their designs run wild.

Their programming, sadly, had not drifted nearly so far from the ideal.

"Mutants," came the high-pitched, clattering voice of the chicken Sentinels, several of them speaking at once in rough harmony. *"You are advised to surrender or face immediate termination. This is your only warning."*

"I think they look kinda cute," Rogue said, glancing over her shoulder at Doug and Hank, who'd cautiously taken up a position behind her.

Before Hank or Doug could answer, the chicken Sentinels opened fire. The roar of their muzzle fire was deafening, but the slugs flattened harmlessly against Rogue, the kinetic energy of the impact absorbed by her nigh invulnerable skin without leaving mark or blemish. Some of the slugs, hitting at more oblique angles, ricocheted off, lancing through the foliage nearby, shredding leaves and branches from the trees.

Somewhere nearby, a flock of tropical birds, alarmed by the noise of the gunfire, squawked loudly in protest and then, as one, took wing. The smell of burning gunpowder reached Hank's nostrils, wafted on the light jungle breeze. And suddenly, Rogue was gone.

She moved so fast she blurred practically into invisibility. It took all of Hank's concentration and not-inconsiderable visual acuity to follow her motions at all, and even then he was tracking her progress more by the destruction in her wake than by any glimpse of her movement.

Where before eight chicken Sentinels had perched before them, none taller than three and a half or four feet tall, now there was only a gently raining shower of debris, falling in a rough line from left to right, clouds of dust drifting languidly on the light breeze.

In less time than it took to blink, Rogue was standing before them once again, smoothing back her white-streaked hair with a gloved hand. Only then did the last of the dismantled Sentinels strike the ground. The whole operation had taken on the order of a few seconds.

"I gotta say, I feel a little guilty 'bout that," Rogue said, smiling sheepishly. "Poor little fellahs."

Doug grinned broadly, looking up at Rogue, eyes full of hero worship. Hank didn't know that he could blame him. As a kid who was good at little more than reading, and then got to be good at running and jumping and swinging, to say nothing of clinging with his bare (and now oversize) feet, Hank had still felt flatly amazed the first time he saw Scott let loose with one of his optic blasts. To say nothing of Jean with her telekinesis, or Bobby with his ability to extract all the heat from a limited region of space. And Warren, who could *fly*? Forget about it. Doug seemed like a nice kid, but Hank knew from experience that having a more sedate power like the ability to read and write in any language left one feeling more than a little inadequate in the face of some of the more demonstrative mutant abilities.

Which was not to say that Hank had not shown off with his acrobatics, from time to time. But one always had to try to get one's own back, whenever possible.

"Come on," Hank said, pointing toward the large opening in the wall between the Master Mold's feet. From this distance, it seemed about the dimensions of a typical house's garage door, but he knew that it was actually large enough to admit the *Blackbird* with room to spare—sideways, even. "These little feral Sentinels could well be just the first line of defense, and we might run into more interference once we're inside."

They set off across the clearing, which rose at a gentle slope toward the base of the Master Mold facilities.

"Um, Mister McCoy . . . that is, Hank?" Doug hurried his pace to keep abreast of Hank, while Rogue trotted a few steps ahead. "I've never heard anything about Sentinels of that configuration before. Had you?"

Hank shook his head. "No. But then, I'm not sure that anybody has."

Doug tilted his head to one side, confused, and tightened his grip on the leather satchel over his shoulder. "Sir?"

"That is to say," Hank continued, "that this Master Mold facility has been sitting disused for some time. And while the central core might have been off-line throughout that time, there would doubtless have been Sentinels in operation throughout, if only for automated defense systems like those we've just encountered. And absent any additional instructions, they'd have continued to carry out their functions. And, knowing what I do about their programming, Sentinels are equipped with the ability to repair themselves, as needed, using whatever resources are at hand; likewise, each is instilled with the instinct to adapt and improve whenever possible. Over the years, they'd have needed to repair themselves for any number of reasons, whether routine wear and tear, or environmental damage, or accidents, or what-have-you. And when they repaired themselves, with an ever-dwindling supply of resources and parts, the second imperative would have come to the fore, and naturally . . ."

Hank paused, and glanced over at Doug, who was nodding in dawning understanding.

"They would have evolved," Doug said, a trace of wonderment in his tone. "Adapted to their environment, eliminated unnecessary design elements, introduced novel designs and features to see whether they improved their efficiency. Perhaps even reproduced, in a sense, experimenting by creating duplicates with varying characteristics."

"Exactly." Hank sounded like a schoolteacher praising a star pupil.

They were now approaching the wide opening of

the factory itself, the space beyond the threshold dark and foreboding.

"But an evolutionary process," Doug went on, "suggests evolutionary niches. Designs adapting to perform specific tasks, adapted to specific environments."

"Yes," Hank said, raising an eyebrow. "What of it?"

They passed through the threshold, into the dark, cavernous space beyond.

"Well, then what if the chicken Sentinels were just scavengers, or something else at the lower levels of the pecking order. What if there was a top predator, higher up the chain?"

Just then, lights flared high above them. They looked up and saw what appeared to be a Sentinel's helmet, lacking a face, perched atop eight immensely long, segmented legs. Where the helmet and the legs met, huge pincers clacked open and closed, like the mouth of some enormous animal.

"Well," Hank said, taking off his glasses and slipping them carefully into his shirt pocket. "There's a fine contender for top predator, if ever I saw one."

"Ah, don't go givin' away any blue ribbons just yet," Rogue said, and pointed toward the shadows.

Another feral Sentinel, this one looking like a giant snake with arms, slithered toward them, undulating across the pitted concrete of the factory floor, the arms which jutted from beneath its Sentinel helmet on either side bristling with weaponry.

"Fans," Rogue said with a thin smile, "we just might have a horse race on our hands."

33

The *Blackbird* skimmed over the waves for the last few miles, approaching from the west. By the time Scott nosed her forward, touching down for an amphibious landing on the far side of Julienne Cay, the fuselage had been gliding bare inches above the waves, more like a cigarette boat at high speed than a supersonic spy plane puttering along at a fraction of its top acceleration.

Scott's gamble was that the foliage of the atoll, and the gentle curve of its sandy hills, would hide them from the sight of the alien city, positioned as it was on the eastern side of Julienne Cay. That they were not surrounded by super-powered Exemplar troops on hover-platforms the moment they stepped out of the *Blackbird* and into the shallow surf at the shore's edge suggested Scott's gamble had paid off.

It was approaching the middle of the afternoon, local time, and the sun bore down on them from behind, sending long shadows angling across the pure white sands of the atoll as they walked inland. All three X-Men—Scott, Kurt, and Peter—were dressed for action in their uniforms, and carried nothing with them but the small handheld device that Scott had tucked into his belt. The *Blackbird,* its hatch securely closed, idled silently on the waves, anchored in place, the autopilot at ready.

"Let's go," Scott said, setting off for the tree line. "And keep out of sight. If they spot us, this'll all have been for nothing."

"Splendid motivational tactics, Scott." Kurt smiled, showing razor-sharp canines. "Perhaps you should do a lecture tour, hmm?"

Peter smiled, but Scott said nothing, plowing into the underground, a man on a mission.

A short while later, they reached the opposite shore, keeping well hidden behind the trees and underground, peering at the alien city from cover.

"Are you sure this is going to work, Scott?"

"What are you worried about, Peter?" Kurt laughed, mirthlessly. "I'm the one that's got to do all the heavy lifting here, *nicht wahr?*"

Peter shook his head, far from convinced. Hank McCoy had drawn up their plan of attack that morning, around the kitchen table in the Xavier mansion. It was simple and straightforward, but for all that he was a simple man, who preferred matters straightforward whenever possible, Peter had long since learned that the circuitous and devious was often the more effective strategy. That was one of the things he admired about Logan and Kurt. Even Katya, to some extent, had a penchant for approaching a problem from strange angles, of doing what was least expected, at the most unlikely moment, and turning it to her advantage.

That was not Peter's way. He was a farmer, not a strategist. If there was a stump in the path of your plow, you didn't change the plow's course to account for it. You simply pulled up the stump and got on with business.

The problem was, of course, that few problems in life were solved as simply as was a stump in the path of a plow. Would that they were. Then men like Peter would run the world, making sensible, straightforward decisions, ones that required no contemplation or additional scrutiny. But this was not that world.

In this instance, the problem was a simple one. There was an impenetrable dome surrounding the alien city, and they needed to penetrate it. Peter's solution, were it up to him, would be simply to punch a hole in the dome. Which, of course, was not possible; or, at least, not directly.

The hallmark of Hank's plan was its simplicity. They *would* poke a hole in the dome, it was true. But where Hank's plan differed from Peter's simpler approach was in *where* they would punch it.

Hank had theorized that it was unlikely that the invaders, these Kh'thon would have the energy resources necessary to maintain a completely impenetrable level of force at all points on the dome at all times. Therefore, he reasoned, there must be some mechanism that redirected the energy as needed. A concentrated, persistent attack on one point, then, would necessitate a momentary weakening of other points. That was were the *Blackbird* came in.

Scott had already programmed the attack patterns

into the autopilot. Once he sent the signal with the remote device on his belt, the *Blackbird* would lift off, circle around to the north at a considerable distance, and then approach the alien city from the east. Then, as soon as it was in range, the *Blackbird* would concentrate its fire on a single point, pouring out a maelstrom of firepower for a span of several minutes.

When the attack reached its peak, at the moment when Hank theorized that the opposite side of the dome would be at its weakest, the X-Men would make their move.

"I'm not so sure about this." Kurt narrowed his yellow eyes, rapping on the trunk of a palm tree with his knuckles.

"We've been over the math, Kurt," Scott said, a hint of impatience underlying his words. "It's well within your tolerances."

"Well, Scott," Kurt said, his tone sharp, "it isn't *my* tolerances that concern me."

The distance from the shore of the atoll to the edge of the alien city was no more than a mile. Kurt could easily teleport twice that distance . . . if he was traveling alone. But the plan called for him to teleport himself *and* both his fellow X-Men. The strain of displacing himself and two others, considering their respective masses, would leave all three of them feeling weakened and profoundly ill on their arrival. It would likely be some minutes before they'd be in a position to move.

Kurt could only teleport to a place he'd seen before. And while he'd visited the strange city years before, with the rest of the X-Men, the only locale he could bring to mind with any clarity was a sort of artificial grotto or pool near the city's center. There was a long, irregularly shaped body of water, lined with varicolored stones, beneath a towering statue of some inhuman creature, a man and a woman draped in postures of worshipfulness at its feet. The image of the place had stuck with Kurt all this time, since he'd never been able to puzzle out just what the relationship between the creature and the humans was—were they slaves, pets, supplicants, or worse?

This was to be their destination, then. Provided Hank's theory was correct. If it wasn't . . . ?

Kurt tried not to think about that.

Scott held the remote in his hands, tracking its miniature readouts and tells carefully. It had been close to ten minutes since he'd sent the *Blackbird*'s autopilot the signal to begin, and if all was proceeding according to the plans he'd input, the attack should begin at any minute.

"Um, friends?" Peter began, uneasily. He shuffled nervously from foot to foot, kicking up little clouds of sand, his expression that of a child worried about an impending visit to the dentist. "Just what *will* happen if Hank's theory isn't correct?"

Scott pursed his lips, but didn't answer, preferring instead to concentrate his attention on the remote.

Beside him, Kurt sighed heavily. "*Mein Freund,* if Hank's theory is incorrect, and the force field is active when we attempt to traverse it, then we will most likely be repelled, pushed back into the under dimension through which my teleports take me."

"Then we will simply teleport back here?" Peter asked hopefully.

Kurt shook his head. "Displacing as much mass as you and Scott combined represent, I won't be able to 'port for another few minutes. But the dimension to which we'll be shunted is a timeless limbo, in which there is no perception of the passage of one moment to the next. Though we will never realize it, frozen always in that single instant, we'll be stranded in that sunless void forever."

Peter shuddered, but Scott shook his head sharply. He tucked the remote back into his belt.

"That's not happening."

Scott reached out, and took Kurt's hand in his. It so resembled a pantomime of an affectionate gesture that Kurt had to stifle a laugh.

"Come on," Scott continued. "It's time to go."

Kurt nodded once. Holding Scott's hand with his left, Kurt took Peter's hand with his right.

"Okay, gentlemen," Kurt said with a sly smile. "I will see you on the other side." He paused, and then added, "And if I *don't* happen to see you again, allow me to say what a pleasure it has been knowing you both."

"And I you, *tovarisch*." Peter smiled sheepishly, and it looked for an instant as though he might begin to cry.

"Come on, you old women," Scott said with a bravado he clearly didn't feel. "We're not getting any younger."

Bamf.

• • •

Bamf.

Kurt had miscalculated, but only slightly. They arrived a few feet in the air. And while he and Scott fell unceremoniously onto the hard, unforgiving stone at the pool's edge, Peter plunged with a huge splash and spray into the clear blue waters themselves, sinking like a stone.

No one could have faulted Kurt for that. It was otherwise a flawless bit of teleportation.

Nor, to be fair, could he be faulted for the fact that they were, to a man, exhausted, haggard, and ill, able to do little more than lift their heads and moan. He *had* warned them, after all.

And if anyone was to blame for the fact that they'd teleported in, in full view of the quartet of Exemplar who lounged at the water's edge only a few short yards away, it wasn't Kurt. But then, by that point, the determination of blame was farthest from anyone's mind.

34

Once, when she was a girl, Lee Forrester had gone with her mom and dad to the stockyards. It was during the All-Florida Championship Rodeo in Arcadia. In later years, looking back on it, she could never quite understand *why* her parents had opted to take their precocious daughter on a road trip halfway to Tampa, to attend a rodeo, of all things. But in all the years that followed, Lee had never been able to forget the image of the stockyards, of the cattle herded into pens, seeming either resigned to their fates or else so numb from fear and shock as to make no difference. They lowed, on occasion, dispiritedly, but put up no active resistance.

That was how it was in the prison to which Lee and her crew had been brought. Though instead of cattle, placidly awaiting their fate, these were men and women, some of them *super-heroes*.

This would not do.

Lee approached the three Xavier students first. Even though she'd never met them, they would, at least, have friends in common.

Magneto had told her about these three, and their classmates. She couldn't remember their names, but she could remember their code names. And, on reflection, she supposed that in the world in which superheroes moved, that was as it should be.

One, the slight Scots girl with the bright red hair, whose somewhat mousy appearance did not hint at the fire she carried within, went by the code name of Wolfsbane. Though one would never guess it to look at her in this guise, this young girl possessed the ability to turn into a full-grown wolf, able to stop at transitional states along the way: a werewolf.

Another, a normally angry young Brazilian, with dark skin and short, wavy black hair, went by the code name of Sunspot. Though at five feet tall he was only a couple of inches taller than the red-haired Scots girl, this intense young man was capable of storing solar energy for long periods of time, and then converting it into superhuman levels of physical strength.

Finally, there was the determined Native American girl, who accessorized the yellow-and-black Xavier uniform with a silver-and-turquoise belt and fringed moccasin boots, who answered to the code name Mirage. This resourceful young woman, the oldest of the three, possessed the uncanny ability of creating lifelike three-dimensional images drawn from the minds of herself and others.

At the moment, though, none of the three appeared particularly fiery, or angry, or determined. Each seemed just as listless as all the other prisoners who wore the silver collars, like cattle resigned to their fates.

It was up to Lee to change all that.

None of the three resisted as Lee dragged them together to a fairly empty space at the side of the chamber. The room into which they had all been ushered, which had already held some dozen or more regular men and women, was large, the walls, floor, and ceiling featureless and unbroken. Once they had been ushered through the aperture in the wall, the silvery material of the wall had flowed back over the opening, sealing it up. But, more importantly, the prisoners had been left alone, without any manner of guard.

It was possible that their captors were watching, even now, whether through some sort of hidden cameras or perhaps through a section of the wall that could act like a two-way mirror. But for the moment, Lee had to assume that they'd been left to their own devices, at least until their captors once more had a use for them, or until they arrived with more prisoners.

If Lee was able to set her plan in motion, though, the prisoners would be ready when the door opened once more.

Next, Lee approached the Japanese hero, Sunfire. He sat slumped against the curved wall, his eyes on the middle distance, his mouth hanging slightly open. Neither she nor any of the Xavier students had met Sunfire before, but she had seen footage of him a few years before, from his first appearance in Manhattan, to his later action as the national hero of Japan. Sunfire's mutant ability was to ionize matter into superheated plasma, like the flames on the surface of the sun itself. This plasma could be fired in bolts at will, or used to create heated air currents around his body, allowing him to fly. Both were powers that, if Lee's plan were to come to fruition, would prove useful.

Finally, Lee approached the two students from the Massachusetts Academy, the Hellions. Xavier's students were helpful in identifying who the two were, and what their capacities were.

One, a young Arab of Moroccan origins, was code-named Jetstream. He possessed the ability to produce large amounts of energy, which he used to propel himself through the air like a rocket.

The other, a tall Native American, went by the code name Thunderbird. His abilities were simply stated, and easily understood. He was very fast, and very, very strong.

It was clear that there was animosity between the Xavier students and their rivals from the Massachusetts Academy, though Lee could not fail to notice the significant glances that Mirage and Thunderbird exchanged, even in their subdued states. Lee could not say whether there was a history between the two, or whether both simply wished that there were.

Now that she'd been able to get the attention of the six mutants, she gathered them together, along with her crewmen, and outlined her plan.

35

As they wended their way through the corridors and chambers of the Fathership, it seemed to Kitty less like an interstellar space craft, and more like some unearthly, foreboding catacombs, as though they were not hanging in space between the Earth and her moon, but instead deep underground in a network of tombs and oubliettes. The atmosphere, though breathable, was oppressive, and from time to time Kitty would shiver as a chill ran down her spine.

Kitty realized she'd felt this way before. Some time ago, and far away, when she walked through narrow streets and felt an inescapable chill in her bones, though the tropical sun was high and shining overhead.

"This is just like that city in the Bermuda Triangle," she said, her voice barely above a whisper.

"Dis," Betsy said, not turning around.

"What?" Kitty glanced over at the telepath, confused.

"The name of the city is Dis." Betsy slowed, and turned to meet Kitty's gaze. "Another fact I pulled from the memories of our Exemplar prisoner. Dis was one of seven major Kh'thon cities, scattered around the globe.

If the Kh'thon and their servants are successful, they plan to restore the other six as well." She paused, and then added, "Once they've razed all human civilization to the ground, of course."

"Naturally," Kitty said.

"Another one up ahead, Bets," Logan said, his voice low and even. He pointed a gloved finger at the turn in the corridor up ahead, where a green-robed servitor was just rounding the corner, carrying some sort of large tray in his hands.

"Already 'heard' him coming." Betsy smiled, and tapped her left temple. "He won't see or hear us."

"Marvelous," Raphael said admiringly, looking at Betsy as though she were a choice cut of lamb hanging in a butcher's window. "What I wouldn't give for a few of you in my employ."

"No, thank you, Mr. Raphael," Betsy answered, a slight sneer curling her lip. "I'm afraid I wouldn't approve of the work requirements." She paused, then added, icily, "Or of management."

Kitty cracked a smile. She wouldn't want to work for the spook, either. At the same time, she could understand why Raphael found the notion so appealing. Though the Fathership seemed almost deserted, by their standard, from time to time they came upon one of the Kh'thon's servitors, whether singly or in some groups. When they did, with little apparent effort Betsy was able to cloud the servitors' minds, creating a mental "blind spot" that prevented them from noticing the interlopers. It was the next best thing to being invisible, without the awkward business of not being able to see your hand in front of your face.

"Are you quite certain you know where we're going?" Colonel Stuart eyed the passing servitor warily, fingers wrapped tightly around the grip of her automatic pistol.

"More or less," Betsy replied.

The servitor continued by, oblivious to Kitty and the others passing just a few feet away, heading in the opposite direction.

"I don't like this," Colonel Stuart answered, jaw set. "I don't like this ship, this plan, or this whole bloody circumstance. Something is . . . wrong."

"Hey, it gives me the creeps, too," Kitty objected, "but don't take it out on Betsy."

"Nah, she's right, kiddo." Logan was walking a few yards ahead, taking point. "Somethin' ain't normal in this joint. Smells are all mixed up"—he reached out a brushed a hand against the dark, oily material of the nearest wall and his finger tips came away wet—"and there's some kinda weird buzz right on the edge of hearing. Making me queasy."

"It's not auditory," Betsy said, eyes on the middle distance. "That buzz you're perceiving—it's psionic. Your brain just doesn't know how to classify the input."

"What is it?" Kitty asked.

"A sense of wrongness." Betsy closed her eyes momentarily, looking pained.

"Yes, that's it precisely." Raphael snapped his fingers, his expression excited, as though Betsy had just answered a trivia question he'd been struggling to answer himself. "A wrongness."

"What is it?" Colonel Stuart asked.

"It's the presence of the Kh'thon themselves, I believe." Betsy opened her eyes, and turned to look at the others. "They communicate on telepathic wavelengths, and what we're picking up is the psychic spillover of their conversations. But since they're operating so far beyond the normal range of human mentation, it comes across to us as a kind of static." She winced, and pinched the bridge of her nose. "Just be glad none of you has any sort of aptitude for psionics. What you're getting is just a mild vibration of the ether. I assure you that the full impact of the interference is"—she blinked rapidly, and grimaced—"considerably more noisome."

"Come along, then." Colonel Stuart pushed ahead, and continued up the corridor. "No reason to spend a single moment on this hellish ship beyond what is absolutely necessary."

This can't possibly be right.

Alysande stared at the strange, pulsating thing before them, willing herself not to be sick all over the floor.

Not possibly right at all.

"This is it," Betsy said, seeming to take the whole thing in stride.

"It's . . . it's just . . . it's a . . ." Alysande's tongue felt thick in her mouth, and she had trouble forming a thought.

Logan stood to one side, eyes scanning the entrance through which they'd come, and the valvelike doorways on the opposite sides of the room. He glanced over his shoulder at the thing, his expression one of supreme disinterest. "It's a brain."

"Eh," Kitty said with a shrug. "I've seen bigger."

Alysande was sure they were having her on, playing a little joke at her expense, but she couldn't muster the concentration to object. Her every energy, at the moment, was devoted to regarding the pulsating thing before her with commingled fascination and horror.

"Fascinating." Raphael stepped closer, and reached a tentative hand out, as though to touch the thing. Then, remembering himself at the last minute, he blushed, like an art lover so overcome they almost laid hands on a masterpiece in a museum. Holding his hands behind his back, he leaned in close, bringing his nose within inches of the things subtly vibrating surface. "It's organic, clearly, but there appear to be technological elements incorporated into the design as well."

The thing looked precisely like what it was: a gigantic brain. It was almost five feet tall, a little more in diameter, roughly spherical with irregular pits and prominences here and there. Bits of metal and crystal were everywhere, protruding from the dark, fleshy surface, or just visible below it. The worst of it, though, Alysande was convinced, was the arrhythmic pulsations that shook the brain from time to time, like a bowl of gelatin set to quivering by passing footsteps.

"It's an immense, artificial brain," Betsy explained, stepping forward to stand beside Raphael just short of the thing, "an amalgam of technology and organics."

"And this is the dingus that controls the fleet's defenses?" Logan asked.

"Down to the smallest cannon," Betsy answered.

Kitty walked the perimeter of the giant brain, her expression thoughtful. "Is it . . . alive?"

"In a sense." Betsy stretched out her hands, holding them with palms only inches from the brain's surface. "It has a kind of sentience, though perhaps not like you or I would understand the term. I suppose you could say that it is *aware* and leave it at that."

"Is it aware of us?" Alysande's mouth felt dry, and she tightened her grip on the pistol.

Betsy shook her head. "No. It's funny, really. Its 'senses' come from countless points on the hundreds of ships of the fleet, but it can't 'see' this room at all."

"So we're in its blind spot, then," Kitty said.

"In a manner of speaking."

"Just like the slaves in the hallways." Kitty rubbed her lip for a moment, and then looked up, her eyes meeting Betsy's. "Could you do to it what you did to them?"

"How do you mean?" Betsy cocked her head to one side, perplexed.

"Well," Kitty answered, "just like you clouded the minds of those slaves, could you kinda . . . I don't know . . . hypnotize the brain into thinking its defenses are active, while shutting them down at the same time."

Betsy thought for a moment. "I suppose that it's possible."

Alysande nodded, and glanced at the young American girl with burgeoning admiration. "Then the Kh'thon wouldn't know that they were vulnerable until after the Sentinels had struck."

"That's what I'm hoping." Kitty gave a slight smile.

"Well," Logan said. He turned around and popped a single blade from the back of his right hand. "I'd planned on bein' a bit more hands-on, but that works, too, I guess."

"Whatever we do," Alysande said impatiently, "we should do quickly and be gone. I don't relish the notion of being onboard when those Sentinels arrive. Assuming, of course, that your friends are able to hold up their end of this bargain."

Kitty put her hands on her hips, her chin held high. "Don't worry about *our* friends, *colonel*." She grinned slyly, and pointed with her chin to the far side of the room. "Might be better to worry about your own, eh?"

Alysande turned to see Raphael poking around at a mix of organics and crystals on the far chamber wall. The spy stopped, glancing up to see the attention suddenly turned on him, and shrugged. "Just thought I'd see what could be seen. No harm done."

Alysande narrowed her eyes. "Don't. Touch. Anything." Then she turned her attention back to Betsy. "Ms. Braddock, are you ready to begin?"

Betsy, her hands still held with their palms facing the brain's surface, her eyes closed, took a deep breath and sighed. Then she opened her eyes with a slight smile. "Begin? Darling, I'm nearly through."

Betsy turned her attention away from the others, and back to the enormous brain. She closed her eyes again, and reached out with her thoughts, brushing against the cool, alien intellect of the enormous organ.

It was unsettling, the brain that controlled the fleet's defenses. Just as its corporeal self was con-

structed of organic material intermixed with metal
and crystal, so too did its consciousness seem an uneasy blend of mind and machine. The brain's
thoughts were simple but quick, rarely rising above
the level of awareness one would find in a house pet,
but processing more sensory input than Betsy could
sort through in a lifetime.

As she became gradually more at ease touching
minds with the consciousness of the Fathership brain,
Betsy began to recognize something almost like a per-
sonality, in amongst the metallic protocols and crystalline thoughts. Something simple but devoted, quick
to anger but eager to please.

You're a fierce guard dog on the outside, Betsy thought, *but
nothing but a cuddly puppy on the inside, aren't you?*

She reached out with her mind, her thoughts fluttering against the brain's consciousness.

Good boy, she sent to the brain in wordless concept-
images. *You just want approval, don't you? Well, we'll see
what we can do about that.*

Moments passed, and then Betsy pulled her hands
back, in a motion that wasted no energy, and opened
her eyes once more.

"Okay," she said, turning to the others, the strain
only slightly audible in her tone. "I should be able to
keep the brain occupied a while, but we shouldn't waste
any time."

"What did you do?" Kitty asked.

"Would you believe that I'm tickling its belly, and
keeping it distracted from its watchdog duties?"

"That makes about as much sense as anything in this place," Logan snarled. "Come on, let's get out of here."

"Can't go that way," Logan said, jerking a thumb over his shoulder and heading back the way they'd come.

"Um, but isn't the landing bay that direction?" Kitty asked, pointing farther up the corridor.

Logan had been scouting ahead, making sure their route was clear.

"Yep," Logan said simply. "But that deserted intersection up ahead ain't so deserted anymore." He glanced over at Betsy. "You've got some pretty impressive mojo, Bets, but I'm guessin' that even you can't keep the Fathership's brain buffaloed and still cloud the perceptions of a few dozen servitors at the same time."

Betsy recoiled a fraction, her hand flying protectively to her throat. "Um, no, I'd rather not try, thank you."

"Then we can't go *that* way." With that, Logan continued walking down the corridor, heading to the next juncture.

They were halfway to the landing bay when everything went horribly wrong.

Using the memories she'd gleaned from their Exemplar prisoner as a guide, Betsy had directed the group along an alternate route. This path, however, required them to make use of a kind of elevator, a roughly spherically shaped chamber that descended from one level to the next.

"I don't like it," Logan said warily. "Enclosed space,

no way out, nowhere to run if this thing goes somewhere we don't like."

"Yeah," Kitty said with a half-hearted shrug, "but what are you gonna do? This is the only 'lift' in sight, and we don't know how long it'll take to make a circuit and come back this way."

"Are there not any stairs?" Alysande asked. Though she was loathe to admit they shared anything in common, the diminutive Canadian's concerns were her own. "Our options would improve immeasurably on a stairway."

"No, I'm afraid not." Betsy shook her head. "It's this or the rush-hour pedestrian traffic back that way." She jerked her head back, indicating the way they'd come.

Raphael stepped forward, and examined the walls of the chamber. They appeared to be made out of some highly durable, completely transparent material. "A glass elevator," he mused. "I believe I read about that in a story, once upon a time."

"I read it too," Kitty said, shouldering past him, "but unless you think we're more likely to find a giant peach somewhere around here that'll get us back home, this is our only way back to the ship. So move it or lose it."

Raphael treated her to a smile that didn't reach his eyes, and followed her in. Betsy went next, followed by Alysande. Logan lingered for a moment outside.

"I still don't like it," he said, shaking his head. Then he gritted his teeth and stepped onboard.

The door, so transparent and clear that it was almost invisible, slid shut behind him, and the chamber began to sink through the floor.

"Woof!" Kitty doubled over, her hands on her knees. "Wasn't expecting *that*." She looked down through the transparent floor of the mobile room.

Where before they had been on the solid, and opaque floor of the ship's deck, now the lift was descending through a vast, cavernous space. It seemed to extend in all directions, apparently limitless, crisscrossed with a network of walkways, ramps, and landings.

The transparent lift, which seemed to be following a vertical track identical to the horizontal walkways that skeined the open space, was rapidly descending toward a wide, gray plain below them.

"First floor, coming up," Betsy said cheerfully. "Ladies' sundries, jewelry, electronics, and long-way-round to the landing bay."

Visible straight down below their feet, the gray floor rose up to greet them, an aperture irising open just as they reached it, just large enough for them to pass through.

And *that* was when everything had gone wrong.

The door to the lift flowed open, and Kitty phased, instinctively, for all the good it would do her.

There, in the wide open space before them, towered seven inhuman figures, each stranger and more grotesque than the last. They were each a hundred feet tall if they were an inch, looking like a cross between a man, an octopus, a Thai dinner, and a nightmare.

"Um, hi?" Kitty gave a little half-hearted wave.

"Friends," Betsy said, her voice level but strained, "meet the Kh'thonic Collective."

As Kitty's eyes adapted to the gloom, she noticed in addition to the seven inhuman creatures before them a human wearing robes that appeared to be made out of golden light, while in the wings more human shapes lingered, hefting what appeared to be strange, alien weaponry.

"You bitch," Colonel Stuart said, wheeling on Betsy. "You set us up?"

"What?!" Betsy's mouth gaped, and her eyes went wide. "What *possible* benefit could there be in it for me to do so?"

"I don't know," Colonel Stuart snarled. "You tell me."

"Ladies," Raphael said behind his hand, his eyes on the Kh'thon, whom he then flashed with a careful smile before continuing. "This is neither the time nor the place for bickering."

"I gotta say, I agree with Raph on this one." Logan popped his claws with a *snikt,* and gave a feral grin. "Now's the time for scrapping."

"I'll have to disagree, friend," Raphael said, and stepped out of the lift. Arms held wide, he began walking toward the Kh'thon, a broad smile on his face. "Now is the time to *negotiate.*"

36

Doug Ramsey was caught in the middle. It was the same old story, really. Scylla and Charybdis, a rock and a hard place, the devil and the deep blue sea. Or, in this particular instance, two giant, feral Sentinels, one of them shaped like a humungous snake with arms, the other like an impossibly enormous spider. And both of them programmed to kill all mutants.

Which, considering that Doug and his two companions definitely fell under the umbrella of "all mutants," was not exactly welcome news.

To make matters worse, though, more Sentinels were arriving by the moment. Some were small, no more than a few inches long, other as tall as Rogue or taller, but all of them feral, all of them adapted along strange paths of evolution and chance, each design more outlandish than the last.

"Okay, boys," Rogue said, swatting at a winged Sentinel no bigger than the mosquitoes whose shape it had adopted. She sized up the competition. "I figure I can handle Charlotte the Sentinel over there"—she pointed to the giant spider—"but that'll leave the snake without a dance partner."

Hank, who'd already tucked his glasses into his shirt pocket, cracked his knuckles like a concert pianist limbering up for a performance, and shucked off his shoes. "I believe I can address that concern, my dear lady. Though my preference is always for matters cerebral, I've had my fair share of experience in the corporeal realms as well."

Rogue flashed him a lopsided grin, and then glanced over at Doug.

"That means it's up t' you, boy," she said.

"Yes." Hank glanced his direction. "If you can get the central computer up and running, there should be a way to override the Sentinels' command protocols."

"Erm, sure?" Doug managed a weak smile. "It'll be a piece of cake, right?" He winced, hoping that neither of them noticed how his voice cracked like a kid about to be booted from the boys' choir, but if they had noticed, they gave no sign of it.

"'Atta boy," Rogue said, and punched him lightly on the upper arm. "Now, if you'll excuse us, I believe we're keepin' our hosts waitin'."

With that, Rogue spun on her heel, and launched into the air like a missile, aiming for the towering spider Sentinel.

"After you, my dear." Hank doffed an imaginary hat, and crouched low, collecting energy in his legs like coiled springs. Then, in one fluid motion, he exploded into the air, twisting around in midleap so that he hit the nearest wall feetfirst, then pushing off and rebounding straight at the snake Sentinel, his arms held wide, enormous hands open and grasping. The snake

Sentinel fired round after round from its arm-mounted weapons, but Hank's movements were too quick and erratic for any of them to strike home.

Which left Doug swatting away minuscule mosquito 'bots, while in the shadows scavenger Sentinels and lower-ranking predators eyed him hungrily. Swallowing hard, and hiking the strap of his leather satchel higher on his shoulder, he set off into the gloomy depths of the facility.

Only minutes after first being told that he was a mutant, Doug had been asked to establish a meaningful dialogue with a potentially hostile extraterrestrial. He'd been sleeping, before that, so this came as a pretty rude wake-up call. A short while after that, he'd found himself halfway across the galaxy, on a megastructure called a Dyson sphere, where he had to decipher the controls of an ancient stargate to prevent the complete destruction of Earth. He'd even traveled to Asgard, the other-dimensional home of the Norse gods.

And yet, none of that led Doug to expect that he'd one day be standing inside a giant robot head, as big as the capitol dome in Washington, D.C. Much less on a hovering platform, hundreds of feet above the ground.

Tricking the floating platform into carrying him up from the factory floor had been the easy part. It had its own independent operating system, requiring a simple security authorization code to unlock all of its features. It had taken Doug only a matter of moments to convince the platform that he was a fully authorized repair technician, put the platform's operating core in a diagnostic mode, disable all of its onboard security procedures, and then slave the command system to his voiceprint. When he was through, the platform would take him wherever Doug wanted with nothing but a word, his own high-tech flying carpet.

Which he would need, since a brief survey of the area suggested that the Master Mold's operator core—the central computer that could regulate all of the factories processes, and remotely operate any Sentinels, whatever the make and model, whatever the distance—was located high overhead, inside the hollow "head" of the Master Mold itself. It was fitting, Doug supposed. After all, the operator core was the facility's "brain," and isn't that where a brain was *supposed* to be found?

Once he had the floating platform on a leash, as it were, it was time to take it out for a walk.

"Platform," Doug said, stepping onto the middle of the disc, keeping careful hold on his satchel. "Elevate."

With a whispered hum, the platform began to rise up in the air, buoyed by some variety of suspensor fields whose functioning was far beyond Doug's kin.

What do I know? Doug ruminated, feeling butterflies in his stomach, and trying not to look down. *I'm a software guy. Floaty-disc tech? That's hardware.*

Gradually picking up speed, the platform rose higher and higher, remaining so perfectly level that, if Doug had closed his eyes, the only way he'd have known they were in motion at all would have been the whisper of wind on his cheek as the air rushed past.

But Doug wasn't about to close his eyes. Heck, he was afraid even to blink, for fear that he'd miss the moment when he'd have to tell the platform to stop and they'd career into the ceiling above at high speed.

The ceiling that, at the moment, was approaching fast.

"P-platform," Doug said, breathlessly. "Stop. Stop! *Stop*!"

The flying platform stopped, with only inches separating the top of Doug's head from the massive array of computational equpment above him.

"Um, thanks?" Doug let out a ragged sigh of relief. Far in front of him was a broad, gently curving purple wall. He slowly turned his head, peering over his shoulder, and was so startled he almost tumbled off the platform.

"Cripes!"

It took a moment for Doug to understand what was before him. His first instinct had been that it was an enormous, expressionless face staring right at *him*. Which was, while impossible, no less terrifying.

Gradually, though, he realized what he was seeing. It was like one of those optical illusions, where one looks at the inside of a plaster cast made of a human face. Seen from just the right angle, the inside of a face cast looks like the *outside* of a face, not concave but convex. It had something to do with the way the human brain processed the visual imagery, or played with expectations, or closure, or something like that. Whatever the case, it meant that a face in reverse looked just like the face itself, and vice versa.

Which meant, of course, that the Master Mold wasn't staring at *him*. Its expressionless gaze was still directed out over the Ecuadorian jungle at the volcano of Tungurahua. What Doug was seeing was the hollow interior of that foreboding, emotionless visage.

And above him, a massive bulk of gray cylinders connected by snaking conduits and cables, was the Master Mold's sleeping brain.

"Time to wake up."

Doug reached into his satchel, and pulled out his portable computer. He squatted down and, opening the LCD, laid the computer on his knees. With a familiarly reassuring chiming noise, the computer woke up from suspend.

"Okay, darlin'," he said, patting the computer's case affectionately, "time to go to work."

Balancing the computer on his knees, Doug reached into his satchel and pulled out a coil of cabling. One end was a standard connector, while the other was a kind of oversize alligator clip, with long, sharp, serrated "teeth."

"Platform. Elevate six inches and stop."

With a quiet hum, the platform raised up. Doug plugged the cable's connector into his computer.

"Okay, now where is . . . ?" Doug squinted up at the conduits and cabling of the operator core, now just within arm's reach. The light was dim, so he pulled a small flashlight from his satchel, and played its beam across the snarl of massive electronics. "Ah, there it is."

Keeping careful hold of the computer, he straightened and, with the cable in hand, reached out and clamped its alligator clip end onto a particular conduit overhead. The long serrated teeth of the clip bit deep into the conduit, and when Doug pulled his hand away the cable held firmly in place.

"Now, Mr. Master Mold." Doug smiled, fingers flying over the computer's keyboard. "Let's talk, shall we?"

Elsewhere in the factory, things were not going so well.

At some point along the way, Hank and Rogue had switched partners, he taking on the spider Sentinel, she taking on the snake. Then Rogue had managed to wrap the snake in knots, and force fed the Sentinel its own guns.

Then Hank had managed to trip the spider up, getting it tangled in its own legs, careering into a wall at speed, knocking out its own sensory mechanism.

Which seemed, for a moment, like a good start.

But then the two X-Men had discovered, to their dismay, that the spider and snake did *not* represent the apex of the Sentinel evolutionary ladder, but were at least one or two rungs down.

Higher on the Sentinel food chain was—

"A giant gorilla?" Rogue said in disbelief. "Ya gotta be kiddin' me . . ."

"Oh my stars and garters." Hank gaped, eyes wide.

It was taller than a typical Sentinel model, perhaps one hundred thirty to one hundred fifty feet tall, but its habit of walking on its knuckles made it seem deceptively short. Its forearms were massive and lengthened, while its legs were short but powerful. It was topped by the familiar Sentinel headpiece, but there was something strange about the lower half of the expressionless Sentinel face.

"Uh, Hank . . . ?" Rogue began, but before she could

finish her thought, the lower half of the gorilla Sentinel's face swung open, jaw distending, revealing a row of laser cannons. These roared to life, spitting out thick beams of pure energy, lancing toward the two X-Men.

Hank danced out of the way just in time, the leading edge of one of the laser blasts singeing the side of his face, his right sleeve smoldering. Rogue had the ability to move faster, but her reflexes were not as highly attuned as Hank's, and so she was caught by a direct hit, the blast impacting on her chest and knocking her backward off her feet. If not for her near-invulnerability, she'd have been incinerated on the spot. As it was, the breath was knocked from her, and she fell with a thud to the hard concrete floor, stars dancing in her eyes.

"Ouch."

Hank rushed to her side, and helped her to her feet while the gorilla Sentinel recharged its mouth lasers.

"I believe, Rogue, that we have met the top predator of the Sentinel world. One can scarcely imagine anything preying on *that*."

Just then, a kind of distorted, electronic roar sounded from somewhere in the factory, followed by a deafening thud, then another, then another. Footsteps, and approaching fast.

"I wish you hadn't of said that, Hank," Rogue said, shaking her head wearily.

Another Sentinel lurched into view, equally as big as the gorilla. But where the gorilla Sentinel had long arms and short legs, this one had tiny, almost vestigial arms, but massive, powerful legs. The torso extended into a kind of tail, which the Sentinel used to maintain balance, and its oversize headpiece was segmented, the lower half swinging open to reveal a set of wicked pincerlike grabbing mechanisms.

Hank looked at it, wide-eyed with amazement. "It's . . . it's . . ."

"It's a blamed dinosaur, Hank." Rogue let out a ragged sigh.

"Could it be some kind of convergent evolution?" Hank absently pulled his glasses from his pocket, and setting them on his nose peered up at the approaching Sentinel in wonderment. "Morphologically it's . . . well, it's a *T. rex*. Which is not impossible, however implausible. But how would . . . ?"

"I think you'll have to puzzle it out later," Rogue said, and grabbing hold of Hank's arm lifted him up into the air just as the massive pincer jaws of the dinosaur Sentinel smashed into the space they'd just vacated. "Looks like Rex here is hungry."

"Just remarkable."

For a moment, it looked like the gorilla and the dinosaur might turn on each other instead, but whatever strange evolutionary paths their command protocols had taken, apparently the imperative to eradicate mutants still took precedence.

Carrying Hank under her arm like a football, Rogue zipped from one side of the cavernous space to the other, managing to keep ahead of the laser blasts from the gorilla Sentinel and the massive jaws of the dinosaur . . . but just barely.

"I don't know about you, Hank, but I'm bushed. Don't know how much longer I'll be able to keep this up."

"Oh, I shouldn't worry about that," said a voice behind them.

They turned, and saw Doug standing atop a flying platform, floating in midair.

"*T. rex* and Kong, huh?" Doug nodded approvingly. "Cool."

The dinosaur roared, and the gorilla swung around, bringing its mouth cannons to bear.

"Doug, look out!" Hank shouted.

Doug just smiled, and raised his hand.

"Stop," he said simply, and the Sentinels ground to a halt, frozen like statues.

"Um, Doug?" Hank said uneasily. "Am I to take it that you've established communication with the Master Mold?"

Doug smiled more broadly. He reached into his satchel and pulled out a cellular phone.

"You could say we've established communication."

Rogue zipped over and landed gracefully on the flying platform. She released her hold on Hank, who straightened his shirt, fussily.

"Doug, you're my hero," she said with a grin. "I'd kiss ya . . . if, you know, it wouldn't mean suckin' the life outta you and stealin' your powers and memories. Those blamed Sentinels dang near had my number."

"Aw." Doug shuffled his feet, blushing. "It wasn't anything, really."

"So have you convinced the Master Mold to activate all the decommissioned Sentinels?" Hank asked eagerly.

"Well," Doug answered, prevaricating, "we may have run into a teensy-weensy *problem* . . ."

37

Scott and the others weren't dead yet, but it wasn't from lack of trying.

"I've got an idea, Kurt, why not try to teleport us into a vat of molten iron next time? That might be quicker."

"I'll forgive that comment, Herr Summers, because I know you are trying to make a small joke, and I can't hold your complete lack of a sense of humor against you."

"Tovarisches," Peter grunted, as an Exemplar pounded into his organic steel frame with a force that could have shattered mountains. "Perhaps now . . . is not . . . the best time."

Kurt sighed dramatically. "You should be grateful we brought Peter along, Scott." He leapt six feet in the air, just narrowly missing the latest sweeping attack by the superspeedster Exemplar, a yellow-clad blur of movement almost too fast to see. "After all, he's the only one of us more humor-impaired than you."

Scott, to Kurt's surprise, managed a small grin, and fired an optic blast at the Exemplar wearing the dark cloak, who maddeningly went invisible and intangible just as the beam reached him, phasing back into visible corporeality only after it passed harmlessly through.

The fourth member of the Exemplar quartet whose amusements their sudden teleportation into the alien city had interrupted was a short distance away, watching the combat with a detached expression. On his forehead was some sort of red gem, though whether it was decorative or served a purpose—a weapon, perhaps?—Scott couldn't say, since the ruby, as Scott thought of him, had yet to make a move.

"This is getting us nowhere," Kurt said, lunging to one side, catching a glancing blow as the yellow-clad speedster zipped by again. "We need to think of a new plan."

Scott fired an optic blast at the ruby Exemplar, who promptly disappeared. For an instant, he assumed that this was another phantom, another able to phase invisible and intangible, but in the blink of an eye the ruby reappeared on the far side of the pool, in the same posture and pose.

A teleporter, Scott realized. That gave him an idea.

"Kurt, you up to teleporting, yet?"

Rebounding off the wall, wrapping his prehensile tail around one of the outstretched stone tentacles of the giant inhuman statue and swinging to the far side, Kurt scratched his head thoughtfully. "I think so. Why?"

"The shield's bound to be back up," Scott answered, not chancing a glance at the remote on his belt, "but you should be able to scout out a path for us through the city. Feel like giving it a shot?"

Kurt, hanging head down, just out of the speedster's reach, crossed his legs, as casually as if he were perched on a park bench, and shrugged. "Why not, *Mein Freund.* I'll be back in a moment."

Bamf.

Scott glanced over, and saw that as soon as Kurt had 'ported, the ruby Exemplar had likewise disappeared. If the ruby was a teleporter, as Scott surmised, then Kurt's little scouting mission would serve a dual purpose. He'd be able to scout out a path for them, possibly even finding the prisoners themselves, but he'd also be leading the ruby teleporter on a merry chase.

Of course, Scott thought with a slight smile, *it might have been better if I'd actually told Kurt that part of the plan.*

Scott almost felt as if he'd made a joke. Well, if so, Kurt would only have himself to blame.

"Verdammt, Scott!"

Kurt leapt into the air, lashing out with a kick that connected with the yellow blur of the speedster. Then, just as the ruby-wearing Exemplar teleported above him, ready to grab hold of Kurt with a telekinetic fist, Kurt 'ported away.

And somehow our four-to-three odds, Kurt thought, *have turned into two-to-one odds against me alone. I do hope Peter and Scott appreciate this gift I've given them.*

Kurt had not been born yesterday. He'd seen Scott glance at the ruby Exemplar across the pool, and had seen the ruby teleport a short distance moments before. So when Scott had asked Kurt to scout ahead, he'd had a fairly good idea that a secondary objective would be to lure one of their foes away, for a brief while at least, on a wild-goose chase.

What Scott had failed to take into consideration, and Kurt had been too overconfident to consider, was that the yellow-clad speedster had clearly taken some sort of personal dislike to the furry blue elf, and that in addition to the ruby teleporting after him when Kurt *bamfed* away, the speedster would likewise come and hunt him down. And so now, while trying to find a path through the city, or better yet locate the prisoners they sought themselves, Kurt was forced to contend with, not one, but two Exemplars out for his blood.

To which he could only repeat, "*Verdammt,* Scott!"

In the years since he'd left the family farm in Siberia, Peter Rasputin had traded blows with aliens, gods, and monsters, with giant robots, cyborgs, and Mandroids, with heroes, villains, and friends. And none of them, to the best of his recollection, had hurt quite so much as this thrice-damned Exemplar.

Hairless, like all the servants of the Kh'thon, this one wore skin-tight vestments of silver and blue, with a stylized thunderbolt emblazoned on the chest. Much shorter than Peter, he was only an inch or so taller than Scott, but easily twice as wide, thickly muscled with a disproportionately large upper body. His massive arms, like pistons, swung back and forth, his large fists like jackhammers pounding into Peter again and again and again.

Not that Peter wasn't giving as good as he got. For every blow that the thunderbolt Exemplar struck, Peter responded with one of his own. Their battle carried them from one end of the long reflecting pool to the other and back again.

By the white wolf, but he's a tough one.

Even in his armored form, the punishment Peter's body was taking had begun to take its toll. Still, he was grateful, knowing that had he been on the receiving end of even one of the thunderbolt's blows while in his flesh-and-blood form his body would likely have been liquidized.

Peter was reminded of the last time he'd gone toe-to-toe with an opponent as strong and as tough as this one. It had been on the moon, years before, facing off against Gladiator, the leader of the alien Imperial Guard. It did not escape Peter's notice that, on that occasion it had been the other combatant who had been the victor, not Peter.

Of course, a building fell on me, so it was hardly a fair fight.

Peter hoped that, assuming he could keep from being buried under falling masonry *this* time, he might come out the winner.

But he wasn't willing to place any bets on his chances just yet.

Scott, meanwhile, was finding out just how frustrating it could be to fight an opponent one could neither see nor touch.

"Kitty could learn a thing or two from you, friend," Scott said, firing another optic blast, only to see it pass through empty air as the phantom disappeared, then reappeared a few feet away.

He considered trying the same shotgun approach that Hank had suggested he use against the Capo of the Judgment's Watch Cohort in Manhattan, but a brief attempt proved fruitless, as the phantom simply went intangible and breezed through the randomly placed blasts.

"Arrant of the Lightning Factor Cohort is no friend to you, degenerate," the phantom said, his voice high and reedy, "but I'll happily teach you and yours a lesson in subjugation."

With that the phantom surged forward, his dark cloak flapping behind him, moving directly toward Scott.

Scott had spent too much time training Kitty in the Danger Room to underestimate the destructive capabilities of someone able to pass through solid matter. If this phantom was able to bring other objects along with him, he could very well phase Scott halfway through solid rock and then leave him there. And Scott knew from experience that any object, or person, that suddenly returned to solidity inside another object fared none too well.

Of course, if the phantom's powers worked anything like Kitty's, he would have to lay hands on Scott before taking him anywhere. Which mean that Scott's optic blasts would be of much less use in this instance than plain old hand-to-hand combat.

Which was fine with Scott. It had been a while since he got a workout.

Sure enough, as the phantom got closer, he grabbed for Scott, hands outstretched. Scott, falling back on years of martial arts training, blocked the grab, ducking down and under the phantom's arms and stepping to one side. Scott lashed out, hoping to land a punch to the phantom's side, but at the last instant the phantom went invisible and intangible.

Scott danced away, and an instant later the phantom returned to visible corporeality, and came by for another pass.

This time Scott tried a different approach, meeting the phantom head-on, shoulder forward, hoping to plow into the phantom's midriff and knock the air from him.

The phantom, taking a defensive posture, went intangible just as Scott barreled through the space he'd previously occupied.

Scott's momentum carried him forward a few yards, and when he spun around, he saw the phantom holding his ground, eyeing him wearily. From the crisp outline of his shadow, Scott could tell the phantom was solid, and Scott assumed that he was planning his next move.

Bamf.

Kurt teleported in immediately behind the phantom, and before the Exemplar could react, clodded him across the back of the head with a two-handed blow. The phantom, rendered senseless, fell to the ground.

"These games bore me, Scott," Kurt said, landing nimbly on his feet. "Shall we move along now?"

Kurt explained quickly. He'd managed to shake the two Exemplars who'd been tailing him, but was sure that they'd be along any moment now. He could use the brief respite, though, as he was just about 'ported out.

Then he explained that, as he and the two had been playing their game of tag back and forth across this strange city, he had caught sight of a group of human prisoners being led down a ramp into some sort of sub-surface chamber. It was only a short distance away from the reflecting pool where they now stood.

"That'll be where Lee and the others are being held," Scott said thoughtfully.

"My thinking exactly." Kurt leaned over, resting his hands on his knees. "And I thought it best to fetch you and Peter before effecting a rescue, since I didn't want you to feel left out."

The barest hint of a smile lifted the corners of Scott's mouth. "Very thoughtful of you." He turned and, cupping his hands around his mouth, shouted. "Peter, it's time to go!"

His combat with the thunderbolt having continued ceaseless since their arrival, Peter straightened, and regarded his opponent, a little wistfully.

"I regret that I'm forced to draw our contest to a close," Peter said apologetically. "But I'm afraid I must be going."

With that, he lunged forward, surprisingly fast, and caught the thunderbolt in a crushing bear hug, his arms pinned to his sides. Before the Exemplar could wriggle free, Peter walked to the edge of the pool, reared back, and then flung the thunderbolt end over end through the air.

The thunderbolt splashed into the far end of the pool, and even though he thrashed mightily, quickly sank to the bottom.

"Let us go quickly, *tovarisches*," Peter said, setting off toward Scott and Kurt at a jog. "He'll take a moment or two to get out, but if we're still here when he does I'm afraid our departure will be again delayed."

Scott looked to Kurt, who only shrugged, and the three X-Men set off running.

They reached a broad courtyard. On the opposite side was the ramp down which Kurt had seen the prisoners being led. They had only to cross a distance of a hundred yards or so, and they could descend.

But there was a slight problem.

"Kurt," Scott said through clenched teeth. "I don't remember you mentioning anything about an army of Exemplar before."

With a rakish smile, Kurt scratched his head. "I didn't? I'm pretty sure I must have."

Peter shook his head, his hands clenched in fists of steel. "I think I would have remembered that."

Kurt glanced at Scott and winked. "There seems to be a bout of forgetfulness going around, *meine Freunde.* Why, first Scott forgot to point out our teleporting friend, and then only a short while later the existence of this horde of Exemplar between us and our goal completely slipped my mind."

"This. Is not. Funny." Scott's jaw was clenched so tightly he could scarcely get the words out.

"Oh, you're only saying that because you have no sense of humor." Kurt gave a little salute, and grinning like one of his swashbuckling heroes, plunged into the fray. "Trust me," he called over his shoulder, falling to blows with a green-skinned, four-armed Exemplar, "it's *hilarious!*"

38

Vox Septimus was the hinge on which Lee's escape plan turned. That, and a fair amount of luck.

Lee, her crewmen, and the inhibitor-collar-wearing mutants were all in position when next the door in the wall flowed open. The next few moments would tell whether Lee's plan had any chance of success.

Clearly, though, Lee was in the catbird seat, as the first figure through the door, crystal rod in hand, was Vox Septimus. Behind him trooped a number of prisoners, most of whom seemed to be regular humans, men and women, except for one in a uniform of black and white, a haughty expression on his elfin features, even subdued as he was by the inhibitor collar. Lee recognized him as Northstar, the Quebecois hero and member of the Canadian super-team Alpha Flight. If Lee's dim recollections were correct, his powers included flight and superspeed, both of which would come in handy, assuming that their escape plans advanced past the first stage.

It was time to see if Lee's strategy would work. She motioned to the others, and took her position.

The tall Native American code-named Thunderbird had been tapped to play the role of the heavy. He was the most physically imposing of all the mutant prisoners, and even through the miasma of the inhibitor collar, was able to work up a sufficiently convincing rage. Lee was sorry for the punishment he'd endure, if her plan were to succeed, but Thunderbird shrugged it off. It was worth it, he'd said, if they could regain their freedom.

Just as the last of the newly arrived prisoners was entering the chamber, and the pair of crystal-rod-wielding servitors in the rear crossed the threshold, Lee went into her act.

"Vox!" she shouted, rushing forward, hands out in an imploring gesture. "Help me! He's gone crazy!"

Just then, on cue, Thunderbird lunged after her, teeth barred, hands out and grasping, bellowing with rage.

Lee scrambled to Vox Septimus's side, and pointed at the charging mutant.

"He's augmented, Vox, and he plans to *kill us!*"

There was a moment's hesitation on Vox Septimus's part, and for an instant Lee thought that her stratagem had failed. But then the servitor glanced at her, drew his mouth into a tight line, and turned back to face Thunderbird.

"Not this time, augment!" Vox Septimus snarled, surprisingly vicious, and then blinding white light shot from the tip of his crystal rod, lancing into Thunderbird.

Pinned by the white burst of energy, Thunderbird hurled back his head and howled.

Just then, the other mutant prisoners, who had arranged themselves in a wide arc around the opening, raced forward, screaming bloody murder and charging directly at the pair of servitors in the rear of the train.

Eyes wide, the servitors raised their crystal rods, just as Vox Septimus had done, and fired off bolts of white light at the attacking mutants.

Then Lee made her move.

She began by bringing her foot crashing down on Vox Septimus's instep, the heel of her boot impacting with an audible crunch. Then, as Vox Septimus began to double over in pain, she brought her hands down in a two-handed chop, smashing into the servitor's wrist. His grip on the crystal rod loosened, and the rod clattered to the floor.

Lee dove after it. On hands and knees, she scrambled for the crystal rod, and just as she wrapped her fingers around it and turned, Vox Septimus was standing over her. He looked down at Lee, a confused, betrayed expression on his face.

"I'm so sorry," Lee managed, and then squeezed the crystal just as she'd seen the servitors do, and a bolt of white light lanced out, splashing into Vox Septimus's face and chest.

Still on her back, Lee lifted on one elbow, and as Vox Septimus crashed to the floor, neck and face scorched, his eyes rolling back in his head, she fired off energy blasts in rapid succession. Her aim was no better than her control, but after a half-dozen blasts she'd managed to connect with both of the other servitors, who now lay writhing on the floor, alive, but just barely.

Lee climbed to her feet, as Paolo and the others helped the mutants to their feet. Those who, like Thunderbird, had been on the receiving end of one of the energy blasts, had a rougher time of it than the rest.

"Okay," she said, dusting off her jeans. "Time for step two."

Lee's gamble had paid off. She'd gathered, from her conversations with Vox Septimus, and from watching the way that he interacted with his fellow servitors, that he harbored some degree of resentment for the "augments," those servitors who had been given special abilities. He'd also seemed to have developed some affection for or attachment to Lee herself. The presence of terrestrial mutants in the prison chamber, whether their powers were inhibited or not, provided Lee the opportunity to stage a little drama for Vox Septimus and see if she could use his resentments to her benefit.

It had all worked flawlessly, of course, going off without a hitch. So why did Lee feel so lousy? Sure, Vox Septimus had been happily leading Lee and her men to the slaughterhouse, along with countless other human prisoners, but he didn't seem such a bad sort, for all of that. But in the end, it had come down to him or the prisoners, and Lee had know immediately what side she was on.

Still, she couldn't help feeling sorry for the poor guy. From the look on his face when the energy blast had knocked him out, it was clear he just hadn't seen it coming.

•   •   •

It took a bit of trial and error to work out how to remove the inhibitor collars, and Lee came very near to blowing off a few heads in the process. In the end, though, all seven mutant prisoners were free, slowly regaining their powers and abilities, leaving Lee, Frank, and Paolo armed with the crystal rods previously wielded by their jailors. The mutants were still a bit dazed from the exertion of rousting themselves to action, and rested here and there, regaining their energy.

"Okay," Lee said, turning and addressing the two dozen or two other prisoners, all of them regular men and women, with a few older children scattered here and there. "Here's the deal. That door"—she pointed to the aperture in the silvery wall—"is open, but we have no idea how long it's going to stay that way. So my friends and I are going out, and we aren't coming back. The problem is, we also have no idea what sort of resistance we're going to run into. The plan is to get off this island, however we can. But there's a chance we won't make it." She paused, and took a deep breath before continuing. "But if we *don't* make it, at least we can make things as difficult for these alien bastards as we can. No one invades *my* planet and gets away with it. Now," she surveyed the crowd, swinging the crystal rod like a truncheon. "Who's with me?"

To Lee's very great surprise, every man, woman, and child leapt to their feet, ready to follow her into the jaws of danger.

I must have hung around Scott too much, she thought, with a tight smile. *This hero stuff is wearing off on me.*

•   •   •

"One side, woman," said the mutant Northstar, shouldering past Lee. "I take orders from no one, and particularly not an *American*."

Lee shrugged. "After you."

They had found the landing beyond the entrance deserted, and no one in sight on any of the intersecting walkways or the ramps. Though Lee had no intention of becoming any kind of leader, most of the others had looked to her for direction, even the mutants. But, considering what they must have been through, and that most of them were little more than children themselves, Lee supposed it wasn't that surprising.

But not Northstar. And not, apparently, Sunfire, after seeing the example of his Quebecois counterpart.

"Let it not be said that a son of Japan hides behind women's skirts while a Canadian *gaijin* ranges ahead." Sunfire raised his hands before him, and solar flames danced at his fingertips.

"Look," Mirage said, hands on her hips, "I don't care *who's* walking in front, so long as we *all* get out of here. Or is that just too complicated for you muscle-brains to get?"

The Japanese and Quebecois heroes looked at each other, eyes narrowed, and then back at the young Native American woman. They shrugged in tandem. "It's pointless to fight amongst ourselves," Sunfire agreed. "There will doubtless be more than enough opponents to choose from above."

He was not half wrong. As Lee and the others walked up the ramp into a large courtyard lit by the slanting

light of the late afternoon sun, they found themselves in
the midst of a pitched battle.

On the one side was a massed army of Exemplar, led
by an imposing figure with skin the color of silver and
flashing white eyes, from which optic beams lanced
out, to devastating effect.

On the other side were three familiar figures, a blue-
furred acrobat with four fingers and a prehensile tail, a
towering man made of organic steel, and a lithe, muscled man with a yellow visor wrapped halfway around
his head.

"Hey, Summers," Lee shouted, firing a blast of white
energy from her crystal rod, and rushing into the fray.
"Looks like you could use some help!"

39

Logan didn't need to wait for an engraved invitation. He was ready to attack *now*.

"Hold on there, cowboy," Kitty said in a low voice, her hand on his elbow. "We might still be able to talk our way out of this."

Logan snarled, the adamantium claws on the back of each hand glinting in the low light, but he remained motionless. For now.

Colonel Stuart, for her part, had her weapon drawn, aimed, and ready to fire. Her target, for the moment, was the strangely familiar human in the robes of golden light; but she was willing to change targets, and aim at the back of the secret agent, Raphael, if necessary.

"Greetings from Planet Earth," Raphael said, sounding uneasily like a game show host. "You can call me Raphael. I'm pleased to inform you that I have been authorized by Her Majesty's government to negotiate terms on behalf of all mankind."

"What?" Kitty gaped.

"I smell a double cross," Logan snarled.

"You and me both, Mr. Logan," Alysande answered,

eyes narrowed. Raphael hadn't breathed a word of any of this to her, and her briefing before leaving Earth, however rushed and abbreviated it might have been, had mentioned nothing whatsoever about negotiating "terms." Was the Resource Control Executive playing a game even its shadowy masters in government knew nothing about?

"This one addresses the assembled," sang the golden-robed human servant of the Kh'thon. "This one is not addressed."

Alysande recognized him now. He was the same figure who'd addressed them on the beach of Julienne Cay, some thirty hours, and a lifetime, ago.

"Vox Tertius," Kitty breathed, suggesting she had just recognized him as well.

"This one is Vox Prime, cell-sibling of the Vox some of you encountered on the planet below, this previous day. The thoughts of the Kh'thon are beyond your comprehension, and so the Collective will communicate its will to you through this one."

"That's splendid, lad," Raphael swanned, stepping closer. "Now, if you could just inform your masters that I would like to offer them a deal on . . ."

"Silence!" Vox Prime bellowed, his shout as pure and clear as the tolling of a bell.

"I mean no disrespect, of course," Raphael said quickly, miming a quick bow from the waist. "But this offer does have a time limit, and if your masters don't . . ."

Vox Prime turned his head, glancing to the nearest of the humans in the wings, who carried large, unlikely looking shapes that Alysande could only assume were armaments of some sort. "Guardians. Please do the necessary."

Without warning, light, heat, and sound poured from both sides, belched from the ends of the strangely shaped crystalline weapons, engulfing Raphael completely. Then, as quickly as it had begun, it was over.

For the briefest instant, Alysande thought that Raphael had been completely unharmed. Then she realized that it was not the effects of the bright light on her vision, but that he really was wrapped into darkness. It was as though he, and he alone, were plunged into deep shadows. Then his shape began to shift, and Alysande realized her mistake. It wasn't Raphael wrapped in darkness. It was a pillar of ashes in Raphael's shape. But the pillar of ash could not maintain the form for long, and quickly disintegrated, collapsing to a pile on the floor. Raphael had been burnt, literally, to a crisp, and worse.

"Never could keep his mouth shut," Logan said in a low voice.

Alysande shot him a hard glance, but for just an instant, keeping her attention on the one called Vox Prime, and more importantly on the weapon-wielding humans on either side.

But Vox Prime had not ordered another strike, only glanced up at the inhuman figures towering above him, in silent communion.

Only then did Alysande remember their presence. For several moments, it was almost as if her unconscious mind had edited the grotesques out of her perceptions, finding them too unearthly and unsettling to perceive. But with her attention brought back to them, Alysande could not ignore them any longer. The towering, inhuman creatures were regarding her and the others closely, with senses beyond human understanding, and it seemed to Alysande that she and the others were being found wanting.

It was all Betsy could do to block out the telepathic voices of the Kh'thon. For all their immense power and ability, the aliens were incredibly undisciplined telepaths, broadcasting their thoughts widely, indiscriminately, rather than narrowcasting them directly to the recipient. As a result, a sensitive like Betsy had no choice but to "hear" the voices of the Kh'thon, resounding loudly in her head.

She winced, squeezing her eyes tight, and wished she was anywhere but here.

Kitty stared at the pile of black ash that had been the man called Raphael only moments before. She'd seen people die before, of course, more times than she chose to remember. But rarely were human lives dismissed as casually, as offhandedly, as Raphael's had just been. The servitor Vox Prime had ordered Raphael's execution as easily as one would bat away a fly, and with even less remorse.

"This one is given to explain the thoughts of the Kh'thonic Collective," Vox Prime went on, heedless of the harsh stares and open hostility on the faces of Kitty and the others. "Since returning to the world you know as Earth, the Kh'thon have studied human civilization, such as it has developed. It is not known what fate befell the brethren of the Kh'thon, who in former days remained on Earth while those present left to roam the galaxies. But it is clear that in the absence of authority, the former servants of the Kh'thon have grown wild and uncontrolled. The Collective is especially surprised to find augmented humans on Earth."

Kitty pursed her lips. *For augmented, read "mutant."*

"In aeons past," Vox Prime continued, "only the science of the Kh'thon had been able to trigger the expression of the randomizing element in the servitor race, whether at birth or in later life. Now, however, the feral humans of Earth have unlocked secrets beyond their kin, and such factors as cosmic rays, and gamma radiation, and the free radiation polluting the biosphere in the decades since humanity split the atom, have combined to produce spontaneous triggering of a nontrivial percentage of the population."

Cosmic rays? Kitty thought. *Like those that gave the Fantastic Four their powers? And gamma radiation, like that which gave birth to the Hulk? Is this clown saying that all of those are mutations deriving from the same "randomizing element"—the X-gene—that gave me and the other mutants our abilities?*

"The Kh'thonic Collective has reason to worry that, without supervision, augmented humans could one day pose a threat to the other civilized cultures of the galaxy, not least of which are the Kh'thon themselves. Certainly, recent history suggests that mutants, as you call yourselves, even present a danger to the civilizations of Earth itself."

"Yeah?" Logan said, taking a step forward, but not *too* close. "So what are you gonna do about it, then?"

"This one?" Vox Prime pointed to himself, confused. "This one does nothing." He then turned slightly to one side, and glanced up with a worshipful expression at the inhuman creatures towering over him. "Our masters in the Collective, however, are inclined to eradicate humanity all together, wiping clean the face of the Earth, and starting over with a fresh crop of servants."

"Alright," Alysande barked, and took three long strides forward. "This has gone on quite long enough."

Vox Prime was silent for a long, terrifying moment, and Alysande stiffened, half-expecting to be burned to ashes. When she wasn't, she straightened, and plowed on ahead.

"Look, you lot." She pointed a stern finger at the towering alien figures, ignoring Vox Prime entirely. "Forget what this pile of ashes told you. I am the *legitimate* representative of the British crown, and I'm here to tell you that we reject your claim to Earth and its inhabitants, full stop. No negotiating, no quibbling. This is *our* planet, not yours."

Alysande glanced back at the trio of mutants behind her. Logan, spoiling for a fight, was kept in place only by Kitty's hand on his shoulder.

"Oh, sure," Alysande continued, turning back to the Kh'thon, "you think *you've* got concerns about unsupervised mutants? Well, chappy, just try *living* with them and see how you feel. But it's none of your blasted business. If the mutants are a problem, then they're humanity's problem to sort out. Not yours. Even if everything you say is true, you and your lot gave up any claim on the Earth or its inhabitants when you buggered off millions of years ago, so don't come swanning around now like you own the place, demanding all the back rent. It's our planet, and we'll defend it, so why don't you just bugger off and let us be?"

For a long moment, no one moved, and not a word was said. Vox Prime looked up at the seven monsters towering over him, and Alysande felt strangely nauseated, unbalanced. She remembered the "buzz" that Betsy Braddock had mentioned, the psychic spillover of the telepathic conversations of the Kh'thon, and realized that the aliens must be communicating with one another at a level beyond her perception or comprehension.

At last, Vox Prime smiled, nodded, and turned his attention back to Alysande and the others.

"The Collective has considered your suggestion, degenerate, and rejected it. They will not be buggering off, now or ever. Judgment will be carried out, immediately."

40

"What do you mean, problem?"

Doug, Hank, and Rogue were standing at the center of the facility, the head of the Master Mold towering high overhead.

"Yeah, Doug, I'm with Hank. Seems to me that we're not gummin' up the teeth of a giant dino-bot, so I'm guessin' that you got the computer to listen to you, at least, right?"

Doug glanced up at the mass of conduits, cables, and equipment that lined the inside of the Master Mold's "skull."

"Well, I was able to use my portable computer to hack into the Master Mold's user interface, and while it was still in a suspend cycle I installed a radio frequency transceiver. Then I just had to prep it to receive vocal commands, do a bit of fiddling with its recognition protocols, and we were good to go. More or less."

He held up his cellular phone, almost as though it were a consolation prize.

"But now we can talk to the Master Mold over the phone. That's something, at least, right?"

Doug pressed a number on the cellular phone's key-pad, and a voice buzzed from the phone's tinny loud-speaker.

"Master Mold online and awaiting instruction."

"So you c'n just tell it what ta do and it'll do it?"

"Um, no, not exactly," Doug said, sheepishly. "That's the problem. See, I was able to hack the recognition pro-tocols, so that the Master Mold and all the local sentinels won't be able to detect the X-gene in our DNA. They think we're human. That's why they're not attacking us anymore."

"Their protocols call for them to defend human life," Hank said, his tone suggesting he was remember-ing something long ago and far away.

"Exactly." Doug nodded enthusiastically. Then he added, less so, "But we still can't give them any in-structions."

"Why not?" Rogue asked.

"Because we're not Bolivar Trask," Hank answered.

Doug looked at Hank, impressed. "Yeah, that's it ex-actly. Or a genetic relative, at least. Even as weird as these Sentinels look, this is a Mark I Master Mold, the original Bolivar Trask model. The Cadillac of mutant-killing machines. And it has all of Trask's original secu-rity protocols still running." He glanced at the giant head high above them, and slumped his shoulders, de-feated. "It'll take orders from a Trask, and *only* a Trask."

"Wait a blamed minute," Rogue said, her tone disbe-lieving. "You're saying that you're smart enough to trick this thing into thinking you, me, and him are human, but you can't make it think we're *one* human in particular?"

A blush rose in Doug's cheek, and he averted his eyes. "I . . . I just . . ." He shook his head. "No, I can't." Then, after taking a quick, deep breath, he looked up, defensive and perhaps a touch defiant. "But it's not my fault. It isn't! Without a sample of Trask DNA to use as a model, I've got no idea what kind of spoof to input."

Hank rubbed his bottom lip thoughtfully. "But wouldn't there be a record of Trask's genetic makeup on file? The Master Mold has to be using *something* as a basis of comparison, right?"

Doug nodded. "Yeah, I tried that. And found it. But it's got 256-bit encryption on it. There's no way we could crack it in time." He looked from Hank to Rogue and back again. "Not unless one of you has suddenly developed the mutant ability to guess decryption keys at random."

"No," Hank said, impatient but somewhat strained, like a teacher trying to lead a student to a troublesome answer. "But if you know where the Trask DNA is stored in the system, couldn't you simply replace that file with a sample you *do* have, and then use *that* as your mask?"

Doug's eyes brightened, and his mouth opened wide. "Hey!" He snapped his fingers. "I *could*. It'd be kind of backwards, but it could work." He smiled, and then added, "Heck, I could use *mine*."

Doug punched in a series of numbers on the cellular phone, and then began speaking into the mic, his voice barely above a whisper.

Rogue shook her head, her brows knit. "I don't follow."

"Well," Hank said, professorially, "since Doug doesn't have the information he needs to convince the Master Mold that he is Bolivar Trask, he's instead going to overwrite the file copy of Trask DNA, essentially convincing the Master Mold that its creator was Doug Ramsey all along."

Doug had the phone cradled between his shoulder and ear, fishing in his leather satchel for something.

"Yeah," he said, glancing over at Hank and Rogue. "It won't hold for long, though. The next time the Master Mold does its schedule system restore, it'll overwrite any of my temporary edits and the Trask DNA file will be back in place."

"It doesn't have to work forever," Hank said. "Just so long as it works long enough."

Doug finished up rattling off a sequence of base pairs into the phone, and then said, "Execute."

"I don't like the sounds a' that."

Hank reached over and patted Rogue's shoulder, an avuncular gesture.

"Master Mold," Doug said into the phone, raising his voice and glancing overhead. "Identify."

A long moment of excruciating silence followed.

"Vocal identification: Trask. Prime command protocols search: online: Running protocols: stop. Preserve Trask DNA."

Doug looked over to Hank and Rogue and smiled broadly. "Folks, I think we're in business."

"Well," Hank said, sounding for all the world like a proud father. "What are you waiting for?"

Doug smiled, and shifted the cellphone to his other ear. He held up a finger, asking the others to hold on, and flashed them a sly grin.

"Master Mold?" he said. "I've got a little assignment for you."

41

"Hey, Forrester, aren't I supposed to be rescuing *you*?"

"Ah, you know me, Scott, I've never been very good at living up to other people's expectations."

Scott chanced a quick glance and a smile, then fired off an optic blast at a tall, thin Exemplar with bat wings and huge fangs. Lee, who'd fought her way through the melee and was now standing at his side, countered with a torrent of white light from her crystal rod, hitting an Exemplar with arms like a fiddler crab, sending him spinning back out of reach.

"You know, Lee," Scott said out of the side of his mouth, while he sighted on another target, "most damsels in distress wait patiently in their dungeons, and don't come rushing to their rescuer's aid with their own personal army in tow."

"What, these guys?" Lee pointed to the seven mutant newcomers, who were hungrily laying into their former captors. "I thought they were with you."

Scott laughed—actually *laughed*—and spared a brief instant to look her way. With her crystal weapon in hand, hair flying behind her in a blond nimbus, she looked like some kind of Valkyrie, like a warrior princess. He felt a quick pang, one he'd not felt since he'd seen her last. It had been a long, *long* time ago, before he'd gone to Anchorage and all that had come after, but suddenly it felt like only moments had passed.

"It's good to see you, Lee," he said.

Lee glanced his way, a wry expression twisting her lip. "Was that *sentiment*? From the man of stone himself? Somebody pinch me . . ."

An Exemplar with the head of a man and the body of a tiger lunged at them, and Lee barely managed to repel him with a well-placed blast from her crystal rod.

"Lee, I'm sorry I never . . ."

From the opposite side, a flying Exemplar who seemed to be sheathed in blue flames threw a fireball in their direction, which would have impacted with the side of Scott's head had Lee not pulled him aside at the last instant.

"Apologize later, Scott." Lee wore a weary smile, but her tone was grim. "Assuming we live that long."

The melee was not long contained in the courtyard, however enormous it was, and soon ranged all over the alien city. In the shadow of immense, inhuman statuary, grotesques from out of prehistory, man and mutant fought side by side against the army of Exemplar.

Eventually, at least . . .

"Watch it, Paolo!" Frank shouted, and inexpertly fired a blast from the crystal rod that, though clumsily aimed, was still well placed enough to fend off the Exemplar who was preparing to decapitate his fellow crewman from the trawler *Arcadia*.

"Watch it yoursel', Frank," Paolo replied, and with his crystal rod in a two-handed grip sent a burst of light lancing toward another of the Exemplar.

The efficacy of the crystal rod bursts seemed to vacillate widely, but were still proof enough to keep the Exemplar at bay, even if none were incapacitated for long.

"Aw, heck!" Frank raised his weapon, sighting it past Paolo's shoulder. "There's another'n."

"Hey!" Paolo lunged forward, shouldering Frank's weapon away, sending the burst firing harmlessly into the open air.

"What's the big idea, Paolo?!"

"Ya blamed wharf rat." Paolo grabbed Frank's arm and dragged him near, and pointed in the direction Frank had been firing. "That'n's on *our* side."

Frank sneered. "Yeah? Well he's got blue fur and a blasted tail, so's far as I'm concerned, he ain't on no side a mine."

Bamf.

Without warning, Kurt Wagner teleported within arms reach. Frank's eyes widened with fear, but Paolo remained calm and steady.

"Good hearing." Kurt twanged one of his pointed ears. He inclined his head toward Paolo. "My thanks for deflecting your friend's shot."

"He's no friend a mine," Paolo answered. "He's just part a the crew. But he's a blamed idiot."

Frank narrowed his eyes, regarding Kurt suspiciously.

"Well, your fellow crewman seems not to like my appearance."

Paolo just shrugged.

"And does my having blue fur and a tail not bother you?"

Paolo cocked his head to one side and pursed his lips thoughtfully. "Well, does my bein' an old drunk bother *you*?"

Kurt smiled slightly, and shook his head.

"Well," Paolo answered, and turned back to face the enemy. "I don't figure we'll have a problem, then."

Kurt smiled more broadly. He gave Frank a jaunty little salute, and with a *bamf* teleported back into the fray.

"I don't know, Paolo . . ."

"Shut up and shoot, Frank."

Elsewhere in the raging melee, friends were reunited, however briefly, and acquaintances became cocombatants.

Peter Rasputin hurled one opponent out of his way, and turned to find himself facing a tiny green hummingbird hovering in midair before him. He was startled, set aback at seeing something so delicate, so beautiful, in such strange, forbidding environs. Then, in the blink of an eye, the tiny hummingbird was gone, and an enormous green elephant towered over him instead, verdant tusks aimed directly at his steel heart.

"Perdao," said a voice at Peter's elbow, and a diminutive figure who seemed cloaked entirely in shadow stepped into view. The shadowy figure grabbed hold of

the elephant by the trunk, and with surprising ease yanked the elephant off its feet. Though no more than five feet tall, the shadowy figure, around whom little motes of black seemed to dance like crackling energy, sent the elephant hurling through the air. In midair, the elephant shape-shifted into a small bat, but its flapping wings were unable to overcome its inertia and it slammed into a wall with a sickening splat.

"Sunspot?" Peter said, recognition dawning.

"Sorry to steal your sparring partner," Sunspot said, eyes white in a jet black face. The young mutant, one of the new class at the Xavier school, had the mutant ability to convert sunlight into tremendous strength; while using his powers, his body absorbed all frequencies of light with one hundred percent efficiency, making him appear completely black. "I have been caged, and have some aggression to work out, clearly."

Peter smiled. "I take no offense, *tovarisch*. Come." He laid an arm across Sunspot's shoulders. "Allow me to introduce you to an Exemplar upon whom you might vent your frustrations. He has a thunderbolt on his clothing, and can take an *impressive* amount of damage."

On and on the battle raged, as day turned to evening. Combatants shifted from one side of the alien city to the other, exchanging opponents, altering tactics. Flickering here and there, like fleeting mirages glimpsed from the corner of one's eye, a streak of black-and-white and one of yellow appeared, for the briefest instant, then blurred into invisibility, only to appear hundreds of feet away in the next instant, only to vanish again. The Canadian hero Northstar and the yellow-clad Exemplar speedster engaged in battle, moving so much faster than the rest of the combatants that they occupied a reference and a battlefield all their own.

Wolfsbane, the Scots werewolf, faced off against the lithe, blue-furred acrobat with long bony talons growing from her fingertips. They cut and slashed, each bearing the marks of the other's attacks, but neither yielding ground for long, snapping and snarling like wild animals vying for the same territory.

Thunderbird, the Native American Hellion, found his considerable strength and endurance put to the test when he went toe-to-toe with a woman who appeared to be made of solid stone, like a massive statute of granite towering ten feet tall, but surprisingly fast in her movements and attacks, for all of that.

Others of the escaped prisoners took more defensive postures. Mirage, the Xavier student and member of the Cheyenne nation, used her mutant ability to create convincing three-dimensional illusions to help protect the innocent and injured, those human prisoners who hadn't the strength or will to fight, or the mutants who needed time to rest or recuperate from their injuries. By projecting an illusion of a wall where none existed, she was able to shield these from harm, at least temporarily.

And Jetstream, the Moroccan Hellion, used his power of flight to ferry injured combatants from the field, when necessary, taking them behind Mirage's walls of illusion and tending to their injuries as best he was able.

And on the battle raged.

•   •   •

As the Sun dipped lower in the sky, Scott and Lee still fought side by side, trying to find some way of transporting the freed prisoners from the island.

"The dome's still active," Scott said, firing an optic blast upward as an experiment, and watching it deflect harmlessly off the coruscating field of energy that blanketed the city.

"If we could get it down, we could fit some of the prisoners on the *Arcadia*." Lee grimaced, a thought suddenly occurring to her. "Assuming, of course, that these bastards haven't sunk her."

Scott found time to give her a ragged smile. "I haven't seen any sign of it. But then, I haven't seen any wreckage, either, so there's still a chance."

Lee fired off a blast of energy from her crystal rod, and grunted. "Damn. I *loved* that boat."

Scott shrugged, and fired an optic blast at an airborne Exemplar, and then at another. "Well, it's a moot point for the time being, since we *can't* lower the dome. Not without knowing where it's controlled from." He glanced at Lee, hope flashing briefly across his features. "I don't suppose you passed a helpful sign along the way reading 'Dome Off Switch,' did you? Preferably hanging over a big red button?"

Lee chuckled, shaking her head. "No, I think . . ."

Before she could say another word, a pair of white-hot beams lanced between them, kicking up plumes of dust and debris. They staggered back to either side, singed.

"Degenerate!"

Scott looked up to see the silver-skinned figure of Invictus Prime hovering in midair over them, arms outstretched. "You vex your betters, and I would hold you to account."

Lee raised an eyebrow, and out of the corner of her mouth said, "Friend of yours, Scott?"

Scott's jaw clenched, and his mouth drew into a tight line. "We've met."

Lee shook her head, chuckling ruefully. "Scott, Scott, Scott. I can't take you anywhere, can I?"

42

Betsy Braddock had been hanging back, listening to Colonel Stuart and the hairless slave who called himself Vox Prime natter back and forth at each other like old ladies over a back garden fence. Kitty Pryde and Logan, standing next to her, were tensed, ready for battle, unsure what their enemies would do next, knowing only that they had just pledged to exterminate the entire human race.

It was all so very, very tiresome.

Betsy sighed, dropped her hands to her sides, and stepped forward.

"This has gone on *quite* long enough."

She closed her eyes, and concentrated. The little mental pill she'd been formulating for the last few minutes was tricky to deliver, but once sent she knew that the Kh'thon would not be able to resist it. Or, at least, that's what she hoped.

Kitty turned and looked at Betsy, who stood now with her head tilted slightly back, face pointed directly at the towering alien figures, eyes squeezed tightly shut, jaw set.

Then Kitty thought to look up at the Kh'thon, and all hell broke loose.

The seven towering aliens of the Collective began to writhe violently, their bodies thrashing back and forth, their tentacles and pincers and segmented limbs flailing in all directions. Though they uttered not a sound, Kitty could "hear" their telepathic cries of agony, which felt more like a kind of psychic pressure against her thoughts than anything intelligible, like when one feels rather than hears a high-pitched dog whistle, just beyond the range of sensation.

"Whoa," Logan said, and glanced at Betsy with admiration.

"What the devil?" Colonel Stuart muttered, still gripping her pistol tightly, but allowing its barrel to slowly waver toward the ground.

Betsy let out a ragged breath. Opening her eyes, she turned and took in the questioning stares of her three companions.

"I've spent the last few minutes probing the mental defenses of the Kh'thon," she explained casually. "Which, surprisingly, were virtually nonexistent. It was a matter of relative ease to design a telepathic virus capable of incapacitating them."

"A virus?" Kitty glanced at the still-writhing aliens, and the confused, frightened humans who crouched beneath them, looking up at their masters in horror, unsure just what was happening. Kitty could only imagine that the servitors, so accustomed to receiving telepathic commands from their masters, weren't used to hearing nothing but an unending telepathic scream of pain from the beings they viewed as living gods. "Like a computer virus?"

"Essentially," Betsy said.

"But . . ." Colonel Stuart said, looking a little disappointed that she hadn't been required to shoot at anything yet. "I thought these alien buggers were meant to be omnipotent and all."

Betsy shrugged. "Just because the Kh'thon are utterly alien and unspeakably hideous doesn't make them all-powerful. Right now, it feels to them as if their internal organs are being squeezed out the equivalent of a nostril. It's hard to be all lordly when you've got *that* to contend with." Betsy sniffed, and added, thoughtfully, "For what it's worth, as unlike us as they are, their comprehension of pain doesn't seem too terribly different from ours."

While most of the human servants were still at loose ends, looking up in horror at their incapacitated masters, some of the guards were regaining their senses. Realizing that their masters were under attack, and that the terrestrials before them were responsible, they turned their attention to the colonel and the three X-Men, crystal weapons raised and ready.

"Okay," Logan said with grim smile. "My turn."

As the guards advanced, Logan exploded into motion, growling like a wild animal, laying about him on all sides with his adamantium claws. The guards were left unsure how to respond as their crystal weapons fell to shards in their hands after a single one of Logan's swipe, and they were slow to recognize the animal fury glinting in his eyes.

"Finally," Colonel Stuart said, raising her automatic pistol. "*This* is something I can understand."

Tightening her finger on the trigger, she began laying down suppressing fire, as calmly and clinically as if she'd been at a target range.

Just then, a deafening boom sounded, like a thousand thunderclaps at once, and the room shook as if it had been hit by an earthquake.

"What the blazes?" Betsy said, barely managing to maintain her balance.

"Um, guys?" Kitty grabbed hold of Betsy's elbow and motioned eagerly toward Logan and the colonel. "Have you forgotten about the *entinelsay?*"

Betsy turned and looked at Kitty as though she'd just sprouted antlers.

Kitty rolled her eyes toward the cowering human servitors and the still-twitching Kh'thon. Then, in a stage whisper, she said, "The *Sentinels?*" She sighed, dramatically. "The armada of giant robot mutant-killers being fired at the fleet like guided missiles. *Those* Sentinels?"

"Oh, dear," Betsy said, her hand to her mouth.

"Come *on.*" Exasperated, Kitty started off at a jog, dragging Betsy behind her. "Time to go!" she shouted at Logan and the colonel.

Logan was having so much fun getting a bit of exercise in, he almost didn't notice Kitty and Betsy leaving. Having made short work of the first batch of guards, he was pleased to discover that some of the others had found new reserves of courage, and were now mounting a spirited defense. Not that it would do them any good, of course. But it meant a little more entertainment.

Of course, now that the fleet was coming under attack, even that entertainment would have to be cut short.

But even as Logan started to turn away, there was a little voice deep inside him, a fierce little growl that said, *Stay. Fight. Kill.* That was the animal inside, Logan knew. And if he let the animal call the shots, he would have been dead a long time ago. It could be useful, letting it out of its cage now and again, but when the chips were down, it was the *man* who made all the difference.

"Hey, Colonel!" Logan shouted to the Royal Marine, who seemed to have a bit of that growling voice deep inside her as well. She had found cover, and was exchanging fire with a newly arrived squad of crystal-wielding guards. "I think our ride's takin' off!"

The colonel looked up, gave a curt nod, and then took off running, firing backward behind her with the automatic pistol without even aiming. Logan was impressed to see her shots splatting into the floor and walls in a tight cluster around the guards. *Pretty good shooting.*

As the colonel raced past him, she was ejecting a clip from her pistol, another in her free hand ready to ram home.

Coulda used one like her a time or two back in the old days, Logan thought admiringly. Then he made a final feint and lunge at the guards mounting a defense, and took off running after the others.

• • •

Kitty and Betsy were already strapped in and ready to roll when Alysande reached the space plane, and as Alysande was strapping into the pilot's seat and running through the preflight warm-up sequence, the diminutive Canadian came barreling through the hatch.

"Hey," Logan said, glancing toward the rear of the cabin. "Where's the bald chick?"

Alysande spared the briefest of glances back to see that their Exemplar prisoner was indeed missing before returning to her task. The hatch swung shut, and the engines began to fire.

"Um, my fault, I'm afraid," Betsy said, raising her hand like a schoolgirl admitting some minor infraction. "It appears that when I was busy with the Kh'thon, my concentration was disrupted and our prisoner was allowed to regain consciousness. With her telekinesis she made short work of the straps securing her, it would seem, and quickly made an exit."

Logan settled into the copilot's seat, looking at the control panel appraisingly. "Don't think she dinked with the ship, do ya?"

"We'd better hope not," Kitty said.

Alysande punched the ignition sequence, and the space plane began to vibrate, first gradually and then with increasing frequency. "It scarcely matters," she said, over the rising pitch of the engine whine. "If she did, we're dead. But there's precious little we can do about it now."

The engines reached their highest pitch, and then

fired, blue flame gouting, and the space plane surged into motion.

As they cleared the hangar bay, the next wave of Sentinels slammed into the Fathership. Of all sizes, makes, and models, in all states of disrepair, the massive purple and gray robots, powerful rockets firing from their lower extremities, were pelting into the fleet on all sides.

"Oh, bugger," Colonel Stuart said, as an enormous shape of purple and gray hove into view before them. She slammed her hands onto the control panel, and the space plane listed to one side, just far enough to miss a collision with the oddly shaped, long-armed Sentinel by inches.

"Hey," Kitty said, leaning forward in her and trying to peer around the back of the pilot's seat for a better vantage at the forward view-screen. "Was that just a giant *gorilla*?"

Logan stuck an unlit cigar in his mouth, and punched the view-screen controls. The angle reversed, and they were treated to a view of the Fathership behind them, which was now roiling in flames.

"Well," he said casually, "I figure they know their defenses are down *now*."

43

Hank sat at the controls of the Quinjet, with Doug in the second chair, trying to milk as much speed from the versatile craft as possible. Hank hoped to reach the alien city off Julienne Cay in time to provide some sort of assistance, but it was clear that whatever the outcome there, they would arrive far too late to have any sort of impact.

Rogue was in the back, fiddling with the communications gear. It was all standard Avengers issue, tied into the comm networks of SHIELD, the United States government, and any number of other highly classified frequencies.

"Hey, Hank," she said, out of the corner of her mouth. "I been flippin' the channels on your set back here, and so far every one of 'm is showin' the same blasted program. Here, take a look. You two'll want to see this."

Hank punched the autopilot controls, unbuckled his safety harness, and then climbed out of his seat to crouch in the narrow companionway, Doug following close behind.

"Holy . . ." Hank said in a whisper.

"Um, guys?" Doug asked. "What are we looking at?"

Rogue pointed at the bug in the bottom left corner of the screen. "Live feed from Starcore One."

"Which is . . . ?"

"UN-sponsored solar observatory," Hank answered. "Sits just outside the orbit of Mercury."

"Um, *that* isn't the sun." Doug pointed at the screen.

"Nope," Rogue agreed. "But it's dang near as bright, ain't it?"

On the screen, a dozen small suns blazed, irregularly shaped, while wave after wave of Sentinels slammed into the ships of the Kh'thonic fleet. Earth's moon could be seen in the distance, while the blue-green curve of Earth dominated the lower portion of the screen, which gave some idea of how large the conflagration really was. Dozens of the Kh'thonic ships were exploding soundlessly into flame, the light so bright it cast stark shadows on the surface of the distant moon. And each explosion seemed to ignite nearby ships, a rippling cascade effect, so that dozens of infernos became hundreds, perhaps even thousands. It was as though they were looking through a window into hell itself, spreading rapidly by the moment.

"Guys?" Doug leaned forward, eyes wide. "How many Sentinels *are* there, anyway?"

Hank shook his head, marveling himself. "Clearly more than we'd anticipated, no? A few orders of magnitude more, unless I miss my guess."

Doug looked from Hank and Rogue to the bright flickering lights burning on the monitor, and then back

again. "This is going to do quite a bit more than desta-
bilize their fleet, isn't it?"

Hank's smile slowly faded, and he nodded, his expression gone grave.

"Oh, yes," he said after a considerable pause. "Most
definitely."

44

Scott thought the battle with the Exemplar almost lost, and with it all hope for humanity, when the Exemplar suddenly stopped fighting.

Kurt Wagner *bamfed* in from the far side of the alien city, his uniform ripped and torn, his lip split and bleeding. "What are they playing at, *mein Freund*?"

"I don't know," Scott said warily.

The Exemplar had been pounding away at the X-Men and their allies, seeming on the verge of victory. Then, something seemed to ripple through them, some communication passing quickly amongst the gathered army. And though none of the X-Men were able to hear this silent telepathic message, they were able quickly to discern its varied effects.

Some of the Exemplar began to weep openly. Some howled in pain. Some merely stood in mute shock, their eyes wide and unseeing, hands grasping empty air. None, though, seemed able to focus their energies on renewing their attack upon the X-Men and the escaped prisoners.

"Scott?" Lee said, drawing close and slipping her

hand into his. "You know I've seen some strange stuff before, but this right here is *seriously* freaking me out."

By ones and twos, the other escaped prisoners found their way to Scott's side, taking up a defensive position in a well-protected corner of the grand courtyard, eyeing their erstwhile opponents with confused, but watchful, expressions.

Peter Rasputin was busy helping to move the last of the injured, but once they were safely installed within the protective circle of mutants and human combatants, he came to stand beside his fellow X-Men.

The sun had just set, and its last dying rays painted the western horizon in swathes of pink, orange, and red, the long nimbus clouds appearing as gray as old scars, like badly healed wounds across the sky. After the tumult of the last hours, the hue and cry of battle, the alien city was now strangely calm, the quiet marred only by the moaning sobs and occasional pained shouts of the Exemplar.

"My guess is that something bad has happened," Peter said thoughtfully.

Scott had to stifle a chuckle, but couldn't completely hide a thin smile as he glanced at the stalwart Russian at his side. Peter was perhaps no rocket scientist, but Scott could think of no one he'd rather have at his back.

"Yeah, Peter," Scott said, nodding. "I think you're right."

Invictus Prime, wild-eyed, flew down to the courtyard from one of the city's high towers. He had vanished, moments before the fighting had been interrupted, and only now reappeared. But where before he had been composed and collected, a figure of emotionless precision and determination, he now seemed barely in control of his rage, white eyes darting, hands clenched in silver fists at his sides.

"Why do you desist!" he shouted at the other Exemplar, now scattered across the courtyard and the city beyond. "Do we not have a duty to perform? Do we . . . do we not still have *purpose*. We were instructed to rid the Earth of the scourge of humanity, and so we shall!"

"But for whom?" said a small voice, coming from the ground below him.

All eyes turned to see a pitiful figure standing near the entrance to one of the subterranean ramps. His face and chest were badly burned, his lips split, and the once-regal robes of purple he wore were now little more than tattered rags.

"Vox Septimus," Lee said in a voice barely above a whisper, her hand before her mouth, eyes wide.

Scott looked over at her, and then to the burned figure approaching with slow, painful steps.

"Invictus Prime," the servitor went on, his voice strained but clear, "this one is assured that you Exemplar might well win your battle against those gathered here in the city of Dis." He pointed a finger at the escaped prisoners in their defensive corner, his eye lingering for a moment on Lee. "But without the Kh'thon and the fleet, you could never subdue an entire world of such beings. They are too many, these humans, and have resources of strength beyond what you might suppose possible."

Lee leaned close to Scott and whispered in his ear. *"Without the Kh'thon'?"*

"Yeah," Scott said in a low voice. "I noticed that, too."

He began to step forward, opening his mouth, but Kurt put a hand on his shoulder, stopping him.

"No, *mein Freund*. Let us see how this plays out."

Invictus Prime, trembling with rage, drifted downward until his feet were floating just above the level of Vox Septimus's head.

"But they are degenerates!" Invictus Prime pointed toward Scott and the others, his eyes on Vox Septimus.

"And yet they could still defeat you in time."

"Then we will fight and die!" Invictus Prime's voice boomed, and here and there around the courtyard some of the Exemplar began to nod, while others averted their eyes, still weeping.

"Again this one asks," Vox Septimus replied in a voice scarcely above a whisper, "for whom?" He began to turn slowly in a circle, taking in the other Exemplar gathering around, while from hidden doorways and passages other unaugmented servitors began to appear, listening intently. "All of you, this one would know. Without masters to serve, what use is a servant?"

Vox Septimus stopped, and he and the others all looked to Invictus Prime, some with defiance, some with expectation.

But Invictus Prime merely opened his mouth, shut it, opened it again, and then seemed to deflate. He drifted down slowly, by inches, his feet coming ever nearer the ground.

"I . . . I am not certain."

Vox Septimus turned to face the escaped prisoners. "This one has such admiration for these people." He glanced at Invictus Prime and then pointed at Lee and Scott, standing hand in hand. "Look how they work together, protecting one another, with no thought to their clade or class. They are simply human, and that is enough."

Lee swallowed hard. Before Scott could stop her, she pulled away, and took several steps forward.

"Vox Septimus," she said, her voice thick with emotion. "I . . . you shouldn't think that everyone on Earth is . . ." She glanced back at Scott, then to Frank and Paolo, who stood on either side of Kurt Wagner. "Yes, it's true," she turned back around and looked from Vox Septimus to Invictus Prime and back. "We *do* work together. There are those on Earth who think that mutants and humans—augmented and unaugmented—cannot live together, but I like to think that there are fewer of them every day." She glanced back at Frank, and smiled slightly. "And more of us."

Vox Septimus smiled, as best he could with his face and neck burned and split, and took a step forward.

"There is so much this one would learn from you. There is so much you could teach us."

"Teach us?!" Invictus Prime bellowed. He pointed an accusatory silver finger at Scott and the others. "These are barely above animals, nothing more than feral degenerates left to breed unattended. There is no place even for an unaugmented in such company."

Vox Septimus's eyes widened, and he looked over at

Invictus Prime, who now hovered just inches above the ground.

"So the Exemplar contends that this one belongs at *his* side, and not with these 'degenerates'?"

Invictus Prime's mouth opened in shock, "Of . . . of course," the Exemplar said, as though amazed anyone could have considered otherwise. "Augmented or not, we are servitors of our departed masters, bred for a purpose. This is no fit home for such as we."

Vox Septimus looked at the Exemplar for a long moment. Then he glanced at Lee, and turned to address the assembled servitors, Exemplar and unaugmented alike.

"Then perhaps there is still a purpose for this one . . . for *all* of us . . . after all."

Invictus Prime regarded him, silver lip curled. "And what is that?"

"To find a fit home."

45

It was not until later that Scott Summers was to learn the full details of all that had happened. It was clear that Hank McCoy's plan to use the Sentinels as weapons had worked, but what Scott couldn't have known was that it worked far better even than Hank had hoped. In the wave after wave of Sentinel bombardment, a good many of the ships in the Kh'thon fleet were destroyed utterly, and many more besides fatally crippled. The Kh'thon themselves, the inhuman creatures seen as living gods by their human slaves, had never been too many in number, only some dozens of them in the entire fleet, ruled by their seven-member Collective. The destruction of so many vessels, while taking a crippling toll on the population of human slaves, had an even more devastating impact on the Kh'thon, concentrated as they were in only a handful of ships. When the Sentinel barrage was complete, all of those vessels had been completely destroyed, including the Fathership itself. There were no survivors.

The Kh'thon were *extinct*.

Only a handful of ships in the fleet were still spaceworthy, and these busied themselves collecting the scattered survivors who had been lucky enough to escape the destruction of the other craft, now derelict or destroyed. These few ships, along with the several hundred mutant Exemplar and human servitors on the surface of the planet below, were all that remained of the once mighty Kh'thon fleet.

46

Scott and Lee stood atop a high terrace overlooking the city of Dis, as the late afternoon sun dipped toward the horizon. It had taken a night and most of a day, but as they watched the last of the invaders gather, the Exemplar shuffling with eyes downcast, the human servitors running back and forth between the unearthly towers of the city on final errands. If the news that reached Scott and Lee in recent hours was to be believed, this was the scene the world over, as the former slaves of the Kh'thon gathered together, their strange metal ships *un*blossoming, becoming sleek and unbroken curves again, and then ascending, leaving the Earth as quickly as they had come.

The repairs and restorations following the invasion's damage would, of course, take much longer to address, and some wounds would be long in healing, but thankfully loss of life had been kept to a minimum and the danger, for the moment had passed.

Even so, Scott had been less than pleased that Lee had refused to return to the mainland with the first round of freed prisoners, insisting instead that she stay in Dis at his side to help oversee the prisoners' evacuation. As Lee had put it, the *Arcadia* was her boat to do with as she wished, and if she preferred to give Paolo the helm and her spot on the deck to a refugee, that was a captain's privilege.

Only a bare handful of prisoners remained. Kurt and Peter had been ferrying them to the mainland in the *Blackbird,* and Hank had taken as many as the cramped cabin of the Quinjet would allow. In a short while, the *Blackbird* would appear once more in the skies over the alien city, now no longer encased in a dome of coruscating energy, and with Lee, Scott, and the few remaining prisoners onboard, there would be no human presence left.

By that time, Scott figured, the last of the invaders would be taking to the skies as well, and the city of Dis would be left as deserted as it had been, all these long millennia.

"Scott, I wanted to tell you . . ."

Lee's words were interrupted by the chiming of Scott's satellite phone. Mouthing a silent apology, he pulled it from his belt and held it to his ear.

"Scott, it's Hank," came the voice from the speaker, laced with static. "We've just dropped off the young Hellions at the Massachusetts Academy, and the rest of us are about to touch down back at Xavier's. I wanted to let you know that we've just got word from Jean and the others. They're fine, and should be back in Manhattan by the time you return."

Scott felt a pang of guilt, hearing Jean's name. He mumbled thanks into the phone, and then rang off.

"Everything okay?" Lee asked with genuine concern.

Scott forced a smile and nodded. Where was this guilt coming from? He'd not done anything to cause remorse. Jean was the woman that he loved, he knew that.

So why did he feel so comfortable standing here beside Lee?

"Look," Lee said, pointing. Scott following her finger, and saw that Vox Septimus, now in a fresh set of robes, was ambling toward them.

Could it be, Scott wondered, nothing more than the fact that danger can draw people together? And the end of the world, even more so? After all, he and Lee had first bonded over the death of her father, and then grown even closer when cast up on the shores of a deserted island. It was something of a pattern in Scott's life, he realized, finding love in the face of impending apocalypse.

But the end of the world had been averted, hadn't it? And that meant they'd have to return to their normal lives, their normal relationships, and these crisis connections, however intense, would have to be put aside.

Vox Septimus had slowly climbed the steps to the terrace, and approached the pair.

"The servants of the Kh'thon you see before you are the last to remain in Dis, and the last to remain on your world, and these few will be leaving shortly."

Lee shuffled her feet, conflicting emotions playing out across her face. Scott knew that she'd feared for her life when a prisoner of this man, and yet she'd come to care for him, in a strange way, as well.

"Vox?" she said, at length. "Are you really sure you want to leave? There might be some way your people could remain here, if only . . ." She trailed off, as if realizing how unlikely it was that the nations of Earth would welcome the survivors of a former invasion fleet, however contrite.

"No." Vox Septimus shook his head, smiling sadly. "The ships of the fleet are the only ones such as this one has ever known. This one's fellow servitors doubtless feel the same."

"What about Invictus Prime?" Scott asked guardedly. "He seemed pretty well disposed to the idea of remaining here . . . once he cleared all the humans out of the way, of course."

Vox Septimus pursed his lips and glanced back to where the last of the Exemplar were loading into the flower blossom shapes of the landing craft. Invictus Prime was nowhere to be seen. "Invictus Prime is not happy, but he is resigned. His siblings in the Exemplar class have no stomach for war with the Earth."

As if in answer, the silvery shape of the Exemplar leader arced high overhead, skin glinting in the late afternoon sun, and then swooped down like a hawk diving for a mouse, stopping just short of where Scott and the others stood. He hovered in midair, regarding them coolly.

"The last of the landers will be leaving momentarily," he announced in stentorian tones. "Vox Septimus, if you insist on lingering in conversation with feral degenerates, you'll be left behind. No doubt you can amuse yourself into eternity with their base discourse."

Lee ignored Invictus Prime, and reached a tentative hand out to Vox Septimus.

"Where will you go?" she asked.

Vox Septimus gave a slight shrug. "Perhaps we will simply roam among the stars for all the ages to come. Or perhaps we will search for a new home, one that need not be bought at the price of another sentient's life."

"Perhaps," Invictus Prime rumbled. "But if we do not find one, and someday tire of our nomadic existence, then our fleet may still come back this way, and claim this little world as our birthright."

Lee's hands tightened into white knuckled fists at her side, but Scott laid a comforting hand on her shoulder.

"If you do," Scott said, steel in his voice, "you'll find us ready for you."

47

A few short hours later, and fifteen hundred miles away, Kitty Pryde propped her feet up on the divan, and glanced around the day room of the Xavier mansion.

"I really want a cup of coffee," she said wearily, "but the kitchen is *way* over there. Anybody want to carry me over there to get one?"

"Sugah," Rogue said, sprawled out on the couch, "you are on your own. I ache in places I didn't know I *had*."

"Coffee would be good, though," Hank mused, hands folded over his chest, eyes barely open. "We should look into that."

The three X-Men sat motionless in silence for a long while. Then they glanced at Logan, who lay stretched out on the floor in front of the fireplace, snoring loudly.

"Yeah," Kitty agreed. "We should."

Tired as they were, though, exhausted and hungry, bruised and battered, they were whole. All of them had survived, and none had left anything behind that could not be replaced.

Most of the New Mutants were up in their rooms,

only recently reunited with their classmates. Kitty knew there was little chance they'd be sleeping tonight, though, as tired as they were. They'd be up all night, recounting their adventures of the previous days to one another, story after story after story. Kitty was their age, more or less, but she couldn't work up that kind of enthusiasm. She was young, but had already had experiences even the New Mutants couldn't guess. Her place was down with the adults, recuperating.

Their quiet solace was interrupted by a chiming, loud and persistent.

"Can somebody get the phone?" Kitty moaned.

Nobody moved.

"Anybody?" she said in a slightly louder moan.

Hank opened his eyes a fraction, and glanced her way, while Rogue hid her eyes behind her arm.

"Okay, okay," Kitty said, defeated, and with a groan shoved herself up into a sitting position. "*I'll* get it." Pushing up out of the chair with considerable effort, she crossed to the wall, where a communications array was disguised as an armoire. She swung open the doors of dark-stained wood, and revealed a large flat-panel LCD and keyboard.

"Oh," she said dispiritedly after the screen came to life. "It's *you.*"

"Delighted to see you as well, Miss Pryde."

Hank found the will to move his legs, and came to stand beside Kitty.

"Colonel Stuart, I presume?" he said.

"Brigadier Stuart, actually," replied the woman on the screen, perhaps a little sheepishly. "The Royal

Marines have just given me a promotion, it seems. 'In recognition of your contributions to the recent effort,' they said. I'd have been happier with a bit of leave, myself."

Kitty chuckled. "Well, try to get some rest, I guess."

"Yes, well," Brigadier Stuart answered. "I wanted to call and let you know that I am . . . grateful . . . for your contributions, as well."

Kitty's smile broadened. *Is she* thanking *us?*

"That said," the brigadier went on, "I must reiterate that I meant every word I said to the Kh'thonic Collective about the dangers of mutants. We've enough to worry about with aliens invading from above, without having to contend with the possibilities of one of you lot secretly mind-controlling our elected officials, or setting up an independent mutant state or whatnot."

"Now, see here . . . !" Hank began.

"Consider this call a courtesy," the brigadier interrupted. "I've just received confirmation that Downing Street has accepted my proposal to create a tactical force of scientists and lateral thinkers, to anticipate, detect, and analyze the bizarre mysteries that lie beyond the fringes of man's current knowledge. The next time alien invaders come calling, mankind won't have to look to rogue elements like the X-Men for rescue, as the Weird Happenings Organization will stand ready to meet the challenge."

"I'm so happy for you," Rogue sneered, not getting up off her seat.

"I think I've heard enough, Kitty," Hank said.

"Oh, I'll not keep you any longer," the brigadier answered. "I'm sure you've got plots and schemes of your own to consider. But I wonder, do any of you find it ironic that the Sentinels, which were designed to protect humanity against the threat of an army of mutants, were used for *precisely* that purpose? Except, this time, it was you lot yourselves who pulled the trigger?"

The screen went black as the connection dropped, and the three X-Men sat in silence, considering what the brigadier had said.

"Well," Kitty said uneasily, "she's a cast-iron witch, but she's got a point."

"Does she?" Hank said, unconvinced.

A long moment passed as silence fell over the room.

"Hank?" Kitty finally said. "I've been meaning to ask you. The whole thing about the Kh'thon being the original inhabitants of Earth, and genetically engineering mutants as their servants?"

"Do I think it's true?" Hank raised an eyebrow.

"Well, yeah," Kitty answered.

Hank took a deep breath and sighed. "There's nothing in the fossil record that supports the Kh'thonic assertion. That said, there's little evidence that *disproves* it, either. They clearly did have some presence on Earth in prehistoric times, as the city in the Bermuda Triangle proves, but whether they originated here or came here from elsewhere we may never know. And as for whether they had some demiurgic role in the genetic development of mankind, well . . ." Hank's voice trailed off, and he ended with a half-hearted shrug.

"So you're saying it's a question of faith."

Hank nodded. "Something like that."

"So I can choose to believe that humans were originally the house pets of Lovecraftian monsters from outer space. Or I can chalk it up to more megalomaniacal ranting and get on with my life."

"Essentially, yes."

"Gee," Kitty said with a slight smile. "I wonder which one I'll pick."

Across the room, Logan snored loudly, which seemed the only appropriate response.

48

Hours later, Doug Ramsey sat down at the boathouse, looking out at the rippling black waters of Breakstone Lake. It was early morning, the still-dark moments before dawn, and he hadn't slept at all.

"I was wondering where you were," came a voice from behind him.

He looked up to see Betsy standing over him. She carried a cup of coffee in either hand, a blanket wrapped around her shoulders.

"I . . . I just . . ." He looked away as Betsy sat down beside him gracefully. "I didn't feel much like being around people, is all."

Betsy held one of the mugs out to him. "And didn't feel like sleeping, either, apparently."

Doug took the mug without meeting her eyes. "I don't know if I'll be able to sleep again." He paused, and then glanced at the stars glittering overhead. "I don't guess I should be surprised, though. I understand the sleep of mass murderers is often troubled."

Betsy widened her eyes at that. "Doug, what *are* you talking about?"

"What?" Doug asked, defensively. "Isn't that what genocide is, after all? I was the one who launched the Sentinels, Betsy. I caused the *extinction* of an entire race of beings."

"A race of beings who were prepared to send all of mankind to its grave!" Betsy countered.

Doug looked at her, a pained expression on his face. "Yeah, I know. But that doesn't make it much easier to take."

Betsy set her mug down on the planks of the dock, and put her hand on Doug's knee. "You could just as easily say that I'm at fault, Doug. After all, I was the one who shut down the Kh'thon's defenses, and paralyzed them so they couldn't respond to the attack."

"So, what? We've *both* got blood on our hands?"

Betsy frowned, but shook her head. "Perhaps. Or you could just as easily say that you and I share responsibility for humanity living to see another sunrise."

Doug's expression lightened for the briefest moment, and then fell. Looking away, he said, "I'm no hero, Betsy."

Betsy reached over and put her hand beneath his jaw, turning his head around to face her. "No? You are an ordinary man, Doug, for all of your talents. But an ordinary man who does what is necessary in extraordinary circumstances."

Betsy leaned in close, her face now only inches from his.

"If that does not make a hero, Doug, I don't know what would."

Doug managed a smile, looking into Betsy's eyes. "Maybe," he allowed reluctantly.

Betsy smiled. "Just maybe?"

"Yeah." Doug's grin widened. "Just maybe."

The sun rose over Breakstone Lake. A new day was beginning.

Author's Note

I've been researching this novel for the last twenty-five years.

I was a DC Comics kid. My favorites were Superman, Green Lantern, and the Legion of Super-Heroes. I suppose the science fiction aspects of all three titles appealed to me, and the breadth and depth of their respective mythologies.

Then, in September 1981, I happened to pick up a copy of *The Uncanny X-Men* #152 off the stand at my local comic book shop. I'd just turned eleven years old, was only a few weeks into the sixth grade, and I had no idea what I was getting myself into. Looking back, I'm not even sure what spurred me to pick it up.

Reading that issue for the first time, I had no idea who anybody was. To complicate matters, it was the second part of a two-part story, in which Kitty Pryde had been sent away to attend the Massachusetts Academy by her mind-controlled parents, Emma Frost had switched bodies with Storm, and the Hellfire Club had made prisoners of all the X-Men inside the Xavier Mansion. So the story begins with Kitty and a blond-haired telepath claiming to be Ororo Munroe on the run, while a white haired African woman claiming to be the White Queen swans around with Sebastian Shaw. I was confusion, incarnate, but it didn't matter. These were mysteries to be solved, questions to be puzzled out. I was deeply, madly in love with Kitty Pryde, and wished I were one of the X-Men, too.

For most of the '80s, I bought every comic featuring the X-Men I could lay my hands on. Every one-shot, every graphic novel, every spin-off, miniseries, crossover, and guest appearance. And nearly all of them written by one man: Chris Claremont. Along with his cocreators, most notably Dave Cockrum, John Byrne, Paul Smith, John Romita Jr., Bob McLeod, and Bill Sienkiewicz, Claremont was responsible for an inordinate amount of my reading material during junior high and high school, and between his X-Men and Paul Levitz and Keith Giffen's *Legion of Super-Heroes,* I imagine that I spent more time thinking about super-heroes and their fictional worlds than I did anything I was supposedly studying in class.

These last few years, having been away for some time, I've been reintroduced to the X-Men through the talents of people like Joss Whedon, John Cassaday, Grant Morrison, and Frank Quitely. These were guys who clearly read all the same comics I did as a kid, and their takes on the X-Men reminded me of what I so loved about the characters in the first place. I dug up my old back issues, picked up the fantastic *Essential* compilations that Marvel has been producing, and fell in love with the X-Men all over again.

I am incredibly grateful to Pocket Books and Marvel for allowing me the opportunity to dive back into the world of the X-Men again, if only briefly, and to my friend and editor, Jennifer Heddle, for making it possible. The weeks and months I spent working on this project—and the grueling "research" involved in reading and rereading huge stacks of cherished comics—have given me a new appreciation for the care and attention that Claremont and his collaborators put into constructing the X-Men and the world they inhabit. Having the chance to write a story featuring characters whose adventures I've been enjoying for a quarter century has been a childhood ambition fulfilled, and seeing them brought so masterfully to life under the brush of my friend John Picacio for the cover has only served to make the experience that much better.

Now, if you'll excuse me, I've got a few more stacks of "research" that I plan to enjoy before I'm done.

About the Author

Chris Roberson's novels include *Here, There & Everywhere*, *The Voyage of Night Shining White*, *Paragaea: A Planetary Romance*, and the forthcoming *Set the Seas on Fire*, *End of the Century*, *Iron Jaw & Hummingbird*, and *The Dragon's Nine Sons*. His short stories have appeared in such magazines as *Asimov's Science Fiction*, *Postscripts*, and *Subterranean*, and in anthologies such as *Live Without a Net*, *The Many Faces of Van Helsing*, *FutureShocks*, and *Forbidden Planets*. Along with his business partner and spouse Allison Baker, he is the publisher of Monkey-Brain Books, an independent publishing house specializing in genre fiction and nonfiction genre studies, and he is the editor of the *Adventure* anthology series. He has been a finalist for the World Fantasy Award three times—once each for writing, publishing, and editing—twice a finalist for the John W. Campbell Award for Best New Writer, and twice for the Sidewise Award for Best Alternate History Short Form (winning in 2004 with his story "O One"). Chris and Allison live in Austin, Texas, with their daughter, Georgia, and far, far too many comic books. Visit him online at www.chrisroberson.net.

Not sure what to read next?

Visit Pocket Books online at
www.simonsays.com

Reading suggestions for
you and your reading group
New release news
Author appearances
Online chats with your favorite writers
Special offers
Order books online
And much, much more!